This book is dedicated to
my long-suffering partner
and Muse

Bryony Doran

'MEKANISMO'

is Filipino Spanish
for the English
'Mechanism'

and the Greek
'Μηχανισμός'
(**michanismós**)

and the German
'Mechanismus'

and the Italian
'Meccanismo'

A Thought-Spanning
Series

of

Pain, Greed, Violence,
Separation,
Intrigue,
Murder,
History,
&
Love

'MEKANISMO'

A NOVEL IN TIME

Copyrights

No part of this book may be reproduced or transmitted in any form or by any means, electronic or mechanical, including photocopying, recording, or by any information storage and retrieval system, without permission in writing from the copyright owner.

The right of **Bill Allerton** to be identified as the author of this work has been asserted by him in accordance with the Copyright, Designs and Patents Act, 1988.

Most characters in this publication are fictitious and any resemblance to real persons, living or dead, is purely coincidental.

Where real or recognisable historical characters are featured, they are used in an entirely fictional capacity with no intent to demean or subvert their image or memory.

MEKANISMO

Journal

I

KEEPERS OF THE BELL

WILLIAM ALLERTON

'For every action, there is
an equal and opposite reaction'

Isaac Newton
1687

'Whatever the World's Lathe turns,
inevitably turns the World'

Auguste Godenot
1938

The Universe is under no obligation
to make sense to you.

Neil deGrasse Tyson
1958-

Liturgia Horarum

The Carmelite Order of Sisters

Tocsin: A Bell to signal Danger

05.00 Call to Prayer
05.30 Angelus (Psalm 51) Domestic Bell
05.45 Lauds (Divine Office)
06.00 Solitary Prayer
07.00 Mass
08.00 Terce (Renewal of Vows)
08.15 (Breakfast) (Work)
08.30 (Gardening/Novitiate Sessions)
11.00 Sext (Passion of Christ) Outdoor Bell
12.15 Dinner
13.00 Angelus (Recreation)
13.15 Novena Prayer (to the Infant of Prague)
14.00 None (Litany of Our Lady, St. Teresa de Ávila)
14.30 Domestic Work
16.15 Salve
17.15 Angelus
18.05 Supper
18.45 Compline (Free Time) Great Silence begins
21-15 Matins
22.00 Sounding of the Clappers
22.30 Retire

PROLOGUE:

The Mechanism

Around Easter 1900, Captain Dimitrios Kondos and his crew of sponge divers from Symi stopped at the Greek island of Antikythera to wait for favourable winds. During the layover, they began diving off the island's coast wearing the standard diving dress of the time – canvas suits and copper helmets.

Diver Elias Stadiatis descended to 45 meters (148 ft) depth, then quickly signalled to be pulled to the surface.

He described a heap of rotting corpses and horses strewn among the rocks on the seafloor.

Thinking the diver was drunk from the nitrogen in his breathing mix at that depth, Kondos put on his own diving gear and descended to the site. He returned to the surface with the arm of a bronze statue.

Shortly thereafter the men departed as planned to fish for sponges but at the end of the season they returned to Antikythera and retrieved several artefacts from the wreck.

Kondos reported the finds to the authorities in Athens, and Hellenic Navy vessels were quickly sent to support the salvage effort from November 1900 to 1901.

Together with the Greek Education Ministry and the Royal Hellenic Navy, the sponge divers salvaged numerous artefacts. By the middle of 1901, divers had recovered bronze statues, one named 'The Philosopher', another, 'The Youth of Antikythera (Ephebe)' of c. 340 BC, and thirty-six marble sculptures including Hercules, Ulysses, Diomedes, Hermes, Apollo, three marble statues of horses, a bronze lyre, and several pieces of glasswork. Many other small and common artefacts were found and the entire collection was taken to the National Archaeological Museum in Athens.

The death of diver Giorgos Kritikos and the paralysis of two others due to decompression sickness put an end to work at the site during the summer of 1901.

On 17 May 1902, archaeologist Valerio Stais made the most celebrated find while studying the artefacts.

He noticed that a severely corroded piece of bronze had a gear wheel embedded in it and legible inscriptions in Koine Greek.

The object would come to be known as the Antikythera Mechanism.

Originally thought to be one of the first forms of a mechanised clock or an astrolabe, it is now referred to as the world's oldest known analogue computer.

Although the retrieval of artefacts from the shipwreck was highly successful and accomplished within two years, dating the site took much longer. It was speculated that the ship was carrying part of the loot of General Lucius Cornelius Sulla Felix 138BC to 78BC (latterly named *Epaphroditos, Favoured of Venus)* from the successful Roman siege of Athens in 86BC and was on its way to Italy.

A reference by the rhetorician Lucian of Samosata to one of Sulla's ships sinking in the Antikythera region gives credence to this theory and coins discovered on the wreck in the 1970s were found to have been early Roman.

In 1974, Professor Derek de Solla Price of Yale University published his interpretation of the Antikythera Mechanism.

He argued that the object was a predictive, analogue calendar computer. From gear settings and inscriptions on the mechanism's faces obtained by X-Ray imaging, along with the relatively new science of carbon dating, he concluded that the mechanism was made prior to 87BC and lost shortly afterward.

Bill Allerton

CHRONICLE

I

TOCSIN

ABBAZIA DI NOVALESA
ALTA VAL SUSA
PIEDMONT
ITALIA

1938

**JUNE 4th.
SATURDAY**

POST TERCE

Madre Honoire slides her finger under the Vatican seal.

The letter contains no more than four tightly-scripted lines. She reads them carefully, reads them again, then closes her eyes to enter a silent plea.

'Sister Mirais. Ring the *tocsin*. Gather everyone in the refectory.'

Since the untimely death of Padre Mension, the weight of the convent has settled unaided around her shoulders.

There is a letter for which she has desperately been waiting… but not this one.

'Sisters. I have here a letter from The Vatican. Cardinal Ullman…' She hesitates as the elder Sisters blanch at her utterance of the name. '…is to visit to discuss matters of vital importance to our Abbazia. He is to arrive by Tuesday of next week. Today is Saturday so let us waste no time. Sister Minette, take some of the novices to detail Padre Mension's old room until it gleams. Find new bedding. Air it in the sunlight this afternoon. I want everything ready by tomorrow evening. Go… *now.*'

She motions to the elders where they stand conversing by silent glances along the colonnade. 'My chamber.'

Honoire drops the letter to her table, where it glows like a vellum threat against the age-blackened wood.

'I see you all understand.'

As one, the elders incline their heads.

Honoire takes her favourite chair. 'How can we make the best of this?'

Sister Mirais lifts her face. 'Perhaps there *is* no best of this.'

POST NONE

Sister Mirais' heart trips at the sight of a small dust cloud moving independently of the wind. It resolves into an unfamiliar object moving briskly along, taking the sharp turn from the Susa-Novalesa road that will lead it to the Abbazia

She careers barefoot down the staircase from the bell-tower, her throat filled with a sour taste of apprehension.

Honoire looks up from the paperwork she is addressing.

Mirais clasps the smaller fingers of her left hand with her right, pulling them until the knuckles pop.

'Madre! I think he is here.'

Honoire stands her pen in the inkwell and pushes her papers into an orderly pile.

'Are you sure, Sister?'

'There is a… I think… an automobile. So unless we are expecting anyone else from the town?'

Honoire moves from the table to stand by the door. She takes a deep breath and holds it for a moment as if it were her last act of freedom.

'Then ring the *tocsin*, Mirais. I hope we are ready.'

Mirais stops, half out of the room, as Honoire calls to her.

'Mirais, where do you think we should meet him?'

Mirais laughs bitterly. 'Samarkand?'

The automobile hesitates at the bottom of the path to the Abbazia, its front wheels having already left the main road. Cardinal Ullman occupies a seat behind the glass screen that separates himself and Prêtre Benaud from the chauffeur. There is a sudden jolt as the tyres cross a drainage ditch and the vehicle comes to a halt.

Sun lances the windows, drenching Ullman in carmine and ivory reflections. The gold of his cross glints amongst the upholstery as the machine stands, swaying them all with the motion of its engine.

He taps the glass screen. 'Move on.'

The directness of the sun at this altitude is giving rise to perspiration. The Cardinal's underarms are clammy and he has a growing certainty that, despite their finery, his vestments have become stale.

The chauffeur throws up his hands in despair.

'Your Eminence. The road is…'

Ullman shuffles in his seat. 'I insist…'

Prêtre Benaud, a slight man of fifty-four years, frowns under the cover of a broad-brimmed hat.

'Your Eminence, the Automobilist must know well what his machine is capable of.'

'I don't care.'

Benaud is pushed further along the seat until he is crushed into a corner. 'Shall I open the window?'

'No. There is too much dust. Just insist that he takes us up there!'

The chauffeur lifts his hands, palms uppermost. Benaud points along the path to where a wide phalanx of Sisters is waiting, some five hundred yards away.

'Up there.'

The back wheels traverse the ditch. The Cardinal's head hits the roof as the car spreads across the dirt path to lurch sideways, narrow tyres clawing at the loose soil. There is a loud metallic clang as the chassis rasps over a stone and hangs, one front wheel spinning helplessly in the air.

Benaud pushes the Cardinal away from him. The tilt of the car presses them back together.

'I'm sorry, Your Eminence, but I think we will have to get out here.'

The Cardinal huffs his displeasure.

'A *German* automobile…'

Prêtre Benaud opens the door beside him. It swings wide in an instant, dragging him to the ground. He picks himself up, replacing the broad saturno over his silvering hair.

'I'm sorry, Your Eminence, but I really do think we will have to walk the last few yards.'

He stumbles around to the Cardinal's side and reaches a hand into the interior. Ullman bats him away to climb out unaided. Self-consciously, he straightens his vestments before looking up to where the gathering is awaiting his arrival.

Even from this distance he can sense the collective smile they are hiding.

As the Cardinal draws near, Madre Honoire bows her head in supplication and falls in step beside him. Benaud, smiling beatifically, treads behind them, exchanging nods with the front row of Sisters. At the threshold of the gate, Honoire halts their progress.

'Your Eminence, we welcome you to our humble Abbazia. We have felt your presence amongst us ever since we received your letter. Since that day you have been in our every thought and preparation.'

The Cardinal hesitates beside her, surveying the ranks of sisters, novices and postulants around him. He is aware of the stale odour arising from his clothing, made acute by his discomfort in the presence of so many women.

'I assure you, Sister, my thoughts have been with you also. May we…?' He indicates the gate. 'It has been a long journey.'

'And a path that we have all trod.' Honoire clasps her hands together across her small stomach. 'But would you grace our Order with one last favour?'

Ullman fidgets uncertainly.

Honoire looks down at his feet, at the gold thread slippers he wears. 'Would you please remove your shoes before entering?'

'What?'

Prêtre Benaud nudges him surreptitiously from behind.

'What? Oh, yes. I see. Of course.'

Benaud knocks dust from the slippers as His Eminence treads cautiously into the yard. As they pass through the gate, Ullman glances briefly behind.

The Sisters have closed ranks and are following, sealing him in.

SEXT

Padre Mension's old room bears a slight echo, despite the abundance of chests and boxes that have been carried up the hill by donkey from a second motor car.

In the centre stands a single bed with a rough wooden frame. The wheat-husk mattress crunches beneath Ullman's weight and he hopes he will not be sharing it tonight with too many of God's lesser creatures.

'Benaud!'

Through the opened door, the Cardinal can see the rough cot the sisters have prepared in the corridor for Prêtre Benaud.

'Yes, Cardinal?'

'Is there any hot water in this forsaken place?'

'I am sure there is, Your Eminence. I shall see what I can do.'

Prêtre Benaud returns wheeling a zinc hip bath.

The Cardinal assumes a look of sullen amazement.

'What is that?'

'It is Madre Honoire's own.'

'Then make sure it is well scrubbed before *I* get in.'

LAUDS

Madre Honoire opens the door of her office to find the Cardinal already waiting. His skin is pink and flushed. A night at the Abbazia seems to have done him little harm and in the early light through the niche window he carries a certain rudeness of health that the dust had masked the day before.

In her absence he has seated himself behind the desk in her own favourite chair.

As he shows no sign of relinquishing it, she takes the edge of the supplicant seat she keeps for visitors and tries to ignore the fact that he is pawing through her personal papers.

'Good morning, Cardinal.'

He beams across the desk at her. 'I see the locals keep you busy.'

'The world is filled with woe, Your Eminence.'

'Yes. But some of these...'

'To an ant, a few grains of sand become a great burden.'

'But really... look at this one...'

'Your Eminence, given the weight of responsibility your position carries, how should the world expect your concern over a few grains of sand?'

'Right... right.' The Cardinal pushes the papers into a loose pile. 'I suppose there is a place for you people.'

Honoire sits back into the chair. 'And in everything a purpose... including your visit?'

The Cardinal leans his elbows onto the desk, lacing his fingers in the air. 'Yes. Padre Mension.'

Madre Honoire looks the Cardinal steadily in the eye.

'Forever in our memory. He will be sorely missed.'

'Yes. Yes. Good man, so I heard.'

'Irreplaceable.'

The Cardinal returns her direct stare. 'Hell teems with irreplaceable people.' He sits back from the table, enjoying the moment. 'Which returns me to the purpose of my visit.'

Honoire shudders visibly. The Cardinal's face adopts a look of solicitous concern, but his eyes remain fixed with a dark humour.

'My dear Madre, are you unwell?'

'Nothing that time will not cure, Your Eminence.'

'Then it is time indeed that Padre Mension was replaced.'

'We feel that too. I have done my best, but my Sisters are now long without patriarchal guidance.'

'We shall attend to that need. Assemble them in the great hall this evening and I shall personally hear their confessions.'

'Would it not be better for them to wait until the new Priest is installed?'

'Madre, you have done your best, but while I am here it would be uncivilised of me not to rectify your shortcomings. A matriarchal order should never be left unattended for long.'

'Then it shall be as you wish. After Vespers?'

'Indeed.' The Cardinal eases himself from the chair.

Madre Honoire hesitates, thinking to gain her seat, but Ullman sits down again.

Another tremor runs visibly through her body.

'Madre? Are you sure you are not unwell?'

'I am fine, Your Eminence. Though we are under great pressure perhaps without a priest… so many ants… so many grains of sand.'

The Cardinal nods sagely. 'Yes. A new priest will relieve you of the more important tasks of spiritual welfare.'

'Your Eminence…' Honoire feels the lump rise in her

throat but knows that she must climb over it.

She understands that she is being forced to ask, and that she hardly dare. 'Do you have a particular priest in mind?'

Ullman leans back into the chair. 'Yes, Madre. I do.'

Honoire studies his eyes as they narrow, incipiently porcine where the folds of his fat flesh obscure the lids.

'Madre?'

'I'll be fine. As you say, the rest may be good for all of us.'

Ullman discards her papers across the desk without significance.

'Your new priest will have the willing ear of myself and therefore that of Rome. If there is anything you need he will immediately let me know.'

Honoire straightens in the chair and draws a single deep breath.

'I thank Your Eminence. I am sure we shall find that useful.'

The Cardinal greets her acceptance with a nod.

'Good. Good. But no grains of sand, eh?'

'Certainly not, Your Eminence.' In unaccustomed haste, she adds. 'Is there anything we can do to enhance your stay with us?'

'Yes. You can make it shorter. Please order the motor cars to return from the town for tomorrow morning.'

'As you wish, Your Eminence.'

'I shall leave behind a small box. It is of no great significance but please ensure that the new padre receives it unopened immediately upon his arrival.'

He bellows from the chair. 'Benaud!'

Prêtre Benaud opens the door from the corridor at such speed that Honoire realises he must have been listening to the conversation.

'Benaud! Fetch the box.'

Prêtre Benaud returns immediately with a small box dressed like a packing crate.

Through the slats, Madre Honoire can see the glow of darkly polished wood.

'May I ask Your Eminence what is in the box? If it is of significance I shall place it out of reach of accidental harm.'

'Do not concern yourself with the contents, Madre.'

Ullman taps the box with the tips of his fingers.

'Mere grains of sand.'

POST TERCE

For the two months since his arrival at the Abbazia, Madre Honoire has avoided his unwelcome touch, but today, trapped as she is in her own room, Padre Coraloni has placed a cynical hand on her arm.

She shrugs it violently away. The sight of him alone is enough to set her limbs trembling. Minette stands three paces away, facing her across the table.

'Sister. Do you know why we are here today?'

Minette experiences the sensation of her inner organs tumbling to lodge solidly behind her pelvis, the weight of an old lie pressing her bladder into urgency.

'No, Madre.'

'We are here…'

Honoire glances quickly at the priest's expression… a mask of supreme unconcern barely covering the blatant smugness of his damned soul.

'…because a matter has been raised by Padre Coraloni. Do you have any idea what that matter may be?'

Minette hears the control forced into Honoire's voice and hopes she can do the same now that her time has come.

She stiffens her stance.

'No, Madre.'

Madre Honoire is well aware that this is a lie, but also that this is a game to be played by broken rules, no matter the distress.

'It has been brought to my attention that you have been less than open in your declarations.'

Minette stands more firmly. 'I have declared all to my God.'

Honoire shrinks inside the shelter of her habit. Never has her heart felt this small.

'I meant your declarations to myself of things that may have prevented you accessing the position of Sister.'

'I have made all necessary declarations to yourself, Madre.'

Minette's eyes blaze with an intensity that begins with the growing urgency in the pit of her stomach and is fanned to anger by her sense of personal betrayal. She turns that gaze onto the priest.

'And for all else I have made my confession. And for those confessions I have carried out the disciplines imposed by my priest and now I stand before you shriven.'

Honoire's expression shelters from the light of Minette's glare.

'There are things I find myself advised of that are difficult to forgive.'

'If God can forgive me, Madre, can you not find it in your own heart to do so?'

Honoire sits upright in her chair. 'Child, how can I *know* that God has found it in His heart to forgive you this?'

'May God strike me dead if I am not the true penitent.'

Padre Coraloni stands abruptly from his seat.

'Silence, child! The preordination of God's will is blasphemy. Do you want that on your conscience too?'

Minette returns her gaze to where Madre Honoire sits in silence. Knowing that her soul is already irreparably torn she dares a reply.

'Madre, I would rather my conscience than his.'

Padre Coraloni lurches his black-clad figure towards her.

Not for the first time in her life, Minette experiences the presence of great physical danger within a room.

Honoire fights for calm in her thoughts. She has known from the start that she is in the presence of the usurper, and knows that only by remaining strong will she survive. She rises to confront the priest.

'You may leave us now.'

Coraloni's anger is towering beyond reach of reason.

'*What..?*'

'You may leave.'

'*But this…*'

'… is now my problem, Padre. For good or ill you have made it so.'

'*I will wish to hear…*'

Honoire lifts and kisses the cross suspended around her neck. She clasps it tightly in her left hand and extends it towards him.

Coraloni backs away. '*My Uncle…*'

Honoire stands resolute before him.

'I know your Uncle well. I also know why he has found it necessary to send you far from Rome. Now leave us to deal with this matter that you have so conscientiously raised.'

'Come sit with me.'

Honoire motions to the chair beside her. Minette sits down unsteadily as Honoire takes her hands.

'What you have just witnessed is a thing no child should see.' Honoire's own hands still tremble. 'But whenever we take issue with Evil there is always damage, for that is its purpose.'

She allows herself a wry smile. 'In the many dealings I have had with the vestiges of Satan, I have been shown by Our Lord that there is only one weapon powerful enough to defeat him. God's Honest Truth.'

Minette opens her hands.

'But Madre, I am not perfidious. I am honestly shriven.'

Honoire catches the fingers to prevent them escaping.

'I know you believe that, child… but I fear you were

shriven by the Devil.' She lifts Minette's face gently. 'We have a price to pay for this, you and I.'

'You, Madre?'

'Yes. I have to ask The Lord for guidance with my conscience… for I wish to hear your confession myself.'

Minette rises from the chair in protest.

Honoire's hand on her shoulder pushes her down again. *'Now.'*

1930

**JANUARY 7th.
TUESDAY**

6:04 A.M.

Through the silence of an early morning the footstep clatter of two women shakes reflections from the closed windows of nearby houses.

The older one stops, dragging her niece around by the arm.

'Hold your head up, girl. What do you want people to think?'

The girl turns back a fold of shawl to peer along the street.

'There is no-one to see us.'

'And if they did?'

'I don't know, *Tata*.'

'Then let us hope we never have to find out.'

A small, prominent house sits at the junction of three streets. A gate is unlocked at the rear.

The hinge is worn and silent. It closes gently behind them.

The door opens to a single knock.

'Come in... come in quickly. You are early.'

Inside, all seems black except for a few baleful embers in the hearth, but the darkness is infused with a presence of living things... the soft, almost silence of breathing, the faint rustle of skin under cloth and a whispered. 'Sit down... over there... away from the window.'

They take the long bench beside the door. The older woman is moved to speak but she is brought to silence by a raised finger. As they wait, the fire-glow inflames the girl's thoughts with demons.

Beyond the drawn curtains of faded summer-print cotton, comes the sound of a distant footfall. Each step brings it nearer as they hold their breath. Following the slow crunch of Gendarmerie-issue boots comes the fine ratchet of a bicycle being held back down the steep hill.

'He is gone. Minette, bring me a flame.'

Minette ferrets in the blackened bucket by the fire for a dry splinter. She dips one end into the hearth and shadows veer drunkenly as it passes between them. Her mother lifts the glass of a lamp and applies it to the wick. Minette retreats into a corner where comforting shades still lurk.

Mme Vautour places the lamp in the centre of the table and beckons the young woman to sit opposite her. She reaches across the scrubbed pine and takes the girl's hands into her own.

'Are you sure this is what you want?'

The aunt speaks up. 'Of course it is. She is a foolish girl.'

Mme Vautour releases the girl's hands to address her aunt.

'We have all been foolish girls at some time, Russhell. Some of us were just lucky. If I were to remember all our conversations on the subject?'

She watches the girl's eyes as the aunt huffs into silence on the bench. What does she see here that she has not seen a hundred or more times? Was there ever such a thing as innocence? The girl's eyes are wide, pupils fully dilated, whites haunted by fear. The shawl has slipped from her head and settled around her shoulders as if it were the weight of all things imaginable.

Mme Vautour takes up the girl's hands again.

'I wish to hear it from you.'

'Yes… it is.'

Mme Vautour glances at the aunt sitting pressed against the lime-washed wall.

'Yes… of course it is.'

She smiles comfortingly and sees a hope for salvation ignite in the girl's face, noticing how truly beautiful she is now that she has shed her shawl. Wonders too, how she had missed the fullness of lips and the short earlobes, fit only for piercing, the grey-blue eyes with the split green segment in the left iris.

'How long has it been?'

'Twelve weeks.'

Mme Vautour studies the grain in the table, counting once again the rings around the knothole close to the middle.

She looks across at the aunt. 'You know what this means?'

The aunt nods silently.

The girl looks down to her fingers, studying the broken nails and churn-handle calluses between finger and thumb.

'I did not dare to tell. I thought it would go away if I wished it were not true.'

'And the father?'

Russhell grunts her displeasure from the bench.

'Long gone.'

Mme Vautour finds little comfort in the predictable orbit of a very small world. 'Minette. Boil the water.'

Minette lifts herself from the shadows to limp across the hearth. The kettle is already warming on the iron pivot attached to the range. She pushes it around with the end of a poker until it sits above the embers. Fresh sticks slide into the space beneath and flame leaps to spread, blackening the iron until the water begins to seethe.

The girl reaches for Mme Vautour's hands again. 'My name…'

Mme Vautour snaps her hands away. 'I don't need to know your name.'

The girl lifts her head into the lamplight and Mme Vautour can see the pride that she is attempting to build into her face, the tears that are held brimming by the incline of her neck. There is a prominent vein that pulses the length of her throat, crossing just below the larynx to disappear behind the sharp enclave of collar bone.

The girl knows that she dare not look down. 'I want you to know my name.'

'Why?'

She is shaking visibly now, the shawl tumbling from her shoulders to catch against the stiff, railed back of the chair.

The room is still. The aunt is listening intently. Minette is holding her hands over her ears, tucking herself as far as she can into the corner.

The girl grasps Mme Vautour's hands and the nails press into her palms until she thinks they will bleed.

'Because I want you to *care*.'

'I do care…' Mme Vautour extracts her fingers from the desperation of the grip. '…or I wouldn't be doing this.'

'No!' The girl tips her head forward at last, tears falling to scar the length of her soft, pale skin. 'I want you to care about *me*!'

Mme Vautour takes a small phial from the dresser by the window. Inside it a green liquid swirls, staining the fluting of the bottle. Minette pours boiling water into a bowl and floats a small dish of olive oil in it. She fills a cup and hands it to her mother.

Four drops from the bottle dissolve into the water.

'When this has cooled enough, drink it as one.'

She replaces the bottle on the dresser.

The girl holds her hands around the cup, staring at the liquid inside. She is unable to move further until she steels herself, willing her hands to not even feel the heat, to not even know that they are lifting this poison towards her mouth.

'Wait.' Mme Vautour places a hand on her arm. The girl's face leaps into the light... hoping to be told that it is all a mistake and that the blood will flow again between her legs without...

'It is too hot.'

The girl replaces the cup on the table and whispers.

'*Bella.*'

'What?'

'My name... is Bella.'

Mme Vautour sits down heavily at the table. 'I wish you had not told me that.'

'Why?'

Mme Vautour pushes the cup aside. 'Because now I care.'

The girl smiles brokenly at her. 'Then that is all that I can ask.'

She lifts the cup and drinks it in one simple movement.

Mme Vautour takes the cup from her shuddering hand.

'This will make you ill for four days...' Her eyes hold no sympathy. In this room exists the hairsbreadth between life and death, reduced to a chemical simplicity. '...and during that time you may wish that you could die. But with God's Will and the help of your aunt, you may not.'

The girl wipes her mouth with the back of her hand and stares at the saliva drying there.

'What was it? Is that all?'

Mme Vautour lifts the lamp to the hook in the centre of the ceiling. She takes the girl's hand and lifts her to her feet.

'It was Parsley... and I wish that were all. Please remove your petticoats and your other garments. You may keep on your dress if you please, but it will be easier if you do not.'

The girl pleads silently with her aunt. The aunt shakes her head. The dress has a lace bodice that unhooks at the side. She slips the sleeves from her arms, showing them long and slender; the crease of her elbow is a map of blue pathways leading down to her wrist where a small scar burns across the white skin. She sees Mme Vautour looking and bows her head in shame.

Mme Vautour lifts both arms to examine the wrists. The scar is repeated.

'You will not be the last.'

The girl fumbles behind for the laces that hold her waistband. Mme Vautour spins her around and tugs them free. The girl steps out of the dress as it falls to the floor.

Mme Vautour turns her again, running her fingers down the satin petticoat to the place where the bulge should be, and finds it. She drops to her knees and places a hand either side of the girl's stomach, delineating the shape with a spread of her fingers.

'How many weeks did you say?'

The girl trembles under her hands. 'Twelve... *perhaps thirteen.*'

Mme Vautour looks around.

The aunt shrugs her shoulders.

The girl is shaking violently now, shedding the remains of her self-control, suddenly aware of the level of deprivation within the room... the worn utensils, the dirt-grained table top, the clipping rugs on the cold stone floor and a knife of real daylight slicing under the door from the yard. The child by the fire is in need of a wash and new clothes... her foot splays unnaturally from the corner where she hugs the fire-shadows, her right leg thinner and shorter than the left.

The lamp above leaches red from the bright curtains,

pressing it boldly into the scars on her wrists. A tight, sudden cramp takes her stomach. She half-doubles into a crouch. Wetness appears between her legs, staining the petticoat. Mme Vautour passes it to the aunt who folds it between finger and thumb.

Now she is unclothed, the girl's shivering stops. The cramp recedes into a dim light shining from the lower reaches of her being. She lifts herself erect. She has no protection, but finds her dignity in a room where she is naked and no-one else is.

Mme Vautour presses her ear against the girl's stomach to listen. Stroking the skin with her right hand, she traces the edges of muscles that are giving ground to the reshaping of this landscape.

She holds her fingers still and remembers how she too had underestimated her own body in just this condition.

She hears Minette scuffle by the fire, rummaging for sticks to push beneath the simmering kettle, hears the drag of her lame foot on the solid stone and in her mouth is the foulness of the poisons she herself had taken, the gin she drank, her skin burning still with the scald of hot water in tin baths in front of that same fire.

This close she can detect the scent of the girl's body, a musk of freshly-spilled urine and the pheromone salts of her inner lips. There is lavender too, in the fine blonde hair, powdered like moth wings from the talcum she has rubbed into it. Under her hands the curve of belly where it meets the thigh has become accentuated.

Her fingers sense that this girl is everything that she should be... young, perfect and whole.

Gently, she pushes her backwards to the table.

'How many weeks did you say?'

The girl stops when her buttocks reach the wood.

'Twelve...' She bends to whisper. '...*perhaps sixteen*.'

'Sit up on the table.'

The girl's feet swing clear of the floor as she jumps up to rest on the edge. Mme Vautour lifts them and reclines her gently. She moves around until she is between the girl and her aunt. She places her head closer. 'How many weeks?'

The girl lifts her head to whisper.

Mme Vautour understands. 'Are you sure you want to do this?'

The girl glances across at the figure on the bench. Her aunt's stare is hard and fixed. She nods her assent.

'Minette. Boil my needle.'

Minette lifts the bright steel needle from the drawer of the dresser. It is long and sharp, but its end is hollow and sectioned across like the runner beans that she slips into the evening stew.

She carries it across both hands, palms open, unwilling to grasp, to where she slips it into the spout of the kettle.

Mme Vautour lifts each of the girl's legs in turn. From hooks beneath the corners of the table she stretches two rubber straps, sliding the girls feet into them so that her knees are held high and her thighs wide.

The girl buds open like a flower, inner petals flaring pink in the lamplight. Her musk permeates the room as Mme Vautour examines her.

Minette pours hot water into a bowl and places it between the girl's thighs.

Mme Vautour gently cleanses the delicate folds with a clean cotton cloth, rinses her hands and shakes them dry.

'Pass the needle.'

Minette withdraws the needle from the kettle.

Holding the bulbous rubber end between finger and thumb she passes it to her mother.

Mme Vautour draws a solution of carbolic soap and water into the bulb. She dips her left hand into the bowl of heated oil then slides her fingers into the girl.

The girl starts to rise from the table, her face a grimace of intrusion.

Mme Vautour waits until she settles then, with her right hand, slides the needle through the curled palm of her left.

The girl reaches down suddenly and grasps her wrist.

'Will this hurt?'

Mme Vautour withdraws the needle, keeping her probing left hand still inside. 'I cannot lie to you.'

'Then that is good, Madame, for I have never felt so alone.' The girl reaches for her wrist again. 'Will I die?'

Mme Vautour twists the needle out of reach to keep it clean. 'It has been known.'

She reinserts the needle. The girl writhes as it searches for its mark.

'Madame?'

'Yes?'

'*Do* you care?'

'How can I not? I know your name.'

3:15 P.M.

Spear-tipped railings do little more than encourage the isolation of the tiny village cemetery. The cortege is also small, as if the performance of death has been scaled to fit the landscape.

Minette watches it wend its way through the gate of the stone-faced chapel. From her distance it is not easy to count the mourners. Their skirts mingle black in the dull fracture of the day but Minette thinks there are four. None of them are men. The bearers set the coffin down alongside the grave and step away. The priest lifts his book into both hands, heads bow and the ground under Minette's feet seems suddenly insecure. She holds tight to the railings, the iron stakes pinning her life to the soil until the bearers have lowered the coffin.

Still imagining its shudder to the ground, she turns away to walk down the hill to the house on the junction. The gate is wide open. The back door pushed to the full. Loud voices from the parlour fill the space inside the kitchen.

'And how do you feel now? Tell me that at least.'

'Helpless.'

Just from the sound of her voice, Minette can recognise the distress of her mother. The smile wrinkles around her eyes will have been carved from her face. The skin of her pale cheeks will be pushed taut by the hands that she will have placed each side of her head, her elbows will rest on the table and that only this familiar gesture and little else will be holding her together.

'*Helpless?*'

The Doctor's roar of irony over-rides everything in the room, the heat of the fire, the grey light borne in through the glass, the scent of food in the oven, until Minette shivers where she stands. His face will have become florid, the little veins standing above his usual unhealthy pallor.

'What do you know of helpless? You know these people will come nowhere near me once they have been to you. I hold you directly responsible…'

'For what?'

Minette hears a chair being pushed back violently across the stone flagged floor.

Her mother is rising from her place at the table.

'For trying to help where you do not?'

'Help? How does it help someone to kill them?'

Minette senses the growing anger in her mother's voice as it becomes quieter, lower in pitch and timbre. She moves closer to the door as her mother speaks.

'Do men know what it is like to live with the result of their moment of glory? Are they spat upon by every sanctimonious hag in town?'

Minette clings to the edge of the door jamb. Fingers curling the rebate by the hinge, she leans as close as she dare.

Her mother's voice quietens, her energy failing, used up in regret for the girl and herself.

'And did you help me when I asked, Philippe? No. You did not.'

'You know I could not. You know it is against God and the law.'

'God? What does God care of my existence? And if he cared he would not have allowed Minette…'

'Believe what you will, but it is still against the law, and God made Minette. He must have a purpose.'

'Yes, and that purpose is to remind me every waking hour that I am foolish and sinful. If you had been less rigid my life and hers might have been so different.'

'You know I could not.'

'Then it is up to me to see that other girls are not blighted by children they neither need nor want. And you can believe what you will and the law can go wherever God wishes to shove it.'

Minette hears a chair drawn back to the table, the rustle of her mother's skirts as she sits again. She peers around the edge of the door as the doctor opens his bag and takes out a bottle of medicinal brandy.

'We cannot go on like this.'

The brandy slicks the bottom of two glasses he has grabbed from the dresser.

He passes one to Minette's mother. 'I must report my suspicions to the police.'

'Report what? That a foolish girl has had a miscarriage?'

'No, that your actions led directly to her death.'

Minette hears her mother sigh as if she may never breathe in again. 'She was dead already.'

The doctor drops the glass heavily to the table. 'I don't understand…'

'She was dead as I am dead. Dead for lack of a proper husband. Dead for lack of respect… and about to die again of misery. With me she had a chance to escape that. I am sorry, but I could do no more. You would have sentenced her to a life where every day would bring her the joyless vision of an unwanted child. I gave her a choice. What is *your* best offer?'

The doctor's voice slows as the brandy takes effect.

'I cannot change society overnight.'

'But you can start here. Now. Make an effort. Make small changes. Understand.'

'I understand that what you did is against the law. I have known you half my life and, despite that, I am going to have to take issue with this.'

'With what?'

'The whole town knows you are an abortionist.'

'Do you think they will stand up in court to say so?'

'Of course they will. Any God-fearing woman would.'

'And who would help their daughters if you put me in jail? You?'

Minette hears more brandy being poured.

Her mother speaks quietly. 'And where did I get all these poisonous things?'

'You stole them, when you worked at my surgery.'

'Doctor Beaufort, people may think that I was given them.'

'Ridiculous!'

'Is it so ridiculous for a man to wish to cover his tracks?'

The doctor storms up from the table, his nose reddened with anger. 'Ludicrous! You and I both know who...'

'No. You and I both know who turned a blind eye to keep an efficient nurse. Do you think I don't see the results of your ethics every day? The twist in Minette's leg, the deformity of her foot, the way she can't run with the other children?'

'You cannot say...'

'*We* did that... you and I... me through helplessness and ignorance and you with your blind eye. Well I hope it sees well enough today. If you want to show it something, there is a funeral this morning up the hill.'

'Is it wrong to fear the law and my Creator?'

'Creator? Up the hill is a situation that you and your kind have created. Watching it take place is Minette, who should not be seeing things like this. I think you are giving your 'Creator' some competition.'

'And what if I had been as you ask? Minette would never have been born.'

'What purpose is a life if life has no purpose for it?'

'You cannot play God!'

'But God can play with us, yes?'

'The law…'

'The law of life says that men will see Minette's foot as an abomination.'

The doctor closes his bag with an audible snap.

Mme Vautour places a hand on it. 'Doctor, how old is your wife?'

'What does that have to do with this?'

'More than you will allow.'

The doctor relaxes his grip on the bag. 'Thirty two.'

'And you have no children yet.'

'You know I haven't.'

'Why?'

'That is a long story, and also very private. I cannot betray my marriage by giving you reasons.'

'And for how long have you carried these reasons around with you like a lead weight in your bag?'

The doctor studies her face carefully to see if she is merely prying. 'You know nothing of my reasons.'

'I know that you have attempted to make my life a misery ever since Minette was born.'

'And you think that has nothing to do with you being an abortionist or a… a murderer?'

The doctor sits down heavily in the chair. Mme Vautour taps the clasp of his bag. The doctor slivers more brandy into the empty glasses.

Through the gap between door and frame, Minette sees her mother drink it down at once.

'It should have everything to do with it. You are as disappointed with my kind as I am with yours, yet all we need to do is work together.'

'I cannot!'

'You could if you put down your bag of reasons.'

'I took an Oath…'

Mme Vautour snorts in derision. 'Which I am sure you have broken many times.'

The doctor sits upright in the chair.

'If you have proof…'

'In many small ways, I grant you. Optimistic prognoses… placebo medication… you forget… I used to work for you.'

'To my eternal regret it seems…'

Mme Vautour taps her glass on the table. 'You also forget… that I am the soul of discretion.'

The doctor pours her another measure of brandy. 'Why should I know that?'

'Because without that I could not do what I do.'

The doctor tips more brandy into his own glass and replaces the stopper. 'Then maybe Discretion is the Eighth Deadly Sin.'

'Then…' She gives him the smile that he always found so infuriatingly patronising. '…carrying around a bag of no-good reasons must be the Ninth.'

The doctor removes the stopper from the brandy and hesitates, watching daylight filter the pale liquid as easily as truth slips a mesh of lies. 'And where would I put down a bag such as that?'

'Here.' Mme Vautour spins the empty glass between her fingers, seeming to examine each dimple.

'And leave it with a Sinner?'

Mme Vautour places the glass solidly in the centre of the table and sits back from it. 'Perhaps I too have a bag I can leave with you.'

The doctor pours more brandy into her glass. 'Then we will never be free of each other. Do you wish that?'

Mme Vautour shrugs her shoulders and spreads her hands across the table, pointedly examining the empty third finger of the left. She looks across to the corner by the hearth where Minette usually sits absorbing the stray heat from the fire into her withered foot.

'It is too late for wishes.'

The doctor lifts his brown leather bag from the table and drops it heavily to the floor beside the chair.

'My wife was eighteen…' He shakes his head to dislodge the alcohol dewing his memory. '…and glorious. I was twenty six and going away to college to study to become a surgeon. I had only just found her. We met in July of that year and we wanted the days to September to last forever. She was beautiful. She had legs that…'

'Still is… Still has…'

'Yes, but then she was like a flower before it buds, potent with all things possible. I have made her live a half-life.'

'She loves you. She waited for you to finish college.'

'And I came back to what? A desert of my own making?'

'Yes. But now that you allow that fact, you can begin to deal with it. Make amends. There are orphans…'

'Orphans? Ha. My wife was fertile then. While I was away she miscarried without my knowledge. I should never have done it. *I* persuaded her into bed.'

'She would have done anything you asked. A bright young man going off to college to acquire a skill… one who would be admired by everyone when he returned? Why wouldn't she listen to you?'

'But if I hadn't been so insistent…'

'Then you would not have been a man. But you are right, she was truly beautiful at that time.'

'The miscarriage left her infertile. She didn't tell me until we had been married for three years.'

'I know.'

'You know?'

Mme Vautour nods slowly.

'*You*…?' The doctor rises from the table.

Mme Vautour studies the table top, strokes with her fingertips the familiar whorls and patterns where knots have spilled into the grain, as she has just spilled darkness into the doctor's life.

'She wanted to be perfect for you. She wanted to stay eighteen for all the years you were away. She couldn't stand the thought of you being tied to her that way. She loved you so much she wanted you to fly.'

The doctor grabs his bag, wrenching it up from the floor.

'You butchered my wife?'

'I did as she wished, but if the blame for her infertility now falls on me, then at least you have put down your baggage… and to know that with all your knowledge you have never learned how to be human helps relieve me of mine.'

'You are an abomination.'

'I am a survivor in an unjust world.'

'Then God help you. You are a mockery of all that I stand for.'

'You will never see this, of course…' Her face turns again to the space vacated by Minette. '…but I did you a favour.'

'A favour?' The doctors face drains of all colour. 'You accuse *me* of a lack of humanity. Don't you know that *any* child is better than no child?'

Mme Vautour pushes herself away from the table with both hands. 'Tell that to anyone bringing up a cripple.'

Minette turns to flee the kitchen but the reverberation of angry voices follows her. Her eyes cloud with tears. Her foot splays viciously to one side in her haste. The half-filled bucket tips its contents onto the floor with a loud clatter. Yellow disinfectant darkens the stone beneath her feet. She is momentarily anchored by shame, fear and panic.

The doctor appears behind her in the parlour doorway.

'Minette!'

The sound of his voice shakes her free. She stumbles through the door and into the street.

At the cemetery she makes her way to the newly filled grave, sitting down beside a small bouquet of fresh flowers.

The ground is thick, heavy clay with a mixture of stone shards that make digging difficult. Beside it stands a mound of loose black earth that will be replaced once the clay has settled.

Minette digs frantically with her hands until she has formed a hollow in which she can hide.

A sudden wind shakes rooks from the ash trees that surround the chapel while a brittle whirr of sparrows fight amongst the winter husks of overgrown bushes by the fence. She wishes her eyes closed but sunlight bars across them through broken cloud.

Above her, the fragmented sky begins to heal.

1938

OCTOBER 13th.
THURSDAY

POST SEXT

'Madre!'

The voice of Padre Coraloni shocks Honoire from her reverie. She feels the sunlight fade as he stands before her.

He is waving the envelope of a letter that has recently been passed to him by one of the farm boys.

'Yes, Padre?'

'Does the Abbazia possess an automobile? I must say I have not seen one since I arrived.'

Despite her best instincts, she welcomes for once the cool of his shade. The rains of August and September have failed and Honoire can do little but watch the orchard wither in the constant stream of light.

The weather has remained unseasonal since the padre's arrival and she hopes the year will soon be drawing on towards the damp chill of November when the sun strikes long and lean across burnt-stubble fields and the morning mists placate the growing hollows in her conscience.

'No, Padre. We have little need of one.'

'I see that but...' Coraloni is closely observing the novices preparing the garden in case of an early frost, lifting late onions to lay them on the soil, treading mulch around the stems of abundant brassica. He waves a loose sheet of paper in the air. '... I have business to attend.'

His face carries the bland assumption of his superiority,

but that in itself is nothing unusual.

Honoire tries to guess the lie that is coming. 'What kind of business?'

'I have to visit a relative…' Coraloni sees the look of enquiry still unsatisfied in her eyes. '…who is ill.'

'And this illness is..?'

'Terminal… probably. In fact…yes. Terminal.'

'Then you must go at once, Padre.'

'Thank you, Madre. But how?'

'Where does this sick relative live?'

'France… some miles across the border… small town… distant cousin…. lived there all her life. She has asked for me especially.'

Honoire's smile is complicit. 'Then of course you must go.'

She points into the distance where a dark smudge degrades the bottom of the wide, green valley. A low pall of smoke tints the air above it.

'You can take a train over the border from the town.'

'But how would I get there?'

Honoire's face holds a consummately pious expression.

'You could always walk.'

Coraloni lifts his biretta, runs his fingers through his thick blonde hair before replacing it, tucking loose strands under the rim.

'Yes, of course. But as I said before, my business is pressing.'

'Then I shall obtain a horse for you, though that may take time to arrange. Do you ride?'

'Yes, I do. But do none of the farmers possess a motorised vehicle?'

'None that I know of.'

Madre Honoire closes her eyes to the sun as it breaks from his shadow, tasting the slice of warmth from it on her lips and eyelids, knowing that for her next words she will have to make reparation although, she reflects, He may well understand.

'If your business is indeed pressing… the Abbazia does possess a donkey. I can have it readied for your journey by tomorrow.'

'A donkey? Is that fit transport for a priest?'

'It was good enough for Our Lady.'

POST TERCE

The donkey waits patiently in the small courtyard, head down, as Coraloni's bags are slung behind the saddle. The small box that has remained unopened since his arrival is perched on top. A mounting stool stands beside the donkey.

Padre Coraloni is late. He is fussing into his best outfit in the hope that a show of obvious eminence may over-shadow the mode of his arrival in town.

Deserting their boxes and baskets by the Borrowers Gate in the garden wall, a gather of farm boys are vying to see what is happening.

Coraloni arrives at last without a speck on his black uniform. His biretta is square and sits comfortably on his head, the brim folded into the middle where small laces tie the ends in place. His tunic bears polished silver buttons and he is adorned with a single necklace of polished, brown prayer beads from which hangs a silver cross. He is helped into the saddle from where he scowls ignominiously as his legs protrude either side.

Madre Honoire hands him the reins. 'Go with God.'

He casts a glance at the eager faces surrounding him.

'Thank you, Madre. Be assured, neither He nor I shall forget this favour.'

Honoire bows her head.

'Then be gone with my blessing also.'

The donkey takes a step. The priest pulls sharply on the reins.

'Wait…' He leans down to Honoire. 'How does the donkey find its way back?'

'Leave it at the Albergo della Stazione in Susa. They will look after it until your return.'

'I do not know how long I may be. Her illness…' His head moves slowly in an anticipation of sorrow. '…and I shall return by automobile.'

Honoire fights down her exasperation. 'It will be fine at the Albergo. I will make arrangements. Tell them I said so.'

He sits bolt upright in the saddle.

'If I am to travel in this manner, I have decided that I must be accompanied.'

'Sister Mirais, ask if one of the farm boys will…'

'No.' Coraloni stuns her into silence. 'One of the Sisters will come with me.'

'But it is too far.'

'Too far? Too far?'

The Sisters surrounding him erupt in agitated chatter.

Honoire raises a hand to calm them.

'It is too far for one sister to travel alone. It will be dark before she is able to return.'

The priest scowls down at her. 'Then she will have to spend the night in the town and return with the donkey in daylight tomorrow.'

'I cannot ask that of a Sister.'

Coraloni leans down to whisper. 'If Our Lord spent forty days and forty nights in the wilderness, surely a Sister can manage one in the town?'

He leans back in the saddle, loudly victorious.

'I shall take Sister Minette.'

Honoire stumbles as if she has been struck a blow.

'Surely… you cannot…'

'I have watched her.' Coraloni leers down from his new-found height. 'She appears exceedingly nimble in the garden and perhaps along the road I can find a way to further her redemption.'

'She is not ready.'

Honoire searches out Minette from the crowd of Sisters surrounding the donkey. Minette nods uncomplainingly.

The priest slaps the saddle bag behind him.

'I have money and a letter of credit from my uncle the Cardinal. She shall have everything she needs when we get to the town.'

He kicks the donkey with his heels. 'Ho!'

A hush falls across the gathering as Minette shuffles beside him out of the yard.

The gate is bolted shut behind them.

The *tocsin* bell tolls three times.

The sisters melt away, leaving the yard empty.

Beyond the gates, a wind whips around the hill in brief intensity, spiralling grey dust from the dry fields until even the very air assumes the colour of the donkey.

POST SEXT

Padre Coraloni brings the donkey to a halt beside a small deciduous tree. The leaves are withered and turning but, higher up, small, winged seeds cling hard to its branches.

The priest's eyes are sore with blown earth, his throat parched and dry. He rubs his face with the back of a hand and slides ungraciously from the saddle.

Sister Minette is clinging to the bridle, knuckles white where they break through the dust.

Coraloni rummages inside a saddle bag. 'Take the animal into the shade.'

He sits down with his back against the tree and opens the lunchbox. Inside is a flask, bread from the Abbazia kitchen and a slab of cheese.

He takes a long drink from the flask. 'Put the nosebag on it.'

Minette drops grain from the other saddle bag into a short sack and loops it over the donkey's ears.

The priest empties his mouth of bread and cheese.

'Come here. Now!'

Minette sits in the shade further away, facing him, legs extended in the dirt.

Coraloni stares at her feet. 'Discalced.'

Minette looks at him with great curiosity.

The priest repeats himself, louder this time, as if she were deaf. He points uncertainly at her feet. 'Discalced, I say. No shoes.'

Minette allows her gaze to drift the length of her legs until she finds herself staring blindly at her own bare feet. The right foot bleeds copiously from broken blisters along the edge that scrapes the floor as she walks.

The priest tears another chunk from the bread. 'Stupid Order.'

Minette remains calm while he eats, allowing him to play out his charade, hoping that he will make his point quickly.

'Your foot is bleeding.'

Minette shrugs at the obvious. The priest puts the flask back in the box without offering it to her. 'Does that bring you closer to God?'

'No.' Minette throws the hem of her habit over her feet. 'But it reminds me that while my heart is in Heaven, my feet are grounded on Earth.'

'Do you really think that God created His Earth so that you could bleed all over it?'

'He allowed that of His only Son. Beside that, what I ask is but a small petition.'

'Which it seems He has granted.'

Minette draws her feet beneath her. The donkey moves off to one side, lowering the sack to the ground to reach the last grains in the bottom.

The priest angrily brushes at the dust that covers his tunic. 'You lack civilisation.'

Minette stares at him in questioning silence.

'Nuns! Cloisterers! Either in silence or without shoes! What is the point? You should be out amongst people, understanding how the world works where God is lost.'

'Only people are ever lost.'

The priest rises quickly to his feet. 'Do not debate Theology with *me*, Sister. As a priest I stand above your petty arguments.'

'Yes, Padre…' Minette eases herself from the ground. '…but only by the thickness of a shoe.'

She reaches for the reins where they dangle in the dust.

Coraloni grabs her from behind, whirling her around to face him. His mouth is distorted, his skin florid and rising.

She is abruptly aware of the animal power of his breath. His gaze is directed somewhere above her and she realises that she is only a catalyst… an unfortunate opportunity for his explosive expression of misogyny and frustration. She tries to scramble away towards the donkey, to pull herself up into the saddle.

His foot lashes out and pinions her right leg above the twisted ankle. She screams in pain. He reaches down and lifts her face in one hand, finger and thumb pushing into her cheeks until they are slashed inside on her back teeth. Her eyes bulge with a sudden fear and the pain of her leg crushing beneath his foot.

Fully half her weight is lifted from the floor by his single hand. There is a reek of strong wine around him and she understands why he did not offer the flask.

He throws her to the ground and unfastens his tunic.

'So you wish to bleed in the dirt.' He forces his knee between hers. The rough cloth of the habit rides her legs.

He tears at what little there is underneath and forces his way into her with strong fingers. He prises open her teeth with his nails and pushes his mouth onto hers.

Minette tastes foul wine, the heat of angry breath, shudders away from the rough surface of his tongue pressing into her throat and then... silence, as her mouth fills again with the taste and sensation of blackly-turned earth. It cloaks her skin like a shroud and she realises that she has again become a part of it.

She cries out once, then closes her mind to the pain... remembering her study as a novice... the kindnesses hidden deep within the words of the Ecstasy of Santa Teresa de Àvila that were now helping her feel nothing but the depth of God's love.

I saw in his hand a long spear of gold, and at the iron's point there seemed to be a little fire. He appeared to me to be thrusting it at times into my heart, and to pierce my very entrails; when he drew it out, he seemed to draw them out also, and to leave me all on fire with a great love of God. The pain was so great that it made me moan; and yet so surpassing was the sweetness of this excessive pain, that I could not wish to be rid of it...

There is movement on top of her, inside of her. She is aware that it is bringing pain to her body but not to her soul, for this pain is insubstantial, no more than a flutter of wind-driven birdsong, or a glimpsed wrack of drifting sky, beside the truth she had withheld from Madre Honoire.

Minette awakes to find herself alone in the dust beside the road, arms outspread, fingers gripping the dusty soil.

'Bella?' she asks, for a second time, while the silence of a grave whispers in her ear like the sea in a shell. 'Did death hurt more than this?'

She folds herself into the discomfort of the memory, gathering its wings of darkness around her, sheltering a place where her mother sleeps at the table, head rolling occasionally on the soft wood, drunk on brandy the doctor has left behind.

The sun shifts around the tree to warm her face. Her habit is in disarray up to her shoulders. Her legs show pale in the sunlight.

She rises slowly from the ground. There is a sensation of warmth as a bloody fluid smears the inside of her thigh and as if that were the first trickle from a bursting dam, recent memory floods into her awareness. She adjusts her clothes as best she can, tying a small knot in the ripped seam of her underwear.

Scanning the sky to guess how much time has passed since they stopped, she follows the tracks along the road.

An hour later she finds the donkey standing alone in the shade of a tree, reins dropped in the dust at its feet.

Padre Coraloni is beside the road, urinating into a dry creek. He greets her with silence, dresses himself and climbs onto the donkey.

It moves off as he kicks it violently with his heels. Sister Minette walks along at its hind quarter.

Coraloni leans down to speak to her.

'You know if you say anything about this, no-one will believe you.'

Minette ignores him and walks on in silence.

'You know I have influence at the Vatican, don't you?'

Minette's feet tread the dirt road without sound, her right foot bleeding copiously into the dust.

Coraloni leers down at her drunkenly. 'You know who my Uncle is, don't you?'

Minette moves up to walk beside the donkey's head, holding on to the bridle.

Coraloni hauls on the reins and drags Minette around so that she is facing him. His face is still hot. Shards of anger in his voice carry around her head like a flock of darting birds.

'And… for the Love of God… who is Bella?'

OCTOBER 14th.
FRIDAY

NONE

Rusting metal litters the entrance to a barn-like building on the very edge of town. Behind its wide-swung doors is an automobile with all wheels jacked clear of the ground.

Padre Coraloni shakes dust from his clothes. 'Wait here.'

Numbed by the journey, Minette sits on a wall and allows the reins to slide through her hands. In the valley below her, where river turns are dictated by the twists in the roofs of houses, an occasional plume of smoke drifts downstream in the accompanying wind. Through breaks in the buildings, bright rail tracks catch the light where they ride a man-made embankment.

Coraloni returns. 'We have an automobile!'

The donkey had moved on a little until it was stopped by a clump of grass at the roadside. Minette gathers the reins.

'Then I shall leave you here and return.'

'Oh, no.' Coraloni snatches the reins from her, leading the donkey into the yard behind the wall. 'The donkey stays here. You are coming with me.'

'Padre. You know I cannot. They are expecting me at the Abbazia.'

'Not until tomorrow.' Coraloni hands her the box from behind the saddle. It is surprisingly heavy. 'Do not drop that.'

The boy returns with the saddlebags as the mechanic wheels the automobile out of the workshop. He throws them into the back then climbs in the driving seat. The mechanic swings on the starting handle until the engine coughs into hesitant life. He steps around the car to open the door for Minette, who refuses.

'No. I must find somewhere to stay tonight.'

Padre Coraloni takes her arm, his tightening fingers bringing sharp pain to the nerves in her elbow. 'Get in.'

POST NONE

Coraloni leaves Minette seated on the platform in charge of the box and his bags while he goes into the Casa di Stazione. He returns with a smile on his face.

'We have less than one hour to wait.'

She passes him the box. 'Then I need to find somewhere to stay.'

He places the box carefully on the seat beside her. 'You can find somewhere later.'

'But I need your letter of credit. I have no money.'

'You are wearing your wallet. Surely they will trust a nun?'

Understanding she is to achieve nothing here, Minette walks over to the ticket office window.

Coraloni watches her with great amusement.

The ticket collector is old and bald. On the wall behind him are three hats with different badges. The air that drifts from the slatted window of the kiosk is filthy with tobacco smoke.

'Good day, Sister.'

Minette steps back out of reach of the stench.

'Excuse me, do you know where I could get a room for the night… or how I could get to the church from here?'

'You will not need a room.' The ticket collector taps a cigarette from a pack on the counter. 'The train will be here in…' he glances at the clock behind him. '…forty eight minutes.'

The fumes from the struck match billow through the

screen. The man smiles at her through teeth brown and stumped as a discarded jetty.

Minette watches the lips close around the cigarette.

'But I am not catching the train.'

The ticket collector removes the cigarette from his mouth. Fresh ash streaks the front of his pale blue collarless shirt.

'Then why did he buy two tickets?'

Along the platform, Coraloni sits fanning himself with the pair of train tickets, a huge grin on his face.

Minette confronts him. 'You know I cannot come with you. I must return to the Abbazia.'

'And return you shall… when I have finished with you.'

The ticket collector is listening at the window, his ear pressed to the slot in the glass.

Minette whispers fiercely. 'This is wrong. You know I am ordered to accompany you only as far as the town and I will not go further.'

Coraloni feigns interest in the pale print on the tickets.

'You will do exactly as I say.' He slips the tickets into a pocket under his cassock, picks up the box and thrusts it at her. 'Do not drop this nor put it down.'

The padre heads off along the platform towards a small, blue-painted pissoir.

Minette can see his feet below the bottom of the metal screen where they splay and relax, rocking heel to toe.

Leaving the box on the seat, she walks quickly to the ticket office window. 'Can you help me please? Is there…'

She hesitates a moment, trying to decide who would be first to believe her. The police? No. The local Padre? Definitely not. He would never take her word against a fellow priest.

Coraloni's fingers clamp her shoulder. 'Leave the good man alone. I know you are anxious about your mother, but he cannot make the train arrive any quicker.'

Minette allows herself to be led back to the platform.

Coraloni pushes her onto the seat, replacing the box in her lap. The heel of his boot catches the toes of her right foot as he turns away.

He knows the pain will be excruciating. 'This time… do as you are told.' He presses once, hard, then steps away to stare along the length of the track.

SALVE

The engine that arrives late is short, maroon, and decked out with bright brass. The smoke-box door is hinged and handled, giving it the appearance of small, pinched features that pout with sharp gusts of steam.

The stench of hot grease fills Minette's nostrils and a wave of heat escapes from between the wheels as the fire-grate is riddled of spent ash.

The Guard climbs down from the last carriage and Padre Coraloni hands Minette to him. The Guard catches her arm and helps her on board.

Inside the carriage, Coraloni pushes them along until he finds a space where there are no other passengers within earshot. He nudges her to sit by the window and piles his bags onto the seat alongside. He takes the box and places it in her lap.

'Hold this carefully. Your life depends upon it.'

Minette has never ridden a train before and, under other circumstances, the scenery whirling past as it climbs the valley would fire her interest.

Running alongside the rails is a strip of silvered river, meandering and inconsistent, the water pooling and clear before falling to blue-white pounding spouts and gushes.

Abruptly, the tracks pull them away from the stream, forcing them through a narrow gorge with densely overgrown, flower-enriched sides.

Shadows of the train accompany them out onto a large, high plateau. The steam exhaust quickens and the wheels pick up speed on the level plain. Outside of the gorge, the land has become scrub… starved bushes at acute angles, browned and broken… grasses clinging to the side of the rails where the engine feeds them water and ash and, as far as Minette can see, there are no animals or houses.

This place is as desolate and dejected as her thoughts.

The Guard makes his way along the car. 'Border in ten minutes.'

Minette is snapped back from the wilderness outside. She shoots a glance at Coraloni opposite. Since the journey began he has been preoccupied with his own thoughts, eyes closed, smiles flickering vaguely across his face.

'Border? I cannot go back to France. I have no passport.'

Coraloni nods blindly. 'As I have said before, you are wearing it.'

ANGELUS

Within a few minutes of standing the interior of the carriage heats up from the sun streaming the black-pitch roof. The windows and doors are open but there is no movement of air.

Minette watches dust fall from the soldiers boots as they move along beside the train, searching under the wheels. Two more sit in shade under a canopy opposite her window, rifles sagged loosely against their knees, cigarettes and idle gossip passing between them. They laugh openly, the sound of it splintered beyond the glass.

Someone is speaking to her. One of the soldiers has entered the carriage and is beside her. 'Sister?'

Padre Coraloni's boot comes down uncompromisingly on her right foot.

'Sister? Are you alright?' The soldier searches her face for an answer. Coraloni's foot presses until the bones shift beneath his boot.

Minette reaches inside her heart for a smile. 'Yes, I am fine. Thank you.'

'Then may I see your passport, Sister?'

'I...'

'Here...' Coraloni opens a saddlebag, riffs through an envelope of papers and draws out a folded sheet. '...these are my orders from the Vatican.'

'Wait a minute...' The soldier folds the sheet into his hand and steps off the carriage.

Through the window, Minette notices the arrogance and ease with which the men un-shoulder their arms. She sees the paper pass from hand to hand until one reaches into his uniform pocket and takes out a small pair of spectacles. Holding it close to his face, he reads it carefully, taps the paper with his fingernails and hands it back.

The soldier returns. 'I am sorry, Padre. The sergeant says that the papers only mention yourself.'

Coraloni sits up straight in the seat, his sheer volume dominating the soldier. 'Tell your sergeant that I am on a mission from the Vatican and that I am at liberty to take whatever I need.'

'My apologies, Padre, but he has already said that it does not include personages other than yourself.'

Coraloni's flesh begins to redden.

His boot tightens unconsciously on Minette's foot.

Closing her eyes, Minette recites her personal catechism, the words of Santa Teresa de Àvila forming a barrier against the blinding light of inflicted pain.

Christ has no body now on earth but yours. No hands, no feet on earth but yours. Yours are the eyes through which he looks compassion on this world. Yours are the feet with which he walks to do good. Yours are the hands through which he blesses all the world. Yours are the hands, yours are the feet, yours are the eyes, you are his body. Christ has no body now on earth but yours...

'Tell him that I cannot be expected to carry all this myself.' Coraloni indicates the bags and the box on Sister Minette's lap. 'Nor could I bring the donkey onto the train. So if he wishes to be a replacement for my animal...'

He gazes out of the window to where the men are relaxed and laughing again, the tips of their cigarettes lighting the shade. '...I think he would be admirable.'

The soldier returns the paper to Coraloni. 'You know I cannot tell him that.'

'Then tell him what you will.' Coraloni presses a small gold coin into his palm.

The soldier studies it, turns it over in his fingers. 'I do not know this money.'

Coraloni smiles, adds another coin. 'You do not need to know it. It is Vatican money.' He takes another from his pocket and hefts it. 'Feel the weight. They are solid.'

The soldier snatches it from mid-air, glances out of the window to find the sergeant watching him from the tin-roof shelter. 'There are four of us.'

Coraloni shuffles in his seat and extracts a leather purse from under his cassock. He throws another coin to the soldier and grins at Minette. 'I hope you realise what you are worth.'

The soldier thumbs the coins across his palm, turning them over and over. He stops at the door of the carriage.

'Where can we spend these?'

Coraloni laughs out loud, waves an arm at the scrub and heat beyond the window.

'Anywhere in the God-given world.'

Beyond the dusted glass the soldiers discuss the coins.

Spun in mid-air they catch stray sunlight, sparking gold against the black crescents of fingernails as they are caught.

The one with the spectacles bites down hard on his, examines it, nods, and waves the driver on. As the train begins to move, they stare unashamedly through the window into Minette's eyes.

As the train gathers speed, wheels swaying consistently beneath them, Minette realises that the padre's boot has lifted. She withdraws her feet to the relative safety of the seat panel.

'Where are you taking me?'

Since crossing the border the padre's mood has gained an elevated ebullience. 'My dear Sister, I am taking you nowhere. You are accompanying me...' His features take a darker turn. '...willingly.'

A shudder passes along the train as the steam regulator is throttled back. Outside the window the land accelerates as the train begins its coast down from the high plateau into a wide, unevenly carved, glacial valley.

The Guard shows his face through the connecting door.

'Carpentras in half an hour.'

'Carpentras?' Minette sits up. 'Why Carpentras?'

Coraloni smiles theatrically. 'Such an inquisitive child.'

6:57 P.M.

The Guard opens the door for Minette and helps her down from the train, placing the box carefully back into her hands. Padre Coraloni steps unaided to the gravel surface.

A man strides through the entrance towards them, arm outstretched, eyes screwed against the glare of the sun.

'You must be Padre Coraloni.'

The padre takes his hand firmly. 'Exactly so, and this is my travelling companion…'

Minette lifts her face into the light. 'Hello, Doctor Beaufort.'

The doctor steps back quickly, studying the face inside the sharp delineation of the coif, then notices the distorted edge of the foot protruding from her habit. '*Minette?*'

'Yes, Doctor.'

'Minette! Indeed! How many years has it been since your mother…'

'Eight.'

The doctor dismisses the implication of lapsed time with a shake of his head. 'It seems far more.'

'For me too.' Minette changes her grip on the box.

The doctor holds out his hands. 'May I take that?'

Coraloni steps brusquely between them. '*Sister* Minette has sole charge of the box whilst it is in our possession.'

The doctor withdraws his hands. 'Look here, I am a busy man. I am not a taxi. It is not by design that I am the only person here who has a motor car. I offered when I was telephoned by the railway only because I was told you are a man of the cloth.'

Coraloni touches the doctor's sleeve, smoothing the nap of the rough wool jacket.

'Forgive me. I did not mean to seem without grace. It is just that my mission is most onerous, and sometimes my sense of responsibility for our Sister gets the better of me.'

'Sister? Hand the good Doctor the box. It would be churlish to refuse such an offer.'

Doctor Beaufort lifts the box carefully from Minette's hands.

'The car is this way...'

Coraloni strides purposefully after him, Minette taking her time over the gravel, feeling it lance into her damaged skin.

OCTOBER 14th.
FRIDAY

7:23 P.M.

The smooth surface of the road gives out onto cobbles at the bottom of a steep hill. Above them, along Chemin du Château, the heart of La Roque seems dominated by the large house.

The doctor shifts the gears and they begin the long winding climb, bounced and jostled in their seats. As they near the chateau, the car swings violently to the right, entering a street of tall, once-respectable houses. They halt without warning.

The doctor turns in his seat. 'Where are you staying tonight?'

Coraloni releases his grip on the strap above the side window, shaking the blood back into his fingers. 'I don't know yet. I suspect a man of the cloth shouldn't have too much difficulty. Is there anywhere you would recommend?'

'There is a café bar on the next street. They have a single room above. If that is not proscribed?'

'I am sure the Sister and I can make ourselves at home anywhere. We are, after all, of the people. It will do us little good to remain aloof.'

'No, no.' The doctor climbs out of the car. 'The Sister stays with us. We have a large house and my wife is acquainted with Minette. My apologies, *Sister* Minette. I am sure they would be glad of the opportunity to talk about the past.'

'I wouldn't hear of you being put to so much trouble, Doctor. I shall take care of her personally. I am under orders to make sure she returns unharmed to the Abbazia.'

The doctor sighs, jangles the keys in his pocket. 'As I said, we do have a large house. Perhaps you too would care to..?'

Coraloni opens the rear door, dragging the bags after him. 'That would indeed be most gracious of you.'

The doctor closes the door the padre has left swinging.

'How long do you intend to stay?'

'Not long.' Coraloni hefts the bags onto his shoulder. 'I will tell you better when I find my contact.'

The doctor ushers them inside. 'Anyone I know?'

'Godenot. Do you know him?'

'Ah, yes. Auguste.'

Coraloni looks around for the most comfortable seat.

'Then you must tell me about him… over dinner.'

The doctor taps the box with a sensitive finger.

'And now I know what is in here.'

The padre eases himself onto an overstuffed chaise, discarding an effortless smile.

'You do?'

OCTOBER 15th.
SATURDAY

7:20 A.M.

Minette sits behind a plate of fresh croissants, dishes of butter and preserves, unwilling to eat. Coraloni strokes a hand across the knotted surface of the table, pushing aside his emptied plate. He waves an expansive arm over the kitchen, gathering in the beamed ceiling, bare brick walls, and the wood-burning stove that occupies an alcove beneath the chimney breast where the doctor's wife skillets a pan of scrambled eggs.

'A little… bucolic? For a doctor, I mean.'

'We…' the doctor steals a glance at Minette. '…arrived here quickly, I'm afraid. We had to take what there was. Since then I have been so busy…' He pushes aside his croissant angrily. '…and we do find it has a certain charm.'

'Yes…'

The doctor finds the deprecation in the priest's smile more irritating than he can express. 'I am sure you will be as quickly on your way once you have spoken to M'sieur Godenot?'

'That may well depend on what he has to say.'

The doctor's wife places a large dish of scrambled egg in front of him. 'Help yourself, Padre.'

The doctor sits back as Coraloni works at loading his plate. 'And if you don't hear what you wish to hear, shall I call at the café while I am on my rounds and ask them about the room?'

'Will there be rooms for two?'

'You will not need two rooms. Minette stays here with us.

I need to oversee the treatment of her foot. It may take some time to heal unless she rests it now.'

'Can you not visit her at the café?'

'She can be attended to properly here. My wife is at home.'

The doctor rescues the remainder of the scrambled egg and offers it to Minette who shakes her head.

He pushes the dish across to her. 'You must eat.'

She pushes it back with a slight smile. Her retreating fingers graze across a ringed knot in the centre of the table.

'Today I am not hungry. Perhaps later I will have a little something. I thank you for your kindness…' She glances across at the priest. '…in the circumstances.'

Colour ascends the doctor's throat until it touches his cheeks. Minette notices that the end of his nose is smaller and less roseate than she remembers.

His words stumble. 'I didn't mean… no… certainly you are most welcome.'

Coraloni, replete with egg and satisfaction, watches this interplay with great interest.

'Well, Doctor, that leaves me with a problem.' He strips a croissant to shovel the last of the egg from his plate. 'When we left the Abbazia I undertook a duty of care toward our Sister. I gave the Madre my word that she should have all she required once we had completed our journey.' He reaches for the butter and the rest of the sundered croissant. 'Under these circumstances I cannot allow her to fall under the care of anyone other than myself. As you can see, I am honour bound to keep her by my side at all costs.'

The doctor pushes away his plate in disgust. 'Have you seen the state of her foot? Do you call that a duty of care? If you weren't a priest I'd…'

Coraloni leans back comfortably in the chair. 'You'd what, Doctor? You'd understand that I am perhaps not such a man of learning as I may appear? That I don't know what constitutes the difference between a dermal abrasion and a medical emergency? In the priesthood, we have only the curative properties of faith on which to rely.'

'Then believe in this…' The doctor rises from the table. '…if her foot is left untreated, you will soon learn the difference.'

He picks up a brown leather bag from the dresser, discomfited by the recognition in Minette's face as she stares at it.

He flicks it open and briefly examines the contents. 'If you are finished, Padre? I am already late for my first patient.'

'A few moments more.' Coraloni reaches for another croissant. 'I will pray for them along the way.'

OCTOBER 15th.
SATURDAY

9:15 A.M.

The box sits unopened on Auguste Godenot's workbench. Doctor Beaufort has driven off, promising to return when he can to collect Padre Coraloni and hoping that his business will keep him occupied until very late.

Auguste, slowly deciphering the letter just handed to him, is perched on the padded stool he usually keeps tucked under the bench.

The Padre is still visibly indignant about the doctor.

Auguste peers at him over wire-framed spectacles, then allows them drop to the end of the coarse string around his neck.

'It says here you have the authority to pay me. With what, may I ask?'

'With these…' Coraloni tosses a Vatican coin to him.

Auguste flips it in his fingers. 'Official business, then.' He places the coin decisively on the bench and taps the box.

'This must be a very special clock. To whom does it belong?'

'Let us say…' Coraloni tucks the paper back into its envelope. '…that your orders come from the highest authority.'

Auguste chuckles loudly. 'Ah. *God's* clock. I did not know he needed one. I thought you priests kept time for him with your bell, book and candle.'

Coraloni places a hand reverently either side of the box. 'If there was anywhere else I could have taken this, I would do so now. Do not be facetious. You know exactly who I mean.'

Auguste laces his fingers over his stomach. 'Why have you brought it to me? Isn't Italy full of watchmakers?'

'Mussolini has them all strutting around in brown shirts. For many reasons you are the only one, but do not think to let this affect your price.'

Auguste laughs again. 'See that pile of old clocks? They are all waiting to be mended. If you are going to haggle with me then please put it down behind the pile. I will let you know when I have time to look at it.'

Coraloni ignores the jibe. 'I know exactly what your price will be.' Auguste's laughter tapers to silence at the look on the padre's face. 'And if you do not open this box, it is a thing you will regret for the rest of your life.'

'But if I shall never know, it will be hard to regret an unopened box.'

'Be sure that before I take it irrevocably away, I shall tell you exactly what is in it.'

Auguste gives the box a half-turn on the bench. The sides are equally plain. Boxwood laths and corner pieces, with a hint of hardwood showing between them from inside.

'But if the box remains unopened, then whatever is in it can be nothing more than a probability. It may exist... it may not. Either way you might as well tell me now.'

'Better than that.' Coraloni picks a stout screwdriver from a rack on the wall. 'Open it.'

Auguste prises carefully at the packing. The wood is dry and splinters under pressure. He draws rough iron nails from the top corners. 'How old did you say this was?'

'Soon, you will tell *me*.'

Auguste reaches in to lift out a box some twelve inches tall and perhaps seven on a side, noticing a small hole drilled in the centre of one.

'This is olive.' His fingers caress the surface of the timber. 'See where the oil has preserved the grain.' He turns it around. 'This was selected. No knots, see? It must have been for someone important. Wood of this quality is impossible to find today.'

His fingers trace the edges of the timber. Beneath his touch, a section of the grain sinks almost imperceptibly. One side springs open as a door. Auguste holds the box under the light to peer in.

He lifts a loupe to his eye and peers more closely, recognising the configuration of the dials, the icons and graphics of the solar system and the stars beyond.

He rummages at the bottom of a pile of papers beside the boiler.

Leafing through the crumpled pages of a magazine, he rips one from it and holds it into the light. He peers again inside the box. 'I do not believe what I am seeing. Is this a replica of the mechanism that Valerio Stais found? Is this real?'

Coraloni is breathing hard beside him, straining to see over Auguste's shoulder into the finely wrought mechanism.

'Believe me. This is not a replica.'

'This must be a replica. The one Stais identified was little more than calcified bronze from the bottom of the Aegean. Why don't you take it to the man who made it? He is far better than I.'

Coraloni places a hand on his shoulder. 'But you are alive, Auguste. He has been dead for over two thousand years.'

'I have seen many drawings of this, what clockmaker hasn't, but look...' He shakes the magazine page before Coraloni's eyes. 'In the picture it is little more than a shapeless lump of bronze. It is impossible to see exactly how it would have worked. Where did you get this?'

'You realise...' Coraloni pushes Auguste aside to peer into the mechanism himself, admiring the bronze intricacy of gears and dials. '...that you are subject to secrecy under the threat of eternal ex-communication?'

'I never dreamed that I should see a working Antikythera Device.'

'Ah.' Coraloni steps away from the bench to allow Auguste another chance to examine the mechanism. 'There you find our problem.'

Auguste tips the box at a slight angle. Around the dial the major stars are represented by tiny jewels of differing colours. The elements of the zodiac with their relevant constellations are inscribed into the bronze. Surrounding the outer rim, an annulus carries what can only be the thirteen lunar months of the year described in an ancient Cyrillic script. The moon tracks its phases around a shallow inner ring while inside it, a rotating plate in the centre is engraved with an iconic fiery sun.

Auguste pushes the annulus tenderly with a fingertip. The device appears to be locked. 'Do you understand what this does?'

'Yes...' the padre casts around for a comfortable seat and finds none. '...and apart from anything else it does, it is a machine devised by an heretic. So beware of what it may tell you.'

'He was also a genius. I am not sure that I can emulate his touch.'

'My Uncle is certain that you can. That is why I am here.'

Auguste screws the loupe firmly into the socket of his right eye. 'You realise that I will have to take it apart?' He holds the box so daylight penetrates deep inside.

Coraloni stays his hand. 'We have not yet fixed your price.'

Auguste puts the box and loupe down on the bench.

'You have paid it. I never thought to see such a thing. There is much I can learn here.' He reaches into a drawer and takes out a chamois leather tool roll. 'May I?'

'You may.'

Auguste selects a fine screwdriver and inserts it by turn into the four holes in the base. Slowly, a crack appears where the sides fit to it. He sits the device on the bench and lifts the case away. As he puts it down, he notices a dark smear on his fingers.

He holds them to his nose. 'Pitch?'

He examines the base. There are three dark areas where the sides have been fitted.

He screws the loupe back into his eye. 'This wasn't put there to seal the case. It seems to have seeped in from somewhere, but the carpenter...' He runs his fingers along the bottom edges of the case. '...was a craftsman. For this to happen it must have been under considerable pressure.'

Coraloni picks up the empty case. 'Would forty three metres of seawater do it?'

Auguste does the rough calculation in his head. 'Easily, but this would never survive the sea without becoming a shapeless lump of metal like the one in the picture. Where was it found?'

'In exactly the same place.'

Auguste unrolls a velvet cloth beside the device. He puts the four hand-threaded bronze screws carefully in place on the soft black nap. 'Then why wasn't this one shown? It would have saved Stais a lot of argument and ridicule.'

'The scientific community thrives on argument and ridicule. While scientists are tearing themselves apart they are leaving Madre Church alone.'

Auguste pours himself the last of the coffee. 'You would suppress ingenuity such as this just to perpetuate your own belief?'

'Why not? We have been doing it for centuries. Ask Copernicus and Galileo.'

Auguste returns his attention to the device. 'To what end?'

Coraloni opens his arms theatrically. 'To the preservation of The Glory of God. What else?'

'To the perpetuation of your stipend?'

'That too.'

Coraloni looks around the workshop, under the benches, behind stacked timber.

Auguste watches him, a dark humour playing around the edges of a smile. 'What are you looking for?'

'A seat. Do you expect me to stand all day?'

'No. I expect you to go. I work alone.'

'I cannot leave the machine with you unattended.'

'Why?' Auguste screws the loupe into his eye and picks up the device. 'What am I going to do? Stop it working? You have already done that.'

'You don't understand.'

'Then perhaps you had better enlighten me.'

'The device does not exist.'

'Then there is no cause for alarm, is there?'

'Officially, I mean.'

Auguste points to a large sack of finely sawn kindling for the boiler.

Coraloni drags it nearer the bench and shuffles down upon it. 'You have to remember that this was 1900. Sponge divers were the best they had and, as good as they were… there were so many dangers that…'

Auguste waves the magazine page at him in irritation. 'I have read the story. Get to the point.'

'The point is, most of the things recovered were worthless… spoiled amphorae full of seawater, broken oil jars, statues, jewellery…'

'Doesn't sound worthless to me.'

'Museums are filled with it. Who wants more?'

Auguste waits impatiently while Coraloni fidgets with the stuffing of the sack beneath him.

'One of the injured divers was cousin to a German priest. He could tell from the cargo that these were spoils of war en route to Rome. This priest persuaded the diver to, shall we say. 'set aside' a little something from the wreck. What this diver set aside was an unusual sealed amphora in perfect condition. They returned for it after the dive was declared complete.'

The boiler in the corner sets up a loud rattle. The valve shrieks live steam out through the vent in the wall. Auguste nudges the priest aside to close the damper under the fire-grate.

'You seem extraordinarily well informed.'

'I should be. The priest was my uncle. He took the amphora to Rome and had it cleaned. The surface still had most of its glaze and there were no discernible cracks. Under the glaze was a representation of the night sky, the prominent stars linked by lines of silver, describing signs of the zodiac that we still recognise today, except that there were thirteen.'

'And the thirteenth?'

'Ophiuchus, evidently.'

'It must have been impressive.'

'Even so, the amphora was left untouched for some time. After the Great War it was rediscovered by a priest who was also a scholar of antiquities.'

Auguste laughs. 'You harbour scientists?'

Coraloni smiles in return. "Know thine enemy'. The neck of this amphora was abnormally wide for such a vessel. The scholar noticed that the seal was in perfect condition and began to speculate as to what was behind it. He reasoned that whatever was in the jar could be responsible for the whole being in such good condition and persuaded my uncle to allow him to open it.'

'And found this.' Auguste picks up the device from the bench. 'But that doesn't explain its remarkable condition.'

'It has been cleaned, as I said.'

'But even that does not explain…'

'The pitch?'

'Ah.'

'When the amphora was opened, it was filled to the brim with black pitch. This was how it had resisted the water pressure for two centuries. In disappointment, and in a moment of great lack of imagination, they resealed the top and it was put back into storage.

My uncle, by then *Cardinal* Ullman, began to wonder why the ancient Greeks should bother to fill an obviously valuable amphora with pitch. Unwilling to see his present to The Pope devalued so dramatically, he came upon the idea of boiling it to see if the pitch would pour out, revealing something, if indeed anything, of value.'

'What if it had been empty?'

Coraloni touches the wooden case beside him on the bench with the tip of a finger. It comes away with a dark smudge rubbed into the whorls of his skin. 'He would have found something. My uncle is not without means.'

'What happened to the scientist?'

'Scientists come and go… only Faith remains.'

Auguste picks up the device, moving it defensively out of Coraloni's reach. 'No wonder he is now a Cardinal.'

'He was a Cardinal before this. As I said, he is not without means.'

'All the same, it cannot have done his position in the Church any harm.'

'On the contrary, if you allow this secret to get out, two

things will follow very quickly. One… my uncle and I will be ex-communicated.'

'For repairing the Pope's own device?'

'The Holy Father does not yet know that it exists.'

'And the second thing?'

'I will return and kill you.'

9:31 A.M.

Mme Beaufort clears the breakfast things to wipe the table. Minette takes the cloth from her hand. 'I'll do that.'

The doctor's wife snatches it back. 'No, you must rest your foot.'

'I will be alright if…'

'No.'

Mme Beaufort scrubs the table top, paying particular attention to the place where the padre has stained the bare wood with scrambled egg. 'You are now my responsibility.'

Minette detects an undertone in her voice.

'Does that trouble you? Why did you not say while the doctor was here?'

Mme Beaufort rinses the cloth in a bowl of hot water, displacing pots and dishes, pushing at a stray lock of dyed black hair with the back of a hand. 'Because you and your mother have always been my responsibility.'

'My mother?'

Mme Beaufort glances around the sparse room with barely concealed disgust. 'Yes… your mother. Why do you think we are stuck here?'

'I don't know. I was Novitiate at the time of her death. I was allowed home for her funeral but more than that I do not know, except…'

'Except what?'

'Except that I was the only one there besides the priest… and when I tried to give away her things I found that no-one would talk to me. I had to leave them outside the church.

No-one from the village would take them.'

'I am not surprised. Most people are ill at ease with the leftovers of a suicide.'

Minette flinches visibly. 'Suicide?'

'You didn't know?'

'How could I? I was at the Abbazia.'

Mme Beaufort sits beside her at the table.

'You really didn't know?'

Minette rests her eyes for a moment.

Behind them appears a memory of the closed mouths of villagers who had known her since birth, the averted gaze, the reticence of the priest, the plot in a far corner of the cemetery away from the chapel entrance.

'I should have known. The letter I received said only that she had died after a sudden illness.'

'Was there nothing with it? No letter from your mother?'

'Nothing.'

'Then perhaps your mother left only one letter. We thought she may have sent a second to you at the Abbazia.'

'I received nothing other than the note from the priest telling me of her death. Was this letter for me?'

'I wish it had been.' Mme Beaufort shifts uneasily within the memory. 'The letter was found on the table beside her. The police took it with them. It was only later that we were told what it contained when they came to arrest Philippe.'

'I know about you and my mother.'

Mme Beaufort snaps back into an increasingly uncomfortable present. 'How?'

'I listened. I was not meant to.'

'What did you hear about Philippe?'

Minette decides to allow a little discretion. 'They were old enemies.'

Mme Beaufort looks away, unable to meet her eyes. 'That was not always the case.'

'People change.'

Mme Beaufort studies the newly appearing veins in her hands, the redness surrounding her knuckles, the coarse skin in the worn surfaces of her palms.

'Look at me. I am forty three years old. Philippe is fifty two. We have no children… and it is only children that bring change…' She glares around the room again, at the bare walls, the neatly stacked books, the precision of tins and labels on the shelves, at the whole implacable ambience of the house. '…and for now I see only brick walls. All I have carried for the last twenty five years is a growing anger, when I should have been overflowing with…'

'I am sorry for the things my mother has done.'

'Your mother was not the most accomplished abortionist in the world. Not even in the district. But it is not your fault. It is ours. Myself, your mother, Philippe… we were all to blame and since your mother died Philippe and I wake only with each other in the mornings.'

Minette reaches across. 'Perhaps it is time to put down the anger, for your own sake.'

'It is not that kind of anger… that would be too easy. It is the desperation that is hard to express… perhaps your being here will help me release it. There are things…'

Mme Beaufort stares into the dark grain of the tabletop between them, knowing they both recognise the past that has leached into the heart of the wood.

'There are things I need to say that can only be said to you.' Her face tilts suddenly upwards in a half smile. 'I never thought that we would find you again.'

'You knew where I was. I am here now… and I need to know how my *maman* died.'

The colour drains from Mme Beaufort's skin. Her mouth is drawn, the eyes unforgiving of herself. 'There was a hook above the table…'

Minette closes her eyes to shield herself from the vision, but the darkness reinforces the memory of shadows drawn by the lamp.

'I understand the how… but not the *why.*'

'Because of you.'

'How could I have hurt her enough to do this?'

From a homemade cupboard built under the sink to cover the drains, Mme Beaufort lifts out a wine bottle. The cork is loose and half-entered.

She picks up two glasses from the drainer. 'I didn't say it was your fault.' She hefts the bottle between them.

Minette shakes her head. 'I am not allowed.'

Mme Beaufort pours the glass half full of thick red local wine. 'Then when you next speak to Him, thank God that *I* am.' She wraps both hands around the glass protectively, emptying it in one swallow. 'How do you think it feels to know the wrong woman is swinging from a lamp hook?'

She tips the bottle but nothing comes out. 'Philippe found the last one. That was all I had.'

'I think it might be better if you had no more.'

'I can't do this on my own. I wish Philippe would come home. Why did he leave me alone with you?'

'I mean you no harm.' Minette reaches out to touch the hand that is firmly clasped to an empty glass. Mme Beaufort flinches away dramatically.

Minette withdraws her hand. 'I didn't mean to…'

'You can't help it. Everything you are brings me pain.'

Minette rises from the chair.

'When the Doctor returns he can find me a room over the café. I can make my own way back to the Abbazia.'

'No.' Mme Beaufort grips her by the wrist, panic rising in her grey-blue eyes. 'I cannot turn you away a second time.'

Minette sees relief drain away the pain from Mme Beaufort's features.

A faint smile quivers about her lips as she reaches across the table to take Minette's hands. 'There… I said it.'

Minette retreats into the chair, bemused.

'I don't understand. What have you said?'

'That I cannot turn you away again.'

Through her new understanding of her mother's death, Minette searches for the source of this woman's charity.

'I am grateful, but it may be better if I…'

'You still don't understand.' Mme Beaufort reaches out quickly, snatching Minette's hand before she can withdraw. 'You must listen to me. If Philippe were here…'

'I will come back when he returns. If you let me…'

'No. Not this time. I will not let you go.'

'Mme Beaufort, have you ever prayed to God?'

'Every day for twenty five years.'

'Then perhaps it might help if we prayed together.'

'I have nothing left to pray for.'

'Then perhaps I can pray for you.'

Mme Beaufort dashes her hands away. '*God forbid* you should pray for me. I do not deserve it. Pray for yourself. There is something else I have to tell you. Your mother is not dead.'

Minette stares blankly. 'You said…'

'What I should have said is that the woman you *knew* as your mother is dead.'

Minette feels a chill course its way through her. 'I heard my mother tell the doctor…'

'Your mother would have said anything to hurt Philippe.'

'I know she thought him misguided. Too…'

'She was in love with him, and in great pain for that.'

Minette eases away from the fingers that search for hers.

'Does the Doctor know?'

'Since we got the letter.'

Mme Beaufort turns Minette in the chair and lifts the

bandaged foot into her lap.

'Philippe is still in shock. The letter from your mother destroyed us. He wouldn't look at me for months. He hasn't touched me since it arrived.'

'Why did you not tell him before?'

'How could I? After you were born it was so complicated. With Philippe at college in Milan I would have died had it not been for your mother's care. As it was, your birth left me barren. It took me three years to confess to him and even then I told him a lie. I said I had miscarried. By that time you were accepted as your mother's child and I... well... I hoped that we could begin again. By the time I began to realise that it was not going to happen, it was far too late for me to turn back.'

Minette tugs at the hem of her habit to expose the rigid ankle, the shin bone where it begins its slow half-spiral.

'Why did he not say anything when I arrived? Does he find me unacceptable?'

'You are his dearest wish, but he is still trying to deal with the fact that his wife is a liar. He doesn't know what to do with that knowledge any more than I did. Look at your dressing. You are bleeding again. Here... be still.'

Her hands unroll the last of the stained bandage. The skin beneath is broken and blistered as if the foot has been dragged the length of the country.

'Whatever did he do to you? Why would he subject you to this? It is inhuman.'

'This is nothing. This will heal.' Minette twists her foot to observe the injury better. 'I thought by now the skin would be harder. There are other things that I dare not think about yet.'

'What other things?'

'I will tell you better in another week or two.'

'A week? No. You can't mean... Philippe will kill him!

And you a Sister! What kind of a priest…?'

'There are things at work here that I don't understand. Please say nothing to the doctor.'

Minette sees the look on Mme Beaufort's face, the rejection of yet another lie.

'Not yet, at least. Give me that.'

Mme Beaufort holds Minette's foot between her hands.

'Alright.' Her hand strokes Minette's ankle, pushing back the hem of her habit. 'Look how slender your legs are. You must eat more, get your strength back.'

'You know better than I that strength only comes from within… and sometimes the only things worth eating are words too hastily spoken.'

'Do you know how bitter the taste of a lie is?'

Minette lifts her foot to allow the last of the bandage to be peeled away.

'It seems I have tasted little else all my life.'

OCTOBER 15th.
SATURDAY

10:40 A.M.

Auguste finds his attention returning to a small sleeved cog that he has been unable to put down. Halfway in, a ridge casts the faintest of distortions. He pours his coffee back into the pot and sweeps clear the area around his lathe.

He trims the ends of a turned, slender brass rod until it slides inside the tube. When it hits the annular ridge in the centre it stops. He continues to push until suddenly it slides the whole way through. As it slides, the cog on the shaft is freed to rotate. He turns it with the tip of a finger and finds that it also is now free to slide along the shaft in either direction. As he slips it from the end, six serrated brass circlips, all of which would fit simultaneously onto the nail of his thumb, drop out of the centre. He screws the loupe into his eye.

He doesn't look up at the knock on the door.

'I haven't had time to study it properly yet.'

The knock is repeated. He opens the door impatiently.

'Mme Beaufort? I was expecting someone else. I thought maybe your husband…'

'Philippe? He won't be back for a while.'

'Come in. I see you have brought company.'

'This is Sister Minette.'

Auguste notes the heavily bandaged foot encased in one of the doctor's old slippers.

'Come in. Sit down… please.' He drags up the stool from the bench and places it near the boiler. 'Here.' He moves to help her onto the stool, then stops to look at his hands in bemusement. 'I'm sorry Sister, I wasn't thinking.'

'M'sieur Godenot, we have come to ask about the padre's clock.'

'A clock? A padre?'

'Auguste, this is important to us. the Sister has carried this clock all the way from Italy. We want to know why.'

'Where is the padre? Is he with you?'

Auguste can hear the shudder in Mme Beaufort's reply.

'He says he is visiting a colleague, the local priest at St. Benedict beyond the vineyards. If that is the truth, he will not be back for at least another two hours.'

Auguste lifts the cloth covering the many pieces of bronze scattered across the bench.

Minette takes a sharp breath. 'So many parts. How did they all fit into the box?'

'That remains to be seen.' Auguste picks up the piece of black velvet with the circlips and nests it into his palm. The rings fall across each other, each as fine as hair, and each shaped differently from its neighbour.

'I seem to solve one paradox only to fall into another. I cannot work out how these fit into the space reserved for what seems to be just one ring.'

'Can I see?'

'Your eyes are probably better than mine, Sister. Just don't...' he indicates the dust-strewn floor of the workshop. 'I may never find them again.'

Minette brushes the circlips lightly with a fingertip, separating out each one. 'I think I have it. Show me where they came from.'

Under the urging of a fingertip the bright rings assemble in order, their various serrations engaging into one whole circle. She inserts the completed circlip into the hollow centre of the cog. With the end of the brass rod she pushes it along until it clicks into place.

'Pass me the shaft.' She examines it carefully. 'Look here. This end has a slight bevel. Do you see it?'

Auguste holds it into the light. 'No.'

'Have you thought of taking an apprentice?'

'My eyes are still good. I just make bigger clocks.' He tries to rotate the cog. 'See… it is now locked firmly into place. If I fit it back together like this then the device remains locked in whatever position you assemble it.'

'What happens if you leave out the part of the circlip that locks it to the shaft?'

Auguste shrugs. 'The device will spin freely and all linkage between the different indicators will be lost. It will appear to work but is probably useless. There is something I am missing.'

Minette draws her habit tightly around her, glancing at the door where at some point the padre may appear.

'Perhaps the thing you are missing, really *is* missing.'

'How do you mean?'

'This could be an incomplete device.'

'Then probably we will never know.'

'M'sieur Godenot…' Minette catches and holds his gaze for a long second. '…there is too much intelligence behind those eyes of yours to let this thing go undiscovered… and far too much experience.'

'Ego never knows anything, Sister… it just *thinks* it does.'

'Then look to your hands.'

Auguste turns them palm up on the bench beside the device. Their skin is darkly ingrained with the dust of brass. As he turns them, small particles reflect the light.

'I see only Time…' He chuckles. '…and so much of it.'

'Please forgive me, M'sieur…' Minette reaches up to take the pencil from behind his ear. '…I am not usually this familiar.'

Auguste smiles in the unaccustomed warmth from her

hand.

Minette lays the pencil on the black velvet cloth next to the cylinder they had used to disengage the gearing. It is thicker in diameter than the cylinder and its sides have been grooved in an asymmetrical pattern. 'What happened to your pencil?'

'I tried it first in the hole… before I made the cylinder.'

'And what happened?'

'It locked the gearing again.'

'But in what pattern?'

'Sister… I do not remember. This again is a consequence of age.'

Minette picks up the pencil and the cylinder, placing one in each of his opened palms. His fingers close around them.

'Now, Auguste… what do your hands say?'

Auguste holds them gently, experiencing the way the metal of the cylinder retains the heat of her touch. He takes a loupe from his shirt pocket and inserts it into his right eye.

'They say you should now leave.'

'Auguste?'

'Yes, Sister?'

'Please don't let Padre Coraloni find the key.'

'What key would that be?'

'The one you are about to make.'

'Don't worry, Sister. I hold a key to the one place in the village that Devil's Spawn would never think to look.'

OCTOBER 15th.
SATURDAY

10:43 A.M.

'Good morning, Padre. What can I get you?'

Albert Dernot draws a chair to a table by the café window.

'Please sit here. The light in the square at this time of the day is quite free.'

'Only the light?'

'This is a small town.'

Coraloni takes the proffered chair and arranges his cassock to cover the draught from the ill-fitting door.

'Then, like anything else of stature, the light will be merely transient… and it does your business little harm for the clergy to be seen as a patron.'

'I assure you the thought never crossed my mind… more than once. What can I get you?'

'Is your coffee thick, black, strong and sweet?'

'As always.'

'Then I will take tea.'

Albert Dernot shuffles his swollen ankles up to the counter, and shouts through into the kitchen.

'Bruno! Ask your mother where she has hidden the tea.'

Padre Coraloni stares out of the café window, absorbed for a moment by spouting shafts of water that coruscate into a large dish surrounding the fountain. At the far side of the *place,* the towers of the chateau loom visibly through the luxuriant branches of a single horse-chestnut tree. Above the line of his eye is a reflection of the clock over the counter, the second hand peeling away the moments from the lie he has constructed to distance himself from the open hostility of the doctor's wife.

He sits up as Minette emerges from the far corner of the square. Her sudden presence demands his attention. Relying heavily on Mme Beaufort's arm, she takes the next exit into the small street that winds to the chateau.

Coraloni knows they will branch off to the right before they get there, finding the narrow lane that runs to the door of the doctor's house.

Minette's foot has been freshly bandaged and is encased in an over-large slipper and, from the direction they have emerged, they could only have been to Auguste's workshop.

He scatters a few coins on the table before he leaves.

OCTOBER 15th.
SATURDAY

10:55 A.M.

Auguste hears someone try the handle on the workshop door, but he has locked it securely since the women left. It is followed by a knock that he ignores until he hears the voice of Padre Coraloni.

'Godenot. I know you are in there. Open the door.'

Auguste quickly rolls up the sheets of cartridge paper he had pinned out, sliding them into the long-case clock at the end of the bench.

'Godenot!'

'For Heaven's sake, what do you think this is? A *boulangerie*? You are disturbing an artist at work.'

He slides back the bolt and Coraloni barges in.

'What did *they* want?'

Auguste returns to his stool beside the bench. '*They*?'

'You know who I mean... the doctor's wife and that fool of a nun.'

Auguste reaches into a drawer for a paper parcel and throws it across the room. 'They brought me this.'

The parcel rattles as the priest catches it. 'What is it?'

'Painkillers... along with a little something to improve my demeanour. Perhaps you should try some.'

'I have never felt better in my life... and what is that?'

He points to a complex array of serrated wheels spread across the bench.

'That is your device...'

'And what have you discovered?'

Auguste covers the pieces with a clean cloth.

'Nothing yet, except that my sense of smell is beginning to deteriorate. I used to be able to detect unction at fifty paces.'

'The mechanism…'

'Only that it is a paradox. I am surprised that as a believer you couldn't solve it yourself. A little faith here, a touch of self-delusion there…'

'About you remembering how it fits back together?'

Auguste snorts derisively. 'Did it work when you brought it? No. Will it work when I have studied it? Maybe. That is an improvement in the odds, no?'

'I did not travel a hundred miles to participate in a game of chance.'

'Then you are *certain* there is a God?'

'Of course. Or I would not have become a priest.'

Coraloni throws the parcel of pills on the floor beside the boiler. Auguste bends to retrieve it.

'Then also be certain that your sins will find you out.'

'On the matter of sins… while I am here, Godenot… is there anything you would like to confess?'

'If it helps to preserve my soul, Padre, I confess I will be glad to see the back of you.'

Auguste returns his attention to the device, studying the stripped frame through all angles. 'Is this all that was in the amphora?'

'All that you need to know.'

Auguste returns the device to the bench. 'So… what else?'

Coraloni shrugs. 'Little of importance. A silver coin, a piece of rag… a broken comb.'

Auguste slides the screwdriver back into the tool roll and gets up to attend to the boiler. 'Would you mind…?'

'As I said, it is of little importance to the working of the device.'

'No… you are sat on the firewood. I know it is a position the church favours for those who dispute its philosophy but for now I need some for the boiler.'

He opens the front of a case clock at the end of the bench and places the cloth holding the device and its box inside. 'It will be safe there.'

'No!' Coraloni leaps from the sack. 'You must do it now!'

'I cannot do it now. I need to absorb what I have seen.'

'Then it must be kept safer than this. I must stay with it.'

'There is nowhere safer than this and with you here I cannot work.'

'What if your customer returns for the clock?'

Auguste rummages in the sack for fresh kindling.

'That may be difficult. First they would have to climb vertically through six feet of earth.'

Shavings spit and crack as the heat from the glowing ash bursts them into flame. Auguste stands up straight to find the padre towering over him. He pushes him away with a single finger to the chest. 'I must think.'

'I have no time for your thinking. I have to know why the machine cannot be reset.'

'I need to understand it first. If I just take it apart and put it back together then it will still be the same. I have to understand why the maker set it the way he did. Anything you can tell me now may help.'

'Why must I sit on this sack?'

'Because it is the only other seat in here. My workshop is filled with memories, not chairs.'

'Fetch me a memory then, so I may wait in comfort.'

Auguste leans back against the bench and closes his eyes.

'I have no memories that would bear the weight of your hypocrisy.'

'How fragile is the world of the Godless.'

Coraloni brushes dust from the bench with a hand and leans an elbow.

'If it is of any assistance, the silver coin in the amphora bears a date. The Julian Calendar translates it as 86BC.'

'And what was the original date? Do you have the coin? Show me. Is it Greek or Roman?'

'No, I don't have the coin. As to its origin I am not sure, but evidently it was struck in an important astronomical time. My sources tell me that five conjunctions of planets in four zodiacal signs occurred in that year, making it a perfect time to set an astronomical clock. But we may also assume that it was a warning for someone.'

'So why hide the thing?'

'Are you familiar with the term 'Judicial Astrology'?'

'Should I be?'

Coraloni indicates the boiler. 'If you had been involved at any time during the Middle Ages, you would have joined your kindling.'

'Ah! We are back to the Church's favourite occupation.'

'With so much wealth and power at stake, you would have done the same.'

'Alas, I have never…'

'But now you have.' Coraloni unrolls the rest of the tools for Auguste 'With these, you may turn not only a clock, but perhaps history.'

Auguste slips from the stool and lifts down his jacket.

'Where are you going?'

Auguste shrugs his arms into the sleeves. 'Home.'

'But the device?'

'Has waited since 86BC…' Auguste ushers Coraloni towards the door. '…but *I* can have it ready by Thursday.'

OCTOBER 18th.
TUESDAY

9:53 P.M.

'Ullman?'

'This is *Cardinal* Ullman…'

The telephone fits uncomfortably against his ear. The earpiece is cold and his fleshy lobe rejects its smooth hardness, as his ego rejects the imperative tone of voice passing through it. '…and I am waiting.'

The telephone is silent for a moment, except for the distant hiss of electrons traversing miles of undulating wire. Another voice answers.

'*Ullman?*'

'Cardin…'

'*Ullman! Where is it?*'

Slowly, his unwilling brain recognises the lack of patience that only undisputed power brings.

'Signor Mussolini! I hope you are…'

'Shut up and listen, Ullman. Your nephew did not appear as arranged. My man has waited now in Milan for six days. I have no patience left for this charade. I have a Conference to attend and an agreement to sign tomorrow and you are playing cups with the ace up my sleeve.'

'Your Greatness, there has been a short delay. I assure you…'

'I assure *you*, Ullman, that you and your nephew can count yourselves amongst the Saints unless the package is delivered to me by tomorrow morning. I did not promise to deliver to the Pope ninety million dollars so I could be treated this way by the *Mafia di Dio.*'

'Signor Mussolini, I have no involvement in the Lateran Agreement and I ask you to remember that we are not dealing with the Vatican directly here. We are merely acting in its best interests.'

There comes the loud clatter of a misplaced telephone. As the hiss of electrons continues, Ullman slowly realises that he is talking to himself. He stops to listen to the distant voices on the line...

'Claretta... Why does the world send me such idiots as this priest?'

'Cardinal... Benito.'

'Cardinal... Priest... Pope! They're all idiots. Can't see beyond the veil of superstition...'

'But Benito, they're just...'

'...and if they can't see that, they make it up.'

'...they're just trying to make a living, Benito. Don't you know that?'

'How? By perpetrating the world's biggest hoax?'

'Your own friend, Herr Hitler, he says that if you are going to tell a lie, make it a big one.'

'That's good, coming from him.'

'It's in his book.'

'Then it must be true, eh? And these 'priests'? What do they do? They promise you Eternal Life and when you're old enough to need it they let you die and then bury the evidence of their failure...'

'Benito...'

'And this... this... telephone... A bell is rung when people call their servants...'

'Benito... come to bed... now! Or must I buy a bell?'

OCTOBER 24th.
FRIDAY

TERCE

Ullman (Cardinale)
Stato della Città del Vaticano
Sancta Sedes
Italia

18th. October 1938

Dear Madre Honoire,

It is a matter of little consequence, I understand, but please forgive my writing to you with this simple request. I am enquiring after my nephew, Padre Coraloni, who I hope has been serving well your needs.

I have written to him myself within the last two weeks, but I have had no reply to my letter. Indeed, I had written to set up an appointment of some importance for him in Milan. An appointment, I was informed last night by the use of the telephone, he never attended. If his ministration to your flock is keeping him so well occupied that he has had no time to write, then I beg of you, Dear Sister, to allow him a moment to communicate his attentions directly to myself.

Yours,

Ullmann (C)

Honoire studies the broken seal on the reverse, returns the single page along its folds and presses it back into the envelope.

Satan's hands are all over this and there is nothing with which she can stop the spinning that engulfs her each time she closes her eyes.

Many days have passed since the padre disappeared, taking Sister Minette into this apparent abyss along with him.

All that binds her to the problem now is hope. Within her drawer are several sheets of writing paper, a small bottle of black ink, an unused envelope waiting for her Madre's seal, and a skeletal pen…

Honoire (Matre)
Abbazia di Novalesa
Alta Val Susa
Piedmont
Italia

October 25th. 1938

Your Eminence,

It is a source of great regret that I have little idea of the whereabouts of your nephew, Padre Coraloni. Since he took the position created by the untimely death of Padre Mension he has kept little counsel with myself though I am sure that he has discharged his duties in a satisfactory manner, as my sisters have dared little by way of complaint.

A short time ago, Padre Coraloni received a letter delivered by hand at the appellants gate. I know not from whence this letter came. I do know, however, that it is not the letter to which you refer, for I have that beside me unopened.

In a most imperative manner, the padre demanded that we provide transport to the station for himself and the box you left in my care. He also insisted that we allow one of our Sisters to guide him and return the transport provided. We had little choice but to agree with this. It grieves me to report that since that day, neither Padre Coraloni nor our Sister have returned.

On the second day of absence, I asked that the local police attend us at the Abbazia. They found the transport that we provided at the local coaching house. It has subsequently been returned to us in good condition.

The police returned to us shortly thereafter to report that Padre Coraloni and Sister Minette boarded a train together scant hours after their arrival in town. The Station Master reports that Sister Minette appeared willing to travel and indeed seemed anxious that the train arrive on time. She accepted the assurances of the priest and thereafter waited patiently until it arrived.

The padre bought tickets to a place by the name of 'Carpentras', one hundred and twenty miles across the border into France.

According to the police these were single tickets and, from this, I was forced to speculate that they had little intention of returning in the near future. When Sister Mirais detailed the Novices to clean his room they found he had taken with him all of his belongings, meagre though they were, and I have to accept that as confirmation of my earlier suspicions.

We are as concerned for the well-being of our Sister as you so obviously are re that of your nephew.

We would welcome any assistance or information that you can provide in this respect,

May God continue to guide you,

Honoire

Her seal breaks the light of the candle. The flame flutters around it in mockery of her heart. This is not the direction from which she would have sought help but she has nowhere else to turn.

She slides the ink and pen away, closing the drawer. From the niche window above her the light streams down to the remaining paper on her desk… empty and waiting for words she does not have. She tucks the letter into the sleeve of her habit and opens the door.

The cloisters… arcing like the sundered ribs of the empty carcass of her hope… suck her soul into the vacuum of the courtyard. Her Sisters are all there… observing their hour of silence and contemplation… yet it feels empty.

Minette had been such a reverberation through her spirit that those now left around her seem formless… a mingling fluid of perpetual devotion amongst the fingers of doubt lately penetrating her thoughts.

A *tocsin* bell has rung persistently in her head and heart since the letter arrived from Cardinal Ullman. Its echo is driving her to the edge of insanity and shows little sign of waning.

A prayed-for early November mist would be welcome right now.

She wraps her fingers around the edge of the well and casts a glance into the empty depths… the bucket is wound clear and tight up to the handle… all she has to do is let go…

She turns her face to question the unending blue of the sky. Then… from the clearest of moments… through the held breath of no wind… the first drops of autumn rain reach down to touch her skin.

OCTOBER 25th.
MONDAY

8:44 A.M.

'I think we should give it more time… another month at least.'

'Philippe… we cannot leave it. You know better than I this thing will never go away.'

'I will ask at the Abbazia. At least I know it will be *honest* advice…'

'How can you say that while the Devil Incarnate is under your own roof?'

'He will answer for the things he has done.'

Mme Beaufort's hands shake as she gathers the coffee pot and cups. 'And who shall ask the question? You?'

'There are higher authorities.'

'And what of Minette's life then? It will fill the newspapers for weeks. Do you want to find her only to lose her to the clatter of a press?'

'I was thinking of a higher authority still…'

'Oh… then that's alright… let's make a pact. I shall not provide for you until we hear the Judgement from God. What would you prefer I did with your remains after I have starved you to death?'

'Allow me time to think.'

'And while you are thinking, this Devil's issue is growing inside your daughter and the demon that put it there still draws breath. How can you call yourself a man and still…?'

The doctor turns away from his wife. A place inside him stirs sluggishly with the remnants of lies he has discovered, clouding his sense of belief.

'I cannot see the truth through all of this.'

'The truth?' His wife takes him by the shoulder to spin him around. 'Your daughter is violated and you look for truth?'

'All my life I have searched for truth. However unpalatable disease may be it exists as a true state... a part of life.'

'That no-one but you wants to touch. Disease is a lie in the body of truth.'

'If that were true then a liar must carry the disease. So how do I cure *you*?'

'You are the surgeon. My heart is open to your hands. All it asks is that you cure your daughter first.'

'She is not ill.'

'No... but she has been invaded by a lie... and by your own conclusion... a lie carries the disease.'

'This is not a disease. Minette has been invaded by Life.'

'Then Life itself is a lie.'

OCTOBER 27th.
THURSDAY

PRE-NONE

'Madre?'

Honoire fights not to return from her brief reverie. As the days have passed with no further sign of Minette, her thoughts have turned to the growing possibility that she will not be easily found.

The police are still seeking permission to travel into France, a remit made difficult by the shadow of conflict spreading across Europe from the political upheaval of Fascist Spain. Once they obtain that permission, Honoire believes in her heart that the mystery will be resolved but, until that time, she has no need to be reminded.

'Madre? Are you alright?'

'Yes. I'm alright. I was just thinking… what is it?'

'You have a visitor.'

'Is it the police? Have they..?'

'No, Madre. It is not the police. It is just a man. He came by motor car. He seems well dressed and mannered but he would not give his name. He will speak only to yourself.'

'Is he young or old?'

'Much as yourself, Madre. Neither one nor the other.'

Honoire winces at the overly-indulged compliment.

'Show him in.'

She arranges a chair beyond the desk, where what little light there is from the high window can settle across his features. She adjusts her habit and slides away pen and ink into the drawer, leaving the table empty.

A tall, heavy man enters, hat in hand, unsure of the required convention.

Honoire shows him to the seat opposite. '*Signore..?*'

The man takes the seat carefully, but finds the rude wood of the chair surprisingly comfortable. He places his hat on a corner of the desk, follows her obvious glance and removes it, placing it on the floor beside him. '*Dottore.*'

'My apologies. But you gave no name. Ordinarily, I would not see anyone under those circumstances, but these are trying times.'

'Then my arrival may be timely.'

'How so?'

'I feel that my visit may set your soul at rest.'

'I wish that were possible.' Honoire slides the arms of delicate spectacles inside her wimple. 'You do not appear as most doctors of our acquaintance.'

'I am a Surgeon.' The doctor casts a deprecating smile, not lost on Madre Honoire.

'And this is a source of pride?'

'My pride was injured by a fall from grace, apparently, many years ago.'

'It is a natural consequence.'

'But that lack of objective pride allows me to openly discourse with you things that I might otherwise have preferred to remain closed.'

Having studied his sincerity, Mere Honoire removes the spectacles and smiles at him across the table.

'Unfettered, we lead many and separate lives, some of which we may be justly proud. My Sisters and I take a simpler approach. We have no life outside of God.'

'It is a life that has fallen outside of God's care that I come to speak of today.'

'No-one falls outside of God's care once they have truly embraced it.' Honoire notes the sudden opening of his expression, the lips that try too hard to remain untroubled, but set within his face are eyes still able to be honest if treated with a gentle hand. 'Do we speak of a close relative?'

She hears his sharp inrush of breath.

'A daughter?'

The doctor looks down sharply at his hat. On the floor beside the chair it is a dome of impenetrable, comforting brown.

'A… friend.' He flinches visibly between the two simple words. 'Perhaps… the daughter of a friend.'

On his left hand is a gold band. Madre Honoire notices the knuckle that holds it in place is more slender than the others. Perhaps the sacraments of marriage have been sterilised too often from this finger in the course of his work, although the deep, brown eyes still carry a simple honesty.

'Is she the cause of your fall?'

He is suddenly aware of the dismissive note that has crept into the edge of Honoire's reply. 'No. No. Not that. I promise you. Not that.'

'Do I know of this person?'

The doctor edges forward on his chair. 'Yes. But not as I do.'

'Evidently.'

'No. You must not think that. This is wrong. This is not how I meant this to be…'

'We must all bear the weight of our Sins, however they may be distributed, until they are forgiven. I can offer you nothing unless you are honest with me.'

'Minette!' The name explodes unbidden from his lips.

'*Sister* Minette?' Honoire sits forward abruptly. 'Tell me what you know of Minette. Do you know where she is?'

'She is with me.'

'Why have you prevented her return? The police…'

'The police would have found her eventually. I am here to set your mind at rest.'

'Where is she?' Honoire peers around him to glance at the door, half expecting...

'Minette is being attended by my wife at our home in LaRoque. I am here to ask if she can be allowed to remain with us for a little time. In order that she... no, in order that we...'

'What is it man? What has happened to her? Tell me.'

'She is our daughter.'

'This cannot be true. I know of her mother. I know the things Minette has seen.'

The doctor clasps his hands together on the desk. 'And that will be the source of my eternal sorrow.'

'Were you party to what was allowed?'

'No. Though through my pride I now hold myself responsible.'

Honoire sits back in contemplation. As yet she remains unsure that Minette can have dealt satisfactorily with the knowledge that the doctor is about to impart. 'Pride is a spur to much dishonesty, especially that of the self.'

'Please do not misunderstand, Madre. Nothing I have done in my life stems from a sense of pride. These things were done by others to protect what *they* saw as pride in me. So often is confidence and ambition misread.'

'How have you come to learn that Minette is your daughter? Are you sure of this?'

The doctor withdraws from his pocket a crumpled envelope, now no longer the incisive implement that had first appeared in the hands of the police, and places it before her on the desk.

Honoire fumbles her spectacles back into place, slides it open and reads. The doctor remains still until she replaces the letter on the desk where, between them, it now becomes a thing of greater understanding.

'This woman loved you very much.'

'And I served her ill.'

'That was not your fault. Nor would it have been your intention had the truth been delivered to you earlier. I see that now.'

'The thing I have found unshakable since I received this…' He points to the letter on the desktop. '…is what these women thought I was. How did they perceive me in such a monstrous fashion? I am not a prideful man.'

'Ambition can assume a proportion from which the wise amongst us are advised to step aside or become damaged.'

'I only wanted it for her… so that she…'

'Your wife wanted it too. But only for you. If either of you had suffered from pride, none of this would have been possible. Bring an end to this self-castigation, Doctor. Tell me of Minette.'

'Minette is well enough for the moment. She has sent you this…' He takes another paper from the pocket of his jacket and hands it across the table. This time there is no envelope and the paper bears many creases.

Madre Honoire takes it as though it carries news of the end of famine. 'Do you know the content of this?'

'No, Sister, I do not.'

Honoire unfolds the paper between them. 'Even though it is unsealed?'

'It is a confidence.'

'Perhaps she intended you to read it.'

'Perhaps I have no wish to.'

'Then may I keep this?'

'It is yours.'

La chirurgie du médecin
Rue du marché
La Roque-sur-Pernes
Vaucluse

October 25th.
Tuesday

Dear Madre Honoire,

It feels strange that I should call you Madre after the events of the last few weeks, but I feel you are more of a mother to me than any other who has laid claim to that title. I do not know why God chose me to be the instrument by which Padre Coraloni has carried out the Devil's work here on earth. I only know that I wish to remain in LaRoque to ensure that the result of that work comes to no harm.

I wish also to remain in the service of the mother church and if that seems hard for you to believe I assure you that, despite all evidence, I remain an innocent in this matter. I had no desire to be such an instrument but I will bear it to the best of my ability. I hope in this to make my saviour accept that I am not beyond redemption. If one can surely be redeemed for the sins of others, then He must be the one to understand my position.

I miss the shelter of my Sisters, the certainty of life at the Abbazia, but most of all I miss your good self and your wisdom. I humbly beg your understanding and advice in this matter.

The Doctor has come to you regarding my continuing infirmity, now that I have made him fully aware of my position. Please help him to understand that I will look to him for the support and wisdom I have previously found in you and, whilst in that spirit, I beg you to allow me to remain in LaRoque. I do not claim to be without sin. You know my history. I see my road to salvation in the protection of this child who will be, after all, the true innocent. Please allow me to walk it with dignity and honour.

Your Loving Sister,

Minette

Honoire touches the breast of her habit before she slips the note into the partially opened drawer.

'Please tell the Sister that she may remain with our Blessing. Until she is well.'

The doctor rises from the chair then remembers his hat, clutching at the brim with both hands.

'Thank you, Madre. My wife will be so…'

'Doctor… I said until she was well. Not forever.'

'Of course not… although it will yet be several months.'

The hat remains tight in his hands until the gate closes behind him.

OCTOBER 27th.
THURSDAY

4:52 P.M.

'It is now Thursday… again. Is the device working?'

'Here…' Auguste prises the edge of the grain with a gnarled fingernail. The door springs open.

Padre Coraloni spins the dials with a finger. 'Yes. It turns. But how do I know that it works?'

'Look…' Auguste inserts his own finger through the door. 'If I turn this dial… the second one moves. If I move this one until it clicks, we have a relocation of the third, fourth and fifth dials. When the fifth dial achieves one third of a rotation, the relationship of the indicator changes, outlining new Star, Sun and Moon positions. What more you ask I cannot know. I am not an astrologer.'

'I see that… but does it *work*?'

'Everything within this device is interconnected.'

Coraloni lifts it from his hands to study the banked series of dials. 'Should there not be a key?'

Auguste leans against the bench, nonchalantly brushing away turnings from the invisibly thin cylinder he has inserted into the device's locking shaft.

'There is no spring. What would be the point of a key?'

'Then I must take your word for it. For I also am no astrologer, although I know a man who is.'

Auguste and the priest are so distracted by the device they haven't heard the doctor push the door quietly open.

'What is this Hell's spawn still doing here, Auguste. I hoped he might be gone by now.'

Coraloni spins around as the door slams shut. The device is in his hands, fingers closing the latch of the cabinet to conceal the dials.

'Ah, Doctor. How good of you to join us.'

'And how selfish of you not to have left.'

Coraloni hands the device to Auguste.

'Wrap it for me. Brown paper will do. I have no wish to attract attention to it. There are dishonest people abroad.'

'About which you would have first-hand knowledge, *Padre.*'

'*Doctor*… I afford you the respect of that title without scorn… even though in a past life you are known to have tolerated a murderer and abortionist within reach of your practice. Some may say that your relationship was much more than… how shall I put it… collusion? I really do not see why you should vocalise my own title with such vituperative candour.'

The Doctor allows the door to swing closed behind him.

'I have just now returned from the Abbazia.'

'Ah…'

'I have also called home to reassure myself that in my absence you have played no further part in the lives of my wife and Minette.'

'The Good Sister. Yes. Have no fear, Doctor. We shall be leaving on the morning train.'

'No… you will not.' The Doctor moves quickly across the room and takes hold of the priest by the front of his cassock, fingers caught in the prayer beads of his crucifix.

'*You* will be leaving *now*… and alone.'

Coraloni pries at the fingers clutching him, at the hand that is slowly lifting his feet from the floor.

'Let go of me. Have you no fear of retribution?'

The doctor shakes him fiercely. 'I am damned already by liars. God will damn me forever if I do not separate you from the good Sister.' He lowers the priest to the floor. 'He may even look kindly upon me if I separate you from your life.'

The padre staggers backwards. 'I am under protection of The Vatican. I shall have you excommunicated. My uncle has influence…'

'I would care little if your uncle was the Pope. Auguste, is this demon's parcel ready?'

Auguste double-ties a knot in the coarse string lashed quickly around the device. Coraloni reaches out but Auguste lifts it beyond his reach.

'My payment.'

'I do not know if it works.'

Auguste continues to hold it high in the air.

'I have demonstrated…'

'Yes, yes. But I do not know if it *works*.'

'Then I cannot help you further because I do not know what you can mean. There remains, however, the matter of payment for the work I have done.'

From under the folds of his cassock the padre brings out a small purse. He takes two gold coins from it and hands them to Auguste. 'As agreed.'

Auguste continues to hold the device aloft, his other hand held out. 'Wrapping and delivery.'

'What?'

The doctor snatches the purse from Coraloni's hand, pushing him violently aside. Gold coins scatter the scarred bench.

'Auguste, take what you need.'

Auguste reaches for two more gold coins.

The padre scoops the remainder into the purse as Auguste waits to lower the device into his hands. He finds the doctor waiting in front of the door.

'Stand aside. I need to gather my things together at your

house. I shall not trouble you for breakfast in the morning.'

The doctor places a firm hand on the padre's chest. 'You shall not trouble me for anything ever again. I have your 'things' in the car outside. I shall take you to Carpentras now and leave you at the station.'

'There are no trains at this time of evening…'

'That is not my problem. Perhaps you can spend the night in silent meditation.'

CHRONICLE

II

ANGELUS

CHAMONIX MONT BLANC
RHÔNE-ALPS
FRANCE

1938

OCTOBER 28th.
FRIDAY

9:36 A.M.

The train is old and uncomfortable. Having waited out the night alone on the slatted wooden seat, Padre Coraloni expresses little regret as it comes to rest against a buffer.

Outside in the sunlight, fellow passengers and men in black uniform are standing around talking and smoking.

Across the platform an electric train waits to take them on into Switzerland, smoke billowing around its wheels from the exhausted French steam engine that has dragged them through the mountains.

Coraloni returns to the carriage to retrieve his baggage, never once allowing the device to leave his grasp. He looks around for someone he can coerce into helping but, as he catches their eye, they turn away without a glimmer of recognition for his position.

10:00 A.M.

The Swiss train is no more comfortable than the French one but, as he is forced to concede, it had departed on time.

Unconsciously, he raises a hand to his chest to touch the missing crucifix.

The stations exist as fleeting fragments of another life... Martigny, Charrat, Saxon, Riddes... as the train makes the long swoop down from the heights of Chamonix Mont-Blanc.

Insignificant between snow-blanketed peaks turned pink and blue with refracted light, the sound of the engine is a high, constrained hiss above the monotony of the rails. It leaps its own shadow through Le Châtelard, where he had first crossed the border some months ago.

The weight of the box in his lap brings a constant reminder that houses and people flashing by are merely ephemera in a wider scheme. War is in the air. He can taste it in their swift stoop from the mountains.

His uncle and Mussolini are fools. How could they believe that an 'arrangement' could be made with Herr Hitler? The meeting he is to attend in Interlaken will be far more profitable… in ways more immediate than his uncle could ever have imagined.

Descending the upper Rhône valley the air becomes thicker, organic, as the carriages beat through agricultural Sion and Sierre, running beside the swift current of the waters to his left.

Far warmer at this altitude, he shakes off the thick blanket borrowed from the Guard at Grenoble and uses it to pad the seat.

1:09 P.M.

A change of trains in Brig-Glis wakes him from the repetitive hiss of the wheels. The new carriage has padded seats and overhead racks onto which he throws his few belongings. He places the box on the rack facing him.

Beyond the station they cross a girder bridge, obliquely spanning the Rhône at a point where the melt from the Jungfrau swells the river, counter-currents writhing against rocks tumbled from the glacier's edge.

The engine suddenly accelerates along the water margin, its shadow a cameo of itself driving hard along the opposite bank. The route now doubles back, taking the incline that leads it above the town. He relaxes and allows it to press him comfortably into the seat.

There is a scuffling in the corridor outside.

The Guard slides the compartment door open.

'Ah, Padre. I hope you don't mind but someone has made a mess of their ticket. They are not of the right date and now they have nowhere else to sit and, as you are alone, I thought?'

Coraloni makes no move to accommodate anyone.

'I fail to see why that is my problem. I require privacy for my devotions.'

The Guard moves aside and behind him is a slender, handsome woman, hair draped to her shoulder, clasped there like a blonde flame by one long-fingered hand.

'But in the circumstances, I think I may take this opportunity to be generous. The needs of the many…?'

As the young woman enters the carriage he offers her his hand, ushering her to a seat at the other side of the small table.

The woman laughs prettily before insisting that Coraloni return to his seat. She sits close beside him, the heat from her body escaping the taupe lace blouse and blue layered skirt to soak through the dark serge of the padre's cassock where it comes to rest like Hell's needles against his skin.

He shuffles uncomfortably, rearranging the cloth as she touches his hand. Her fingers are white as the snow he's travelled through… and inexplicably hot.

She hesitates a moment at his visible discomfort, then pats his hand with hers before addressing him in fluent Italian, her breasts lifting with each accentuation.

'My name is Angelica, and I thank you for your consideration. I was quite losing myself in desperation for a moment.'

Coraloni's attention is absorbed by the rise and fall.

As he struggles to regain the natural movement of air in his chest, she bows her head gracefully in his direction.

'Forgive my presumption.'

Coraloni relaxes back into the seat with a smile.

'A woman in distress has little to forgive. I am Padre Coraloni.'

The carriage walls resonate like his growing expectation while the engine labours up the steepening incline until, without warning, they fly into the mouth of the Lötschberg tunnel. In the darkness, a slender hand steals into his, and he begins to experience each judder of the engine as if it were his own.

A flicker of light illumines the corridor outside.

The Guard inches his way along carrying a storm lantern.

'Do not panic. Please remain in your seats. There has been a small electrical failure... Do not panic. Please remain in your...'

He passes out of sight along the train, taking with him the small, wavering pool of light.

Coraloni is left with a burning image on his retina of the inside of the compartment, much as he remembered it, but with one single exception... the box on the rack opposite him has disappeared.

2.22P.M.

Twenty-five minutes within the confines of the Lötschberg tunnel becomes an eternity of ears numbed by wind pressure and the shout of steel on steel until, with the briefest flash of grey, the tunnel recedes under the brilliant sunshine of the north-western slopes.

The woman releases her grip on his hand.

'Thank you, Padre. I hate to be alone in the dark when there is a man available, and surely no-one could object to my holding the hand of a man of the cloth?'

Coraloni shuffles in his seat as the heat from her fingers leaves his body. He rearranges his clothing, hoping that the inevitable staleness he has acquired during the journey will not communicate itself directly.

She turns to smile at him. 'I see I have made you uncomfortable. It's an unfortunate habit of mine. Your face has turned a delightful shade of pink... no, that's good... you were looking quite pale when I arrived.'

On the floor, Coraloni's scuffed boots are covered in a layer of brown paper and string. The box is uncovered on Angelica's lap.

She lifts it into the sunlight.

'This wood is beautiful... I think it might be olive... but the quality! What is it?'

She holds the box away from Coraloni's reach and strokes the edges with her thumb.

Coraloni leans back into his seat. There is nowhere she can go. He folds the wrapping paper from the floor into a neat shape.

'It's just a clock.' He notices the question in her face. 'I'm taking it to a friend.'

'In Interlaken?'

'Yes. In Interlaken.'

'How convenient. Perhaps as we travel together you will demonstrate it for me.'

She sits the box upright on her knees. Her thumbnail slides around the grain of the plinth. Silently, the door in the side swings open.

'Oh... delightful. A secret catch. How romantic.'

Coraloni sits bolt upright. 'How did you do that?'

She opens the door of the box to allow the light from the window to enter. 'There is a catch to everything, Padre... didn't you know?'

She peers inside at the serried rows of dials and gears, engraved planets, moons and stars.

'Now I understand your reticence. It is quite beautiful, but hardly the thing for a man of the True Faith to be carrying abroad.'

'As I said...' Coraloni reaches again for the box but her grip on the wood is visibly increased. 'I am taking it to a friend. He is a collector of obscure clocks.'

The hard smile in her eye burns into his memory. The blue-grey steel of the irises is marred only in the left by a single, green segment. He reaches again for the box.

She teases it further from him.

'It has a way of making me feel that I can't quite explain, Padre. How are you on analogies?'

Coraloni lowers his hands in a deprecatory manner. 'I have written the odd sermon or two.'

'Well... this makes me feel like I am an empty carriage standing at the edge of a platform... left behind by an engine that steams away into the future, but there is something indefinable that anchors me... as if at one time I might have flown alongside it. Wouldn't that be fun... to fly?' She laughs brightly. 'Wouldn't you like to fly, Padre? With an Angel?'

He reaches out for the box and this time she allows him to take it. He closes the door on the side until it clicks.

'One might always hope for an Angel, but without doubt we are all encumbered by an anchor of some form or other.'

'You find me an encumbrance?'

'I apologise. I meant no offence.'

'And none will be taken, if you allow my moment of fantasy.'

'Perhaps I would prefer it a reality?'

This time her smile is guarded, less openly delightful than before.

'Reality can have its demons, too.'

Coraloni places the box onto the folded layers of paper, reaching out with both hands to stroke the smooth, wooden sides.

'Don't we all.'

3:15 P.M.

Angelica leans across Coraloni to study the flowers overflowing the hanging baskets along the canopy of Mitholz Station until his hand is crushed against the seat beneath her thigh.

She leans further. 'Aren't they beautiful? So strange, that autumn can arrive so much later here than in Ireland. I suppose they don't have fog the way we seem to.'

She takes his hand again, this time holding it between her own.

'That place where I met the train this lunchtime… where was it? Bridge..?'

'Brig-Glis.'

'Yes. That was it. Terribly provincial. That's where I got the ticket messed up. One cannot possibly do anything at short notice in Italy. The bureaucracy is so… so…'

Coraloni nods sagely. 'Italian?'

Angelica flushes. 'I am so tired of apologising that I shall do it only once more. Padre, please accept a sincere apology for my lack of manners.'

Coraloni presses her hand. 'Despite my name being Italian, I consider myself to be of German origin.'

She laughs without a trace of self-consciousness.

'Of course… and in these rather troubled times, asserting one's Germanic ancestry could well be the safest thing to do.'

'Is that why you are leaving? I thought that Italy might remain relatively stable.'

'My dear Padre, Italy has only ever been relatively stable… and as for your famous friend, Mussolini, well… And are you, too, famous? Padre Coraloni?'

'Hardly. Insofar as I am aware.'

Her eyes stare directly into his. He feels his insides being scooped out, leaving him no more substance than a spun-sugar figurine.

'As I look at you, Padre, I see ambition. In fact, I see it buried so deeply that only in the grave shall you rest.'

A shudder runs through him as she disengages her study.

'And how *Grande* shall be my tomb?'

She closes her eyes for a moment. 'It shall be white marble and limestone.'

He is amused by her assertion. 'Fit then for a Pope?'

She greets his probing laughter with a deprecating smile.

'Fitting at least for a German priest.'

OCTOBER 28th.
FRIDAY

3:56P.M.

The engine pulls them swiftly along beside a torrent of glacial-blue meltwater, through Frutigen, Mülenen, Emdthal, all without stopping.

Angelica leaps to the window.

'Was that the sign for Reichenbach I just saw? Can you see the falls from the train? I do so admire Conan Doyle. He imbues Mr. Holmes with a wealth of knowledge about things chemical.'

She turns away from the bluff stone to lean across Coraloni and stare down at the river. Her breasts rise and fall to his conscious delight. A faint scent of lavender emanates from the aura that surrounds her while another air travels deeper, undetectable until it meets those places inside him that he has never been able to refuse. He steadies himself against the edge of the table.

Angelica touches him lightly. 'Am I taxing you with my chatter? It is a well-known fact that I talk too much.'

Coraloni seeks vainly for a degree of genuine concern in her face. 'No. I am fine.'

He removes his hands from the table and reasserts his grip on the parcel.

Angelica slides back the compartment door.

'I shall walk along the corridor for a while. I shall study the lake and leave you in peace. No...' She puts out a warning hand. '...don't get up.'

At the end of the second car along, Angelica finds the toilet compartment.

There is soap of a kind in the basin, a coarsely scented tablet with a pumice grain and a towel that seems little used. It will have to do. She slots the bolt behind her.

Tired now after so many hours without sleep, she rubs her face with her hands then pulls them away quickly. They reek of priest. and so harsh is the smell it's like a layer of ungodly unguent attached to her skin.

Wrenching the rings from her fingers she drops them into her purse. She will flatly refuse the next operation unless someone gives her more time to prepare.

The water returns a pallid glaze to her hands. She cups them to her face and her skin now smells of lemon with a grey hint of pumice. Her reflection in the failing mirror is mottled, infected by the tarnished silver, but still an improvement without the hasty makeup.

Out in the corridor, the carriage sways beneath her feet with the vagaries of the line. She stands to watch the flat expanse of Thunersee stream away towards the horizon as the train begins its long, gliding turn around the lake.

From above, the sliding window allows cool air to flow over her. After the harshness of the soap, its touch is light, calming, and perversely sensuous. She takes several deep breaths before returning to her seat.

The stale scent of the priest is omnipresent in the compartment as she slides shut the door. Coraloni is exactly as she had left him, tightly clutching the parcel. She touches his fingers with hers.

'Padre? I hope that I now find you better?'

Her skin is visibly softer since her return. The travel lines have disappeared from beneath her eyes and he finds her entirely refreshed. He offers a smile in recognition of her concern.

'I am fine, thank you.'

Angelica withdraws her hand and a chill settles over him.

Despite all his misgivings, Coraloni wishes an excuse to maintain that contact, even though it searches what remains of his soul.

'Padre? Wouldn't it be jolly if we found ourselves at the same hotel? Where are you to stay tonight?'

He continues to grip the parcel. 'I am not certain.'

'Then might I suggest my hotel? I could arrange a room for you. Close to mine?'

'In other circumstances that would be…'

'Oh, Padre… please say you will. I would love to continue our discussion over dinner.'

'Dinner would be possible, I think. But my contact… my friend… has arranged accommodation in my absence. It would be churlish of me therefore…'

'Oh, no, you mustn't do that. But wouldn't it be just *perfetto* if it was our hotel?'

Coraloni adopts a diffident expression, yet behind it there is a growing fear that he has never before experienced.

Is this how it feels to be prey? He fights hard to keep his face from changing its apparent diffidence to a savage irony.

'Yes… *perfetto.*'

4:53 P.M.

The railway rises and falls with the undulations of the landscape, each change of elevation accompanied by the clank and whirr of the driving cog on the third rail until they reach the flat green plain where the *Kanal* and the River Aare discharge into Thunersee.

'Padre? You must put your clock on the table. I will not touch it again, I promise.'

Coraloni flexes his fingers, unaware that his grip had been so tight. Angelica is watching his face closely.

'The tension was making you look quite ill. By the way, I am booked in at the Harder-Minerva. I think it is very close to the centre. I shall not know my room number until I arrive but you can always telephone from wherever you are. No... I have a better idea. Meet me there for dinner tonight. I'm sure I have a card in here somewhere...'

Her fingers filter the clutter of her purse until she picks out a card. She repacks her purse, leaving a gold ring in the flat of her skirt.

'You may keep the card.'

Coraloni hides a smile by turning to the window.

'We may find ourselves under extreme scrutiny while sharing a table.'

Angelica's eyes focus on the roof of the carriage and beyond. 'Are we not always under extreme scrutiny?'

Coraloni chuckles darkly. 'Him and my conscience I can live with. My uncle and his friends are a different matter.'

'Can I help?'

Abruptly, Coraloni laughs out loud. Angelica draws away from him.

The sudden lack of heat brings him back to his senses.

'I apologise. There may be a way you can help... if only by distracting me for a while.'

'You may find me a willing distraction.' Angelica presses against him. 'How shall I know where you are staying?'

'There will be a message for me at the ticket office. I shall telephone you...' He wedges the card she gave him under the string of the parcel. '...as soon as I am settled.'

She touches him, fingertips light as the feet of a wasp.

'Then I must leave you for now. My luggage is in the baggage car. In all the confusion the porter simply threw it in. I hope my dresses are not ruined. I shall be mortified if I do not look my best for you tonight.'

OCTOBER 28th.
FRIDAY

5:22P.M.

By the time Coraloni reaches the ticket office, Angelica has disappeared from sight.

'Excuse me… I am Padre Coraloni…'

The man extracts a card from a pigeon hole behind him and slaps it on the counter between them.

'Do you have any identification?'

Coraloni stares at him defiantly, brushing the dust of the train from his cassock.

'Sorry, Padre. It is my job. I spend half the day waiting for trains to leave and the other half wishing they had never arrived.'

Coraloni retrieves the card from under the glass screen.

'Rugenpark Hotel… where is that?'

The man indicates over his shoulder. 'South of here. Four hundred metres. It is a steady walk in the sun. Take the path by the canal.'

'Is there no-one that can help with my bags?'

'The taxicab was taken by a woman who got off the train before you. There is only the one… and I have no porter I can spare.'

Coraloni steps out into the bright sunlight. In front of him, beyond the narrow, alluvial strip on which the town stands, the Jungfrau broods magnificently beneath shredding clouds.

'Padre! There you are!'

A large black taxicab eases to a stop beside him.

Angelica's face smiles at him through the open window.

'I have a spare seat, Padre. Allow me to take you to your hotel… please?'

Coraloni makes a step towards the rear of the cab. The trunk lid has been pulled down and piled high with her boxes.

'You haven't the room.'

The driver reaches for the card in Coraloni's hand. He reads the address and laughs out loud before handing it back.

'I will make room, Padre. It is not far.'

The driver straps Coraloni's bags beside the already large pile of cases but Coraloni refuses to relinquish his grip on the box.

Before the car has managed to achieve fourth gear, they arrive at the Rugenpark. The building leans visibly to one side and the paintwork is long faded. Coraloni waits for the driver to unload his case while Angelica continues to study the incline of the hotel.

'The man who arranged this… you did say he was a friend of yours?'

'I shall telephone later. Thank you for the lift.'

'Dinner will be at seven?'

'Then I am afraid I shall have to decline. My meeting is also for seven o'clock.'

Angelica laughs brightly. 'Then I shall just have to postpone dinner until eight. Do you mind?'

'Not at all.'

'Until eight, then.'

Coraloni drags his box and bags up a staircase that leans across the sunken gable wall first this way then that.

The Concierge, who by way of excuse has affected back pain all the way up the staircase, is now holding out his hand.

Coraloni trips the catches on a case, searching through

for a small black casket. He opens the lid and offers the man a communion wafer.

6:40 P.M.

Washed, changed and in a clean cassock, parcelled box clutched tightly under one arm, Coraloni exits the hotel door.

'There you are, Padre.'

Angelica is waiting by the bottom step, one eye to the clouds swirling the tops of the mountains to the south. She is attempting in vain to release the catch on a perfectly ineffectual parasol.

'I thought we were to meet at eight?'

'Well… you didn't telephone.'

'I know.'

She shakes the parasol in mock annoyance, as if that might dislodge the catch. 'You said that you would.'

'There is no telephone at the Hotel.' With a single-handed flick Coraloni pops the parasol into shape.

She slopes it over her shoulder where it perfectly matches the blue dress she has changed into.

'I do hope it doesn't rain…'

'You will be fine.'

Angelica kicks up her feet as she walks, slender ankles flashing in and out below the swirl of her skirt.

'But no telephone? How on earth does one do business today without a telephone?'

Behind them, the effect of the sinking gable wall and faded paintwork are amplified by the scowl of the Concierge behind a ground floor window.

'I have absolutely no idea. I think there is one, but when I asked he said it wasn't working.'

'Some people have no grace…'

She folds her arm through his to lead him along the pavement of Rugenparkstrasse. '…but I have brought my own!'

Coraloni returns the squeeze. 'This promises to be delightful… but my meeting must be…'

'Oh, absolutely!' She holds tight to his arm. 'I promise I shall keep right out of the way… out of sight even… should that be necessary.'

'It is of little matter… other than if my contact sees you he may refuse to make his presence known.'

She surveys pointedly the azure blue cotton dress with the cream silk trim where it swirls about her perfectly polished, matching boots, and the half-sleeved bodice that accentuates the pale translucence of her skin. 'Even to me?'

'From what I hear of him… especially to you.'

She holds Coraloni at arm's length. 'But you are not…?' She registers the surprise on his face. 'Of course not.' She draws him close again. 'Silly me.'

He extricates his arm from hers. 'I am sorry but this is as far as I can allow you to accompany me.'

She scans the buildings around her. 'Neugasse. Why, I am almost back to my hotel.'

'Would you care to wait for me there while I conclude my business?'

'No.' She takes his arm again and leads him on into Spielmatte, towards the bridge.

'I really must insist…'

'Look.' Angelica points across the bridge. 'There is a small garden outside the Bellevue where I can sit and wait. I really can't see anything from there. It's surrounded by trees. You wouldn't want me walking the streets alone?'

The Hotel Bellevue garden has a seat nestled between rockeries overflowing with tiny alpine plants.

Through the surrounding trees there is barely a glimpse

of the river. She allows her arm to slide from his as she sits.

'This will be perfect. I have no doubt that a waiter will be along in a moment or two. You may feel free now.'

Coraloni hurries back across the bridge, turning left into the narrow cul-de-sac of Unter den Häusern until he arrives at a gate. Beyond it lies a small footbridge that spans an arm of the canal. The lock on the gate is off, hanging open on a rusted steel loop. He pushes it aside cautiously.

The row of sluices that govern the flow of water through the Elektrizitätswerk are contained in their own covered building at the far end. The roar from the released overspill is deafening as he walks on into the shade of a canopy. A man leans against an open door there, watching his progress.

The noise once inside the generating plant is incredible, a whine far harsher than the roaring water. The man stops beside a fiercely spinning dynamo where sparks leap wildly from the carbon brushes riding the huge commutator.

Coraloni is drawn towards its shrieking power until the man reaches out and taps his arm and gestures toward the box. He waits until the man takes a piece of paper from his jacket pocket, then studies it carefully before handing over the box.

The man unwraps it quickly and turns it in his hands.

Coraloni shows him the hidden catch. When the door swings open, the man reaches into the box to spin the dials with his finger.

Coraloni walks alone up the street towards Spielmatte.

7:12PM.

'Padre! I simply cannot allow you to walk past me in such a peremptory fashion.' Angelica is at a small table under the awning of the Altstadt Tearooms. 'The Bellevue had finished serving for the day. How very provincial.'

Coraloni can see that she must have followed him back over the bridge and from here she must have had an uninterrupted view of his meeting.

A large white pot occupies the centre of the table. She passes him a matching cup and saucer and pours it full of pallid, English tea.

'I'm afraid you will take tea English fashion today, Padre. How was your business?'

His fingers smooth the crisply folded paper he has slipped into an opened seam in his cassock. 'Concluded.'

'Good. Then there remains little to come between us.'

'That seems to have been your intention since Brig-Glis.'

'Have I been so obvious?'

Angelica replaces her empty cup on its saucer and pushes them away.

'Padre? What is a man without clothes?'

'I might suggest that he is just a man?'

'Then what is a priest without clothes?'

He muses. 'Probably little more than that.'

'Then who shall tell the difference between them?'

'I'm not sure… God?'

'No… a woman.'

Coraloni reaches beneath his cassock for a bag of small change as the waitress approaches. He drops coins into her palm until she is satisfied enough to go back inside.

'Unless, of course, God is also a woman.'

Angelica shrieks with laughter. 'Heavens, no! What an abominable thought!'

Coraloni is amused by her reaction. 'I don't understand. This very thought has been promulgated by your own sex since time immemorial. Though for myself, I find the idea heretical.'

'I beg your pardon, Padre.' Angelica stifles her laughter with a gasp for air. 'But when I go to the final repose I wish to spend my eternity in the arms of a Man.'

'With or without clothes?'

'As God made me.' She offers her arm for him to take. 'Shall we? Our table is booked and I do not wish to appear late.'

7.30 P.M.

The sun, low enough to crown the mountains to the west, spills gold across the red-tiled roofs of Harderstrasse.

The Hotel Minerva boasts an arched doorway beneath two enormous balconies, their ledges overflowing with fresh flowers. The roadway below is already cast into blue evening shadow.

Coraloni is drawn aside by her arm.

'Padre? Would you?'

Angelica gives him the still-open parasol. 'I'm told that it's dreadfully bad luck...'

With a subtle twist he snaps it shut.

She passes it directly to the hovering waiter who shows them to their table.

The restaurant is almost empty and they find themselves in a small booth against a wall. Between the booths are narrow screens of varnished timber and stained glass.

Coraloni catches her profile repeated in a large, oval, gilded mirror, and is reminded again of her elegance.

She orders for them both in fluent Italian, after asking the waiter for his language of preference.

'Whatever Madame Pedersen prefers...'

Coraloni remains silent until the waiter has moved away.

'Pedersen? That doesn't sound British... unless I am mistaken?'

'You are not mistaken. I wondered when you would ask.'

'About what?'

She holds up her left hand. It is again without the gold band. Coraloni wonders when she had removed it… perhaps while she distracted him outside.

'I was afraid that manners might prevent you from enquiring about my husband.'

The waiter returns to light a candle in the centre of the table and brings back the parasol. He hangs it on the hat rack by the door.

'One is sometimes reminded of how cruel God can be but I was never cut of the cloth from which widows are made.'

Coraloni samples the wine. It is unsurprisingly warm and ordinary, but things will change once he has banked the draft in his pocket. 'And you yet so young.'

She turns her profile into the candlelight. 'Yes… I am… am I not?'

He feels the touch of an un-slippered foot beneath the table. 'Handsome indeed.'

Coraloni relaxes back on the bench seat.

In the darkness, black-stockinged toes slide across his ecclesiastical socks.

'If I didn't know you were a man of God, Padre, I would suspect that you were flirting with me.'

9:23 P.M.

The lighting outside is rudimentary but, as his eyes accustom to it, more than enough to appreciate the effect this insanely elegant woman is determined to have on him.

The air has calmed, shadows are full-blown surrounds to the warm pools cast by streetlights and the wine has begun to sing a recurring theme in Coraloni's head.

Angelica swings her feet wilfully, allowing them to fall short, making only small steps along the pavement beside him. Her face carries a smile that only deepens the more she studies him.

Her arm tightens on his. 'Are you alright? We had left it rather late for dinner.' She gives him the folded parasol to carry. 'Would you hold this a minute?'

Among the chaos of her purse is a small clip of francs.

'I really must pay you for dinner. I thought the waiter would book it to my room.'

Coraloni stays her hand. 'I instructed him not to.'

'That was sweet of you.'

She takes back the folded parasol, finding it awkward whichever way she tries to carry it.

'Why did you bring that?'

'One never knows…' She swings it from one hand to the other, finally bringing it to rest against her right side, away from the padre.

He reaches around behind her as if to grasp it, then leaves his arm there, pulling her in a shade closer.

'You will not need it. I always take the weather with me.'

Angelica's feet resume their hypnotic swing, traversing pools of isolated lamplight along Bahnhofstrasse and into Rugenpark. The hotel sits on the corner of a side street and, even in this light, the lintels and sills lean visibly.

'There is something surreal about this place.' Her feet slow to a steadier pace. 'Almost as though it only… edges into this world. Tell me. Does it have cavernously dark wardrobes?'

Coraloni laughs out loud, his throat harsh from the surprisingly strong wine. His voice sounds brittle in the empty street. 'Why, yes. It actually does.'

He indicates the sweeping lines of his cassock.

'Though I have so few things, I have had no need to delve so deep as to find out.'

Her feet swing them in the direction of the hotel.

'Then may *I*?'

'If you should so wish.'

'Do you not find it fascinating?' She ignores his quizzical glance and continues to stare at the darkened hotel, whose only light shines from the lower ground floor window where the concierge sits, his bulk outlined against the glass.

'I sometimes think I have made it my life… delving into things that belong to others… Anholt… my husband… said that one day I would become lost in another dimension where nothing would matter and there was no way out. He said that I would die there. I even think I might.'

Her frown is reflected clearly enough in the glass of the door for Coraloni to ponder as to its meaning. He touches her shoulders, feeling a rhythmic trembling in his fingers.

'I think not. Tonight you are in God's hands.'

'Then for tonight at least… please do not let Him be a Woman.'

10:08 P.M.

Angelica tries a door set into the side wall of the room. The handle turns but the door is firmly locked.

Coraloni switches on the bedside lamp and raw electricity flickers until the hanging loops of filament swell the room with a sepia light. He tries to rub the sensitivity from his eyes and fails.

Angelica is standing by the door, watching him, eyes glistening.

'How is one supposed to use the bathroom? Do you have the key?'

'What did you say?'

'The bathroom. Do you have the key?'

'No. The bathroom is along the corridor. Three doors to the left.'

'I thought this was a hotel? In my hotel the bathroom is

next to the bedroom.'

Coraloni shucks off his priests boots and lifts his feet onto the bed.

Angelica peers along the corridor. 'I will not be long.'

Coraloni moves to get off the bed.

She puts a finger to her lips. 'No… stay as you are.' She waves him back onto the bed. 'I have a plan.'

Coraloni is still on the bed when Angelica slips back into the room.

She closes the door behind her and slides the bolt. 'I like a man who does as he is told.'

'Always?' Coraloni sits up unsteadily, propping himself against the iron rails of the bed head. 'I'd guessed that your feigned delicacy was masking a desire for the masterful.'

'My feigned delicacy? How dare you?'

A look of approbation flickers in his eye at the strength of her outburst, but she relents.

'Of course, you are right… as you shall see. Tonight I shall be masterful enough for both of us.'

'And what if I prefer..?'

'Prefer what to me? I assure you I am no blue-stocking. Unless that is your own personal mountain to climb?'

'A blue-stocking?'

'A lesbian, Padre. One of my 'sisters'.'

His mouth feels strange. His tongue tingles unexpectedly. He ascribes it to anticipation as she manipulates her clothes so that an erect bud of nipple flares briefly into the light.

'I don't understand…'

She unhooks the waistband of her skirt and allows it to slide to the floor. Her hair flows wildly into the light as she shakes out the silver clasp.

'Tell me, Padre, how many misguided women have you saved with your missionary zeal?'

Blood sings in his ears, his thoughts flow in and around

like dark wings in a rookery.

'I don't know… you cannot ask me that… I am a priest.'

'And that makes you my personal mountain.'

Coraloni swings his legs from the bed to sit up.

Angelica steadies him with a gesture. 'Wait… tell me your name… quickly.' She stops, fingers holding still on the last button of her bodice.

'What?'

'Your name. For Heaven's sake, Padre. Your mother must have given you a name?'

Coraloni rubs hard at his eyes, one lid falling half-shut as Angelica moves around him in a swaying motion, hands manipulating straps and loops. Her bodice appears suddenly over the rail at the foot of the bed, followed by the layered skirt, their movement through the air sending underlying waves of cologne into his unsettled senses.

Beneath that scent is another, a wilder musk, that experience tells he will be unable to resist. He grabs a fistful of the garments, drags them across the bed to his face, drawing her scent deep into his own body.

He drops them to find that Angelica has disappeared.

He scans the room. The bolt is still fastened. There is only one other place she can be. He staggers up from the bed, his left foot holding a little on the carpet.

He consciously lifts it straight.

The scratched oak wardrobe by the wall consumes what small light falls this far from the lamp, sucking-in the colours of the room.

He steadies himself on its edge to gather a breath, tries to push back the numbed eyelid. It falls again, as does one side of his mouth. His lips are wet and he brushes them dry. The touch of his own skin is hot enough to burn. His limbs tremble with a fine vibration as he tugs the doorknob.

As the wardrobe opens, the figure of a priest steps into

the light.

Coraloni stumbles back at the sight of a tall, slender figure, wearing his own cassock, blonde hair tucked tightly beneath his own black Biretta. The vision smiles at him, offering a genuflection that seems to swim from the surrounding darkness.

Her essence pours from the enclosure of the wardrobe into his heightened senses, mixed now with the stale scent of his own cassock.

From somewhere strange in his thoughts comes a confusion of memory, a mingling of past and future.

His tongue has become thick, unpredictable, and bereft of control.

'M… Man… us.'

The hem of the cassock rises until she lets him see that beneath it she is entirely naked.

'Then, Padre… *Manus*… Coraloni…'

His legs buckle and his eyes close as she pushes him to the floor.

She drapes the cassock over his head.

'…welcome to my confessional.'

OCTOBER 29th.
SATURDAY

10:15 A.M.

Coraloni's eyes open as if they are lifting the edge of the world's curtain. They fall closed again… but the image of a pair of stout, oxblood brogues remains in his awareness. He opens his eyes once more. The brogues are close enough to his face that he can make out splashes of coffee on the white spats that overlap them.

Incapable of protest, he is rolled over onto his back. The floor presses up against him, hard and unforgiving. The cold in his flesh and the ache in his bones advise him that he has been there for some time. He tries to move his arms but they are not within his power to control.

Above him, a slight though handsome man of around his own age, stoops to study him. As the man leans down his hair flops in front of dark, deep-set eyes. He pushes it back with a single-handed gesture. The hair is thick, brown and luxuriant between the comb of his fingers… inconsistent with the shabby, creased tweed suit he wears. Coraloni can only observe as the man takes a gold watch from his waistcoat pocket.

'Ah, Padre. I am afraid that you have missed Matins. Terce would seem appropriate about now, but I am no Pilate, for it appears that I cannot wash my hands of you… yet.'

The man's voice washes around Coraloni's senses in that peculiarly Italian-scented German favoured by the Swiss.

His own mouth hangs open, incapable of reply. He licks his lips with a swollen tongue. His palate is cloaked with a thick saliva that drains into his airways making him choke.

His head has been lifted so that he can gasp for air. From that position, Coraloni can see that he has been left naked. The room swims under him. Grip returns to his hands and he clings to the thin, shredded rug until the motion stops.

His head is lowered to the floor and, from the corner of an eye, he watches the brogues turn and pace comfortably across the room to the window. The curtains are whipped back to allow daylight to enter.

He turns his head away. From a single glimpse the room is a mess of thrown bedding, cushions and pillows. The mattress is ripped open and leans drunkenly in the corner by the locked door. The wardrobe has been emptied completely of his meagre effects.

He begins to search his senses for broken bones or contusions, until the man speaks to him from over by the window.

'I am not sure how you are still alive, Padre, your heart must be pure Bezoar stone. And I dare say you are as surprised as I am to find yourself in this position.'

Coraloni's throat will only grunt. He tries to twist himself around but there is no movement in his legs.

'Stay where you are and try to rest. There is no advantage in it for me if you were to die now. With a little time you may well recover completely.' The man looks quickly around the room. 'And then what stories may we hear?'

10:21 A.M.

The concierge braces himself within the frame of the door, a tray of tepid coffee and cups in his hands. He tries to peer around the edge but a brogue shoe holds it so that only the tray will pass through. Krafft relieves him of the tray and tries to close the door. The concierge fills the gap with the bulk of his shoulder.

There is a glimpse of bare flesh on the floor from where

the opened curtains cast a narrow bar of sunlight.

'The young lady… is she?'

'The young lady?' Krafft appears puzzled for a moment. 'Oh, I see. Yes, she is fine. She is just resting. We will be down in a short while then you can see for yourself.'

'I expected the priest to come back before now.'

The man puts the tray on the floor. 'Has he paid you?'

The concierge coughs uncertainly. 'Yes… but only for last night. It is now well past the time for vacating of the room so I will have to ask for twenty francs.'

Krafft riffles the money in his wallet.

'That's scandalous.'

The concierge leers at the collection of notes.

'Priests who walk through my lobby without a word in the middle of the night carrying cloth bundles… fine ladies… mysterious third parties… naked people on my hotel room floor… those are things that sell newspapers. I may have been a little hasty in my first request. Shall we say… forty francs?'

The man gives him fifty in fresh notes. 'For the extra ten I want some of your old clothes.'

'I only have old clothes.'

The man glances from the concierge to the priest.

'Then preferably some of the ones that you have allowed yourself to outgrow.'

10:43 A.M.

Reality flows in and out for Coraloni as coffee is forced between his lips. He laps for it greedily, allowing the excess to run down his chin into the collar of the greasy shirt that has been dragged across his chest.

'Padre.' The man slaps his face with no real force. 'Padre. The shirt I can manage. I can't get you into the trousers without your help.'

Coraloni opens both eyes wide. The right eyelid holds up on its own. He has been dragged into an armchair in an upright position. The coffee has lessened the thick, crawling sensation in his mouth. His genitals lay exposed below a stained cotton shirt. He raises an arm to cover them and watches his hand creep slowly over his thigh.

'That's better. Drink some more of this…'

The coffee cup is pressed against Coraloni's lips again. He lets it drain into his mouth, filling it before swallowing in an attempt to cleanse him of her scent. His stomach cramps, hard and brightly painful. The muscles in his limbs set up an insistent tingling he is sure will drive him insane.

The cup is taken away. The waistband of a huge pair of trousers is being eased under his thighs.

'A minute. Please…'

He puts out a hand to stall the manipulation of his legs.

'Ten minutes… I may be able to do it myself by then.'

He collapses back into the arms of the chair, the effort of speaking having drained him entirely. 'Who are you?'

The man pours more coffee into the cup and helps Coraloni guide it to his mouth. 'I am Karl Ernst Krafft.'

'You… you cannot be.'

'I assure you that I am, Padre. Look…'

There is a Swiss identity card in his wallet.

'At the Elektrithi… Elektrishi…'

'*Elektrizitätswerk.* You have been too long in Italy, Padre. Your mother tongue lies heavy in your mouth. Contrary to your expectations, that was not I. There are factors abroad that meant I had to use an intermediary. But have no fear, he is a trusted colleague. The device is now in my possession. There remains, however, the small matter of the key?'

Coraloni gulps at the coffee. 'There is no key.'

'Come, come…' Krafft chides him gently. 'Who could be so naïve as to take one glance at the device and not see that it is useless without the proper key?'

'There is no spring. It cannot be wound.'

'Agreed, Padre, but with the proper key it can be set. Where have you hidden it?'

Coraloni ignores the request, choosing instead to command all his effort into rebuilding the movement in his legs. Already the tendons in his ankles are tensing with a renewed awareness, driving out the frustration of his nerve endings.

'What did she give me?'

'At a guess?' Krafft moves Coraloni's head from side to side, examining the bright red patches that blotch the skin of his cheeks. He presses hard against one with his thumb. As he releases the pressure, the rosy blush immediately returns.

'I would say Fowler's Solution. Potassium Arsenide. A substance once much beloved of otherwise wan-faced prostitutes, if taken slowly. How very droll. It has very little taste… no odour as such… and is almost always fatal in any worthwhile dose. I could almost convince myself that I am conversing with a ghost…' He picks at the clothes the concierge had thrown through the door. '…except I've never heard of one so shabbily attired.'

Coraloni stands with the aid of the chair.

The trousers fall around his ankles and Krafft bends to lift them up. He tucks the shirt roughly inside and cinches the belt.

'It seems that she has left you intact. You can be grateful for that at least. I hear she is not always so generous.'

Coraloni attempts the buttons on the shirt.

Krafft's hands brush his away. 'I will do this or we will be here all day.'

Coraloni is absorbed in the deftness of the fingers dressing him… his own mind still swimming in and out of focus… suddenly recalling Angelica's hands on his earlier garments.

'You know her?'

Krafft tugs the shirt collar into a semblance of order.

'I know of her and I think I am glad not to have made her acquaintance the way you have. Try to stand without the chair.'

The padre sways into a more upright position. The suit drapes across his frame like soiled washing on a line.

'You will have to do. It is not far to my hotel. I can get you cleaned up better there. Now try to walk. I will help.'

Coraloni makes a stumbling step forward. His stomach cramps suddenly.

Krafft gives a wry smile as he picks up the jacket.

'I had hoped to travel in a more… clandestine manner.'

OCTOBER 29th.
SATURDAY

12:10 P.M.

Coraloni declines the hand with the soap. 'I can wash myself, thank you.'

Krafft drops it into the bathwater.

'If you have a problem being naked in front of me, I can assure you that I do not share it.'

'That has been remarked upon.'

'Do not believe every remark you hear.'

Coraloni holds on to the soap, lathering his arms and chest. 'The way my luck is running at the moment...'

'*Im Gegenteil,* my dear Padre. Your luck is a very insistent Lady. She has protected you against the Archangel. In the past you must have been very pious indeed or... as is more likely... she recognised something of a kindred spirit?' He watches a bright anger transform Coraloni's face beneath the still rosy cheeks. 'Though I can see it may be better not to look too closely into that.'

'Where are my clothes?'

'I think I know where I might find them. The Harder-Minerva is just around the corner.' Krafft chuckles. 'Please don't go anywhere until I return.'

'And if she is still there? You will tell me?'

'Padre, she is long gone... if what I hear about her is true.'

The enamel of the bath is cold against Coraloni's back, jolting alive some of the feral pathways in his brain. 'Then if there *was* a key... she must have it.'

'No, my friend, she does not have the key or we would

not be having this conversation. There can be only one reason that she has left you intact… she could not find the key herself… and you saw what she did to your room.'

'Then why have you brought me away? Are you not afraid that the concierge…'

'Not at all. If the key had been there she would have found it and you would be dead, that much I know. But the rest of the story… and what it is you want in order to disclose the whereabouts of the key… I have yet to discover. However, for you to be of any further use to me, I need your brain alive. So take my bed and get some sleep. With luck, the worst of the ravages as it leaves your system will pass while you are unconscious.'

10:24 A.M.

Coraloni's church clothes spill onto the floor as Krafft unties the coarse string.

'These had been left at the front desk of the Harder Minerva. As I earlier suggested, *der Erzengel* herself is long gone.'

He searches the road outside for anything he doesn't recognise, but all seems quiet now except for a few railway carriages filing slowly past the end of an open alley, windows reflecting sunlight into the street. He turns away to find the padre on the bed, tearing at the seams of a cassock.

'What are you doing?'

'What does it look like I am doing?'

'If I didn't know better I'd say that you were ripping up your only good set of clothes. Are you so tired of being a priest?'

Coraloni slings the torn cassock to the floor and begins on the next one. As he picks it up, the remaining scent of Angelica's flesh traps him in its cloying grip.

He throws it violently across the bed. 'Bitch!'

Krafft swings around in a chair, chin resting on his hands. 'Padre… for what are you looking?'

'For the bank papers. I hid them inside a loose seam in my cassock.'

Krafft smiles whimsically at him. Coraloni's anger flushes out the arsenic from his cheeks, burning brighter still.

'*You* have it!'

The smile lingers around Krafft's face, though neglecting his eyes, which harden at the accusation.

'Would that I had, Padre. Paper like that might be all it would take to prise the key from your grasp. But I assure you

I do not.'

'Then you can replace it? You can stop the original draft?'

Krafft throws socks, gaiters and dishevelled underwear to him.

'It was not a draft. It was access to a secret, numbered bank account.'

'Then you still have the number?'

Krafft wraps the remainder of the clothes in the brown paper and drops them in the chair.

'When is a secret not a secret, Padre?'

'I don't know. My head… I cannot think in conundrums.'

'A secret is no longer a secret once it has been shared.'

Krafft's gold watch appears again from his waistcoat pocket. He dangles it in the air between them. 'You have slept the clock around, my friend, and this particular secret was shared on Friday evening. It is now…' He steadies the watch. '… ten thirty-three.'

Coraloni stamps hard on the floor to kill the return of the tingling sensation. 'So what?'

The watch disappears back into Krafft's pocket.

'On Sunday.'

OCTOBER 30th.
SUNDAY

11:32 A.M.

Padre Coraloni shields his eyes against the lance of sun.

Everything around him seems bent on reflection where it will create the most discomfort. Flashes from the cutlery... little more than coffee spoons and the brash holders for napkins and vinaigrette... follow his eyes whichever way he turns.

Krafft observes him for a moment.

'It will take time, Padre. I might suggest two more days to rid your body of it. Four more days may effect a full cure. Of course... if there has been more permanent damage... then who can truly say?'

There is a sign above Coraloni's head for the Altstadt Tearooms. 'This is where she brought me.'

Krafft pours coffee into two cups.

'Then this is most likely where she began to poison you.'

Coraloni stares reluctantly at the silver coffee pot in the table centre.

Krafft pours him a cup and passes the sugar container.

'They serve arsenic only on Fridays.'

Stretching out his legs under the table, Coraloni massages the ache from his thighs. The short walk from Krafft's hotel has set his muscles on fire with a damnable tingling that permeates to the bone.

'I find myself forced to ask, where does an Astrologer of a *certain* eminence make the acquaintance of such a woman?'

'Ah. Good question, Padre. I have to admit that I

prepared a clever answer for this very occasion, but then I caught sight of myself in the mirror and I thought… do I look like the man such a woman would pursue? And the answer came, no, I do not.'

He opens the jacket to show the waistcoat beneath to be threadbare around the watch pocket. He strokes his chin, fingering a short growth of stubble. 'I am not a man much given to espionage either. All my secrets are open and available… so in effect I have none. It was my colleague to whom you delivered the device who recognised her. What use could she ever have for a man like me?'

The padre runs his tongue across his lips. They are still bloated and coarse, their rims sore and burning in the sunlight. 'I have no doubt she would find something… and she knows you have the device.'

'She also knows that you still have the key.'

'I do not have the key. There never was one.'

'Come, come, Padre. Man of the World I may not be but I do retain a degree of intelligence that resents being insulted.'

The waiter approaches the table to hand Coraloni a slip of paper. Coraloni reaches inside his cassock for a small purse attached to the body belt that is no longer there.

'The bitch took everything…'

Krafft's dark eyes remain hooded in the direct light, the overarching ridge of brow accentuating shadow to the point where they are unreadable. His high forehead caps a heart-shaped face and cleft chin that, as he speaks, carries an almost elfin smile.

'She left you your life. Amongst other things.'

'Barely.'

Coraloni shakes the ache from his fingers and the tingling sensation returns. 'And I hope that will prove her undoing.'

'Have you read my theory of 'Typoscomy'?'

Coraloni's blank look is Krafft's immediate answer.

'No. Why would you have? I only spent ten years of my life developing it.'

Coraloni picks up the coffee cup, then returns it slowly to the table without tasting a drop. 'We all need something in which to submerge our desires. For my own part it was the Church.'

Krafft bursts into outrageous laughter.

'You are priceless. The only thing you have devoted your life towards the progression of is Padre Coraloni.'

'And through that?'

'No, my Good Priest, I assure you, as an avid student of human nature, there is nothing whatsoever beyond that single principle. Given your obvious personality type, my theory, should I wish to apply it, would describe your future in minute detail.'

Krafft reaches for the slip of paper in Coraloni's fingers.

'I see also that I shall have to foot the bill for this consultation.'

He holds the paper in the shade of his hand. 'Ah! Padre. It seems that I was wrong in my initial assumption.'

Coraloni pushes it away. 'I cannot read that. The light… and it is a scribble.'

'It is not a 'scribble' as you call it. It is English.'

Coraloni touches the rim of the cup then withdraws his hand again. 'There is a difference?'

He shies away from the paper as Krafft pushes it back towards him. 'What does it say?'

'It says… Padre Dearest, I am glad to see that you are up and looking so well. The air here must agree with you.'

Coraloni rotates slowly in his chair, examining every window within sight but the sun pours across each pane like a golden blind. He returns to the table where the dark wood soothes his eyes. His voice is little more than a whisper.

'Damn her! Where is she?'

Krafft slides the watch from his pocket to study the dial.

'Who knows? I have to admit that she has run so far contrary to character that…'

'So much for '*Typoscomy*', then…'

Krafft throws a shower of small coins on the table.

'As your God has made of us strange bedfellows, I think a touch of humility will serve.'

The waiter scoops the coins from the cloth. He looks searchingly from one to the other before settling on Krafft.

'Herr Krafft?'

Krafft leans back in his chair. 'I am he…'

'Herr… there is a person from *Der Weisses Kreutz?* Your hotel?'

A young man in burgundy uniform waits at the edge of the pavement, the small round hat he affects as incongruous as the scuffed boots on his feet. Krafft studies him for a moment. The uniform has obviously been thrown on in some haste. The collar is folded under on the left and Krafft wants desperately to reach over and twitch it straight.

'What is the problem?'

The youth clicks his heels more smartly than the uniform might have suggested. 'Thank you, Herr Krafft. There is no problem. There is a telephone call for you at the hotel.'

Krafft folds the napkin onto the table. 'I am expecting no call.'

The waiter comes over to clear the cups. Krafft prods him. 'Stop that!' It makes me nervous. Who is making the telephone call?'

The messenger remains silent, eyes on the waiter. When no-one speaks, the waiter shrugs and walks away.

'You may speak freely in front of the good padre.' Krafft crosses his legs and leans away from the table. 'This is our confessional.'

The messenger's hands move to the collar of his jacket to hide a profusion of old stains.

'He said his name was Hess.'

Krafft muses for a moment.

'Hess..? Walter, the Physiologist?'

'No, Herr Krafft. He said his name was Rudolf Walter Hess. If you were in any doubt, I was told to mention the *Thule Society*?'

Krafft shoots up from the chair so quickly the youth stumbles back out of reach.

'*Herr Deputy Fuehrer*? Why did you not say so?'

He shoves the youth in front of him along the pavement.

'Hurry… tell him I am on my way.'

He turns to Coraloni. 'Stay here until I return.'

The padre indicates his empty pockets. 'I have nowhere to go.'

'Then remember that, my little Church Mouse.'

12:23 P.M.

'Krafft? Is that you? Identify yourself.'

'To whom must I do that?'

'Reichsminister Hess.'

'I am not sure how..?'

'Perhaps I can help. What is the thirteenth sign of the Zodiac?'

'Capricornus.'

There is silence on the telephone line where Krafft had expected confirmation. 'No… wait… I remember your letter now. It's Ophiuchus. Except that it's actually the eleventh… pushing Sagittarius into…'

'That will be enough, Krafft. Do you have the device?'

'Yes, Herr Reichsminister. I have it safe.'

'Is it intact?'

'Except for the key. I am working on the whereabouts of the key as we speak.'

'Leave the key. A key cannot be so difficult to make. You will be contacted at the station in Neuhausen. I need you in Munich as soon as possible.'

'Can I not work from here, Reichsminister? Switzerland is...'

'Switzerland is safe. If you are going to make predictions for me I need you to be near the cutting edge. You will enjoy all the benefits of being so close to the seat of power, I assure you.'

'I am flattered, Herr Reichsminister. I did not know that you were a student of my work.'

'I am a student of many things, Herr Krafft. Tell me... have you ever played Roulette?'

'As a young man... but very little in fact... I do not think that gambling is...'

'But what if you could be a little more certain, Herr Krafft, in which socket the ball would come to rest?'

'Then that would be a rare privilege... but it would also not be honest.'

'Only a fool allows honesty to stand in the way of ambition, and if the *Weldt Politik* is anywhere analogous to Roulette, then I have set the wheel in spin.'

'And my part in this?'

'Is to introduce the ball... exactly where and how I tell you. Now listen to me... go straight to your room and pack... and when you leave this hotel... do not return to where you left the priest.'

Krafft lifts the handset away from his ear and studies it.

'How did you know..?'

'I leave that for you to discover. Take this telephone number from the operator. Use it only if you have a problem.'

Krafft stares hard at the slip of paper handed him by the hotel operator. 'Are you certain?'

At the answering nod, he slips it thoughtfully into his jacket pocket.

12:48 P.M.

A stillness has fallen around Padre Coraloni. Krafft has been a necessary diversion but how much longer he will convince himself that there is a key is open to conjecture, and then what will happen? Perhaps it is in God's hands.

Coraloni shudders away the thought.

Young, pollarded lime trees line the avenue by the river and from behind Coraloni comes the sound of narrow wheels crushing the debris of autumn. A bath chair is drawn up to the wall beside him, its wheels wedged against a folded table.

A stooped, dark-haired woman is helping a large elderly man out of the wicker seat and into the café. Coraloni hears the brass bell on the door ring twice.

Devoting a second's thought to his options, before deciding that he has few or none at all, he closes his eyes against the sun to wait for Krafft to return.

The sting of an insect bites deep into his calf above the ankle. He opens his eyes to swat it away.

'Padre. We meet again.'

As detail filters back into his vision, he notices the tip of a familiar parasol resting against his sock.

'Please don't get up to greet me. In fact, please do not move at all. If you do… well, let us say that what will follow may be quite unpleasant, especially as your system has not yet had time to clear of my last ministrations.'

A cool brightness begins to spread across his skin where the parasol rests. Coraloni moves his head around slowly. He recognises the coat worn by the old woman… the wig is no doubt stuffed into the small round bag she now throws on the floor beside the discarded coat.

Even shabbily dressed, Angelica had been the most entrancing thing he had ever laid eyes on.

'God damn you, woman.' He spits drily on the floor beside the chair. 'I can still taste you.'

'How wonderful! Most people are left with just a painful memory.'

'What do you want from me?' Unable to face the light as the sun moves beyond zenith, Coraloni stares into the dark cloth covering his lap. 'You have already taken everything I had.'

'Then it won't help you to know that you only ever had one thing that I wanted.'

'The money?'

She laughs, overprinting his memory with its brightness.

'Oh, Heavens no. I have enough of that. I just didn't want you to have it. No. I want the key.'

The surface of the river beside them is convex and swollen where it gathers itself before plunging through the twisting rush of the turbine under the bridge.

Coraloni's thoughts emulate the scream and chop of the spinning blades.

'There… is… no… key.'

Angelica nudges his leg with the parasol and the needle bites deeper into his flesh. 'Then why is Krafft still here?'

Coraloni grips the edge of the table with both hands.

'Because he is as stupid as you are.'

With a twist of his upper body he wrenches at the table, but the table remains where it is, feet embedded in a large block of concrete.

Angelica thrusts viciously with the parasol. The hidden syringe empties like cold fire into Coraloni's muscle.

The tremor begins in his foot, spreading until the whole

of his left leg vibrates uncontrollably. His hands begin to shake with a rapid violence that he can't contain. His mouth drops at the corner, along with his left eye and the skin of that side of his face.

'You bitch…' is all he can manage. Spittle drools from his lips and down his neck.

Unable to resist, Coraloni is lifted from behind. Strong hands drag him from his seat and wrestle him into the bathchair.

Every touch sets his skin on fire. His own weight on his thighs has become unbearable. He would scream but his throat is empty of sound.

Angelica wipes his face with Krafft's discarded napkin.

'There… there… and you were looking so much better when I arrived.'

OCTOBER 30th.
SUNDAY

1:15 P.M.

Through the unsprung wheels of the chair, Coraloni experiences each joint in the paving as if it were a precipice. His eyes are fixed in their orbits but he can see anything that passes within his field of vision.

The platform of the Bahnhof is immediately familiar.

Angelica nudges the bathchair against a small step that bars her progress. 'Can you help me, please?'

The ticket officer comes from behind his screen to lift it over. 'What is the matter with him? He was fine the last time I saw him.'

'Our cousin has had a small stroke.' Angelica waits.

The information sinks slowly through the ticket officer's mind until he nods enthusiastically. 'Ach! You are taking him home to die!'

'Oh dear, no!' Angelica steers the chair away from the canopy and out onto the platform where the sun scorches into Coraloni's immovable eyes. 'I am taking him to the Klinik at Neuhausen. They have new treatments there.'

'Then he is fortunate to have you in his time of trouble.'

Angelica reaches over the handle of the chair until the pale flesh of her calves comes into view.

She pats the priest's shoulder. 'Yes, he is, isn't he. We are cut from the same cloth and I have sworn that his future will be as eventful as I can make it.'

The sun picks out the lace trim of her blue and taupe travelling suit. The ticket officer looks her up and down with little sense of shame. She stands upright and the hem of the skirt drops almost to the ground, leaving only her slender, polished boot heels on display.

'Then you will be needing tickets.'

'I have them.' Angelica rummages in her bag. 'I bought them earlier when I brought in my luggage.'

'Then there is only one problem. The chair will not fit into a compartment. It will have to go in the brake car. Can you take him out of it?'

'I cannot lift him myself, if that is what you mean.'

'Then he will have to ride in there with it.'

'That is no problem.' Angelica smiles broadly. 'I shall ride with him.' She smoothes the cloth of Coraloni's cassock where it falls across his lap. 'I can see to his every need.'

'There is only a seat for the Guard in there… and this is a six hour journey.'

'We will be fine. The Guard can use my seat in the compartment. Is it possible that the door can be locked?'

She taps the commode bowl suspended beneath the chair. 'Just in case?'

'I will see what I can do.'

The rocking of the train nauseates Coraloni. Acid swills around his empty stomach but his gorge will not rise to expel it. It forms a slow burn behind his ribs and that, along with the sunlight burned deep into his retinas, are not the only things he can feel. His entire skin is alive with needles of pain.

Angelica moves in and out of his vision, occasionally sitting on the Guard's seat from where she studies his face, staring into his eyes as if she were flaying him, layer by layer.

The Guard enters through the door behind Coraloni.

'Is he alright?'

Angelica peers theatrically into the depth of Coraloni's eyes. 'Yes. He is still with us. Aren't you, cousin dear?'

The Guard unties a length of string from a postal sack.

'It would be safer if we tied the chair to the rack on the wall.'

'Maybe later… when we reach the mountains. Until then I want to be able to help him. You understand?'

'Would you like me to lock the door?'

'Just leave the key in this side of the lock. I will see to it myself.'

The Guard fits the key in the door before moving off along the train. Angelica turns the key until it clicks.

'Now, Padre. Remind me where we left off.'

Opening her bag on the Guard's desk she places two slim, silver cases in the pigeon holes in front of her, along with three small phials, two of them clear, the third half-filled with a black viscous fluid that ripples with the motion of the train.

In the first case is a surgical blade, fitted into a handle where a simple twist makes it secure. She dabs a colourless liquid from one of the phials onto a snatch of cotton wool and holds it under Coraloni's nose where the odourless sting of alcohol brings tears to his eyes.

She raises the hem of his cassock, hitching it up until she can tuck it under his chin, rearranging his head so that he is forced to look down into his own lap.

'I do so love an audience.'

Angelica applies the contents of a second phial to a swatch of cotton wool. 'This will stop the bleeding.' She examines his badly shaven face. 'You must have used some yourself this morning.'

Coraloni can resist nothing but inside him a violence is building that shows only in the flush of his cheeks and in the depth of his eyes. He is acutely aware of every inch of his skin and in the places where Angelica is performing her rudimentary surgery it burns like a bright star. As long as she leaves him alive... someone will pay for this.

Angelica takes off his Biretta.

'I sometimes think that Catholic Priests lack adornment, don't you?' She smiles beatifically at him as she brushes away loose strands from his forehead. 'Such beautiful hair... such a shame it will always be hidden under a cap.'

She slopes his head back until it rests against the wicker of the chair and wipes the skin of his forehead with a swab.

The cold intensity of the alcohol lights a pyre in his brain. He knows will never forget that particular smile.

2:18 P.M.

Angelica stands with her back to the compartment door, fingers deftly closing the lock behind her.

'Frau Pedersen... an unexpected...'

'A word to the wise, *Herr* Krafft... do not ever call me *Frau*. You Germans...'

'Swiss...'

'Whatever... you make it sound so utterly bovine.'

'I assure you no slight was intended.' He indicates a seat diagonally across the compartment from himself.

'Be seated.'

Angelica sits opposite him.

'Herr Krafft… how do you know who I am? We have never met… so far as I recollect.'

Krafft tips his head in slight deference. He makes the motion of identifying her perfume but also… beneath that… the something else he had heard the priest speak of.

'Your identity followed you into the compartment.'

'Ah. The priest.'

Krafft turns up his hands as if expecting to see coarse, fibrous weave still clinging to the sweat now lining his palms.

'I folded his cassock.'

Angelica reaches across to touch one palm with a single finger. Krafft recoils immediately.

'If I didn't know better, Herr Krafft, I would think that you were a little afraid of me.'

'Should I have reason to be?'

'Not so long as we can reach an agreement.'

'Like you did with Padre Coraloni?'

'The padre had his own agenda.'

'Had?'

'I shall correct myself… *still has*… although I suspect that his perspective may have changed somewhat. Whereas you, Herr Krafft, have no agenda to speak of.'

Krafft stares straight into her eyes. 'No more than any other man?'

Angelica returns the stare steadily, smiling only when she sees his eyes flicker to her mouth, her hair… and back again.

'Far less so than most, I suspect.'

'Yet you are exceedingly handsome.'

'And you are as bad as the priest. Is this the new age we are working for? Where it is not enough to be beautiful…

one has to be *handsome* also?'

'You would be beautiful in any age… and were I to find myself occupying your body, in a strictly existential manner, I assure you… I would be consumed by my own ecstasy. As are you.'

'Then how do I storm your particular rampart, Herr Krafft. Afford me some small clue.'

Her eyes are indeed as the priest had said… at once beguiling and terrifying in their almost perfection. The seemingly insignificant green segment amongst the blue of the left placing them in his psyche somewhere between.

'It would depend upon what you thought was behind it.'

'You know what I want.'

'Then I have to say that I do not have it.'

'Herr Krafft, you would not travel to your assignation in Neuhausen unless you had what I seek. I promise you this. I shall not allow you to leave Switzerland with it in your possession.'

Krafft averts his gaze as the train continues to decelerate. Outside, a sign drifts past beside the track. He laughs out loud. Angelica leans toward him.

Her breasts heave into Krafft's sphere of vision.

'You doubt my ability?'

Krafft dismisses her with a sweeping gesture. 'Put away your toys and learn to recognise when you have lost the game. The device is already in Germany.'

Angelica sits up quickly. 'That cannot be. I know you have it with you.'

'Indeed.' Krafft moves up to the window, pointing to the sign on the platform they have that moment drawn up against. 'And it is now clearly in Germany… as are you, my dear *Frau* Pedersen.'

'I was not born yesterday, Krafft. This train does not go into Germany.'

'Then you failed to hear the Guard. There has been a rock fall at the entrance to the tunnel. We have been re-routed through that small, western arm of Germany that penetrates deep into Switzerland. With all the security and identity checks that the German border guards will make this will add four hours to my journey. Unfortunately, it may add much longer to yours.'

Angelica shifts uneasily in her seat. 'I cannot go into Germany. I do not have the necessary papers.'

'And as I have your identity, I am sure I will be well rewarded by *der Vaterland*?'

'Herr Krafft… look at me… you cannot let this happen. You know what they will do to me.'

Krafft tilts forward to stare into her eyes. Buried in the depth, beneath layers of confidence and bravado, there is a real fear.

'I have a suggestion. I assume that you know the whereabouts of the priest?'

'He is in the baggage car.'

'You brought him with you?'

'I had no wish to kill him outright. He is much more fun alive.'

'I am not sure that he would share your sentiment. I am also unsure how to approach this problem now. Shall we find the priest and ask his opinion?'

'Sit back down, Herr Krafft. The priest will be talking to no-one.'

'I see…'

'No, you don't see. He is still alive. If inconvenienced.'

'Then how do I storm *your* particular rampart, *Frau* Pedersen? Afford me some small clue.'

'Tell me why you should, *Herr* Krafft. In your position I would have little interest in my survival.'

'Let us say that while you are alive and free, I find I have something to aspire to.'

'You surprise me, Krafft… or have you seen my fate in your futures?'

Krafft chuckles out loud. 'I'm afraid not, *Frau…*'

'*Angelica…* please! If you call me by that appendage again your crystal ball will be the sole orb remaining.'

'My interest in your future… *Angelica…* is little more than an applied interest in my own. Where I am going I may find myself in need of a weapon and, as a weapon, I think you have few peers.'

'So your motive is not entirely selfish, then?'

'Put away your humour, unless you wish to find yourself the source of endless amusement. The border guards are unlikely to understand the implied nuance of *'handsome'*.'

OCTOBER 30th.
SUNDAY

3:51 P.M.

A stolid figure blocks the whole of the entrance from the corridor. *'Ihre papieren bitte.'*

Through the small side window Angelica notices two others behind him. The trooper waits for her to respond.

Disgusted by the broken skin and grime-edged nails of the proffered hand, she turns her head away.

The trooper moves further into the compartment, reaching for the small purse in her lap.

'Halt!'

The trooper spins around to face Krafft, dropping the rifle from his shoulder in a futile gesture.

Krafft stands, making it impossible to lower the barrel in the confined space.

'Entschuldige Sie mir. I did not mean to shout.' He shows his own travel warrant. The trooper passes it without a glance to those waiting behind him and turns once more to Angelica. *'Ihre Papieren… Bitte!'*

Angelica hurls a look of appeal to Krafft. She hisses at him in Italian. *'Do something.'*

Krafft catches the arm of the trooper. 'Do you have the use of a telephone on the station?'

The trooper dismisses him. 'That is no concern of yours. All I want are the *Frau's* papers. If she has none she will have to leave the train and remain here until she can be identified.'

Krafft sighs, amused by the bright mixture of appeal and fury in Angelica's eyes. 'The *lady* is accompanying me on a mission for the Reich.'

The guard retrieves Krafft's papers from the men in the corridor. 'You can prove this?'

Krafft slides the papers into his jacket pocket. 'Yes, I can prove this. Show me to your telephone.'

3:59 P.M.

'Herr Reichsminister… I apologise for the call.'

'No matter, Krafft. I needed an excuse to leave the rhetoric behind but why have you called? The device is safe?'

'Certainly, Herr Reichsminister and now… perhaps more safe than ever.'

'There is a problem for me in your charts, Herr Krafft?'

'Not at all, Herr Reichsminister, providing you are happy to guarantee safe passage for my companions.'

'You are to arrive in Neuhausen alone, Krafft. You hear me? Alone. There will be no contact made if I suspect you are followed. You have no need of companions.'

'It appears that the priest is on the train.'

'I ordered you to leave that idiot in Interlaken. Are you always so inept?'

'No. But with respect, Herr Reichsminister, it was my other travelling companion who brought him on board. I have only been made aware of this situation in the last moments.'

Krafft waves away the border guard listening over his shoulder. 'I am trying to do my best here in a fluid situation. I also think it is in our interest to add your assurances to the border patrol.'

'Why should I be interested in these people? Do you have the device or not?'

'Yes, Herr Reichsminister… but…'

'Then dispense with your companions, Krafft. I have no need for idiot priests. Germany has its quota.'

162

'I too am unconcerned about the priest. My other companion has made certain alterations that make it unwise to be associated with him.'

'Why would they do that?'

'She thought it would be fun.'

'She..?'

'A certain… Frau Pedersen… Herr Reichsminister?'

'Archangel?'

'The same…'

'I shall not forget this, Krafft. Please pass the telephone to the border guard.'

4:03 P.M.

At the end of the platform, the door to the baggage car has been slid open and the bathchair dragged out into the lowering sunlight.

One of the soldiers lifts the priest's Biretta to show the others. Sharp peals of laughter echo around the empty waiting rooms. The border guard ushers Krafft back onto the train but Krafft hesitates.

'What about the priest?'

The border guard urges him into the carriage. 'He is to remain here. It appears there are plans already in hand for him.'

Krafft takes his customary seat by the window. The border guard sits beside him.

From across the compartment, Angelica searches Krafft's face for an explanation.

Krafft crosses his legs, straightening the cuff of his trousers before reaching into his pocket for his pipe.

'It appears we have company, my dear *Frau* Pedersen. For myself… to Neuhausen… for you… to Munich.'

'Munich? I cannot be found in Munich. Have you any idea how long they have been trying to…'

'My dear Angelica, where there is life there is hope. However… if you feel that your circumstances would be more favourable out there on the platform with the priest… then be my guest. The officer here would be reluctant… but I dare say you have ways to convince him?'

Angelica stares along the platform to where the bath chair sits out in the light. She is aware that every touch of sun on the priest's skin will bring excruciating discomfort. If she leaves him this way, incapable of response, they will quickly tire of him. Beyond that a swift bullet to the head will bring an end to his misery and she hates it when her plans are interrupted.

'Herr Krafft? Can you convince the guard to allow me to wish *auf wiedersehen* to the padre?'

'I think that might be possible… but why would you want to?'

'Why did you wish to save my life?'

Krafft gestures with the stem of the empty pipe.

'Because I think that at some point you may return the favour.'

'And if I told you that a belief in altruism has never crossed my horizon, what then, Herr Krafft?'

'You would still be an interesting study.'

'And the padre?'

'I am curious as to what more you can possibly do to him.'

'With your permission… I am about to make his life much more interesting.'

Krafft smiles. 'Why do I get the feeling that he may not share your enthusiasm for his impending state of grace?'

'If he had ever existed in a state of grace… I would have let them shoot him.'

'Then with my blessing…'

A quick word with the border guard brings a grunted

reply.

'The guard says that he is ordered to accompany you until you reach Munich.'

'Everywhere?' She looks the guard up and down, but a peasant in uniform is still a peasant, the world over. 'That could become interesting.'

Krafft identifies the look in her eye. 'I am sure you will be able to contain yourself.'

Angelica slips from the carriage, clutching at the fastenings of her small purse. Along the platform, soldiers are occupying a seat in the shade of the canopy and laughing amongst themselves. The priest swelters out on the bare concrete, hatred blazing in his eyes at Angelica's approach.

She kneels beside the bathchair. 'Forgive me, Padre... for I have sinned.'

His skin radiates such lividity that Angelica is almost concerned.

'You poor darling. This much sun is not good for one's blood pressure... but don't worry... your very own Angel is here to help.'

From her purse, a syringe slips into the shadow between herself and the chair. 'I am sorry, I have had no time to sterilise this, but I think that an infection will be the least of your worries.'

She lifts his hand as if to kiss it, her thumb holding back the flow of blood until the needle penetrates a prominent vein. 'This will take three or four hours to work, during which time you will reject every ounce of bodily fluid you contain. If they allow you to survive that without putting you out of your misery then there will be little to stop you regaining a full and *interesting* life. All I ask is your promise never to forget me.'

Coraloni's eyes flare with unmitigated venom. She smiles in return. 'I will take that as a yes.'

The tracklayer's labourer who has been sent along the platform for water replaces the padre's cap, adjusting it properly.

'So! Now I see what they were laughing at... but why are you dressed as a priest?'

Coraloni can do no more than roll his eyes. His limbs are vibrating infernally as sensation begins to return.

The labourer shouts along the platform to his colleague.

'Someone is having a little joke here.' He leans down to speak to the padre. 'Do you think it is a joke, eh? *Juden*?'

'Loos... come away before the soldiers return. They may not find it so funny.'

Loos shouts back. 'Of course it is funny... How many *Juden* do you know who try to escape into Germany?'

'I... I... am... a priest.'

'What?' Loos brings his ear close to the priest's mouth, reeling away from the bitter stench of his breath.

Coraloni struggles the words to the surface where they drool from the corner of his lips.

'Priest... on train... please...'

'Loos! What are you doing?'

The plate-layer stands in horror as Loos tips the wheels of the chair over the baggage car threshold before sending the priest inside with a final push. He reaches up to slide the door closed.

Loos makes his way back along the track, jumping down beside his colleague.

'My uncle... he is also a priest.'

The plate-layer cuffs him hard on the side of his head.

'And your uncle is also a dead man?'

4:48 P.M.

The green fields and river rills of Germany etch their way across the window beside Angelica.

Krafft dips in his pocket for his pipe, only to find that he had unwittingly broken it in his earlier frustration.

'Put that thing away.'

'Might I remind you… *Frau* Pedersen… that you are travelling solely at my discretion and if I should choose to smoke…?'

Angelica sits up abruptly. 'May I remind you that the discretion has passed from your hands to that of Reichsminister Hess?'

Krafft nods toward the border guard occupying the corner seat. 'Only for as long as I affirm that to *him*.'

The note of the engine shifts downbeat. The sliver of Germany flashing by the window resolves into a clearer picture as they slow. Krafft checks his watch.

'It seems we have made good time. I did not expect the border again so soon.'

The border guard leaves as they are brought up with a lurch at a makeshift platform. Outside, a small squad of *Heer* soldiers are standing to attention.

Footsteps make their way unhurriedly along the corridor until they stop at the compartment door. It slides back and a tall man, hatless, shocked with dark hair, heavily-browed and square-jawed, enters the compartment. His suit is a pale grey with the finest dark stripe. His shoes are tan, polished and reflective.

'Herr Krafft?'

Recognition rattles through his previous display of arrogance and Krafft leaps to his feet.

He indicates frantically that Angelica should do the same.

Hess holds up a hand to stay the movement she had never intended to make.

'Herr Krafft. I think introductions are in order.'

Krafft stammers, his hands not knowing what is expected of them. He has never been fond of salutes. His fingers disseminate the bits of pipe in his pocket.

'I… I thought that you knew…'

Hess waves him to his seat. 'Perhaps, but we have never been formally introduced.' He smiles down at Angelica. 'And I always find the formalities interesting.'

Angelica holds out her hand for him to take. His face is darkening from the lack of a recent shave, but for now it affords him a certain *kreatürlich* air. His hand is hard and dry like the dark depths of his eyes.

He kisses her hand and returns it gently. 'I am Rudolf. And you must be?'

'Mrs. Pedersen.'

Krafft snorts. '*Frau…*'

Angelica finds her perception locked into the movement of Hess's eyes, while her mind as ever floats free.

'*Herr* Krafft… If your own future ever becomes as clear as your unkindness to me, it will make very short reading.'

Reichsminister Hess motions Krafft from his seat so he can place himself opposite Angelica.

'I had heard… but never thought…' He leans toward her, elbows on knees. 'This should be one of those soul-searching moments, like standing on the ledge of a very tall building, but your beauty is all the more so…'

'Do not analyse me, *Liebherr*, or I may disappear.'

'*Entschuldige Sie mir, bitte…*'

Hess tears himself away from her eyes. 'What is it, Krafft?'

Krafft reaches the box from the overhead rack. 'I have

brought you this.'

He hands it to Hess who slides it onto the seat beside him and returns to his contemplation of Angelica.

'Do you not wish to…'

'All things in their time, Krafft. All things in their time.' He hands the box back to Krafft. 'You have sole charge of this device. From this moment on its safekeeping shall be your first priority.'

'I have other commitments… arrangements…'

'Then I apologise. The device shall be your second priority. Your first will be to find another compartment.'

He points towards the door. '*Geh jetzt, weg!*'

Alone now, Hess returns his attention to Angelica.

'May I ask what you are doing with this… fortune teller?'

'What do *you* intend to do with him?'

'There are those who consider his guidance valuable, but Krafft is no longer your concern.'

'But I am travelling under his protection.'

Hess closes the compartment door, locks it and draws down the blinds.

'That privilege now belongs to me, *Erzengel.*'

6.40 P.M.

Hess enters the compartment Krafft has found at the front of the train, shocking him from his reverie.

'I wish to speak to you about the device that you have brought. My own position has been sidestepped on so many occasions that I now want to know what is happening before it happens. Retrieve this machine of yours and instruct me. I wish to understand it fully before it reaches Berchtesgaden.'

'I have to state, *Herr Reichsminister*, that I resent the attempted use of this machine. It is unprofessional.'

'In what way? Surely anything that helps to see our future

is of use?'

'I have developed my own field of research in which I am an eminent practitioner.'

'In a competition of one… that is most impressive.'

'I see that the benefits of 'Typoscomy' have not yet reached the ears of Berlin.'

'*Im Gegenteil*, Herr Krafft. It has been the talk at all the best dinner parties.'

Krafft sets the box aside. 'You mock me.'

Hess leans forward apologetically. 'I do not mock you. It is the truth. It was your vision of a Unified Europe that first caught the Chancellor's ear, and also that of the Archangel, if memory serves me well.'

'Frau Pedersen?'

'If that is what you wish to call her. I hear of that woman everywhere. It is with little surprise that I find her riding your shirt-tail.'

'I must protest!'

Hess crosses his legs and smiles. 'Not too loudly I hope. I left her asleep in the other compartment.'

'If the Chancellor does indeed accept my vision that Europe can become unified, then why does he pursue such a divisive course. History will…'

'…be written by the victorious, as always, Herr Krafft.'

'But there is no need to conquer. Given time, the whole of Europe will willingly give up their sovereignty to a new and revitalised Germany.'

'How appealing, but why should anyone wish to unify a fractured mirror when it would never bear a true reflection? No. A new mirror must be forged without warp or blemish. Only then will unification become an irreversible process.'

'My calculations prove that Time alone will achieve this.'

'Ha! Time…'

'You scoff? In a world where the planets and their

effects still remain beyond the wit of man?'

'What role do your stars show for the *Englisch* in this Unified Europe of yours? Herr Hitler sees them as a major concern.'

'The *Englisch* will never become a part of Europe. They may say they will, but Time will demonstrate the wisdom of letting that sleeping dog lie.'

'Then without them, Herr Krafft, how do we impose this New Order of yours? With Legislation by Zodiac? I wish to see this in my lifetime, not in Time's good grace and I feel it is now within our grasp.'

'Then why do you need the machine?'

7:04 P.M.

The train drifts to a standstill in Neuhausen.

Hess releases the blinds on Angelica's compartment and stares westward to the dark waters of the Rhein where they gather energy to challenge the falls that provide a constant sonic background. He shakes her gently awake.

'Angelica? We shall alight here. Do you have luggage?'

'A little. In the baggage car. I shall go and retrieve it.'

'Then I shall meet you by the ticket office... or will you need a hand?'

Angelica fastens the clip on her bag. 'No. It is quite modest.'

On her way through to the baggage car she tries the toilet door. It is now unlocked.

7:13 P.M.

'Herr Krafft? You have the parcel safe, I see?'

'It has now become my first priority, as you suggested, Reichsminister. Though I now I thank you for your earlier intervention. There is something about that woman that...'

Hess scans the empty platform for Angelica. She must still be on the train.

'Yes… there is… isn't there. See to it that the device gets safely to Munich. My office there will take it from you.'

'But I thought… *Der Fuehrer?*'

'The line between madness and greatness is increasingly a slender one and you are not adept enough to walk it alone. Unless you continue to press your case, I shall keep you safe.'

Angelica's suitcase has been ravaged… her dresses are ripped and strewn across the floor. Scarcely a stitch is left untouched but one garment alone is missing. Her favourite travelling suit has gone.

She reaches into her bag. The new bank draft is still there, tucked into the liner. She can always buy more clothes.

Hess is out there on the platform, scanning the length of the train to find her. She steps down into his hands in time to see her favourite blue-and-taupe disappearing down the side of the station building, gripped hard between two *Heer* officers.

On the apron of the station a temporary border post has been erected. Hess holds out his Party card for inspection.

The guard examines it respectfully under the light and hands it back with a salute.

He holds out a hand to Angelica.

'*Ihre Papieren, bitte?*'

Hess throws his arm around her shoulders and gives the guard a broad smile as they sweep through the exit and out into the evening light of Neuhausen am Rheinfall.

Angelica kicks her feet gaily as she walks. 'Find me a clothes shop.'

'But I thought… perhaps another short interlude… *mein Engel?*'

'Not yet. Shopping is what I do when I'm on holiday.'

CHRONICLE

III

SALVE

Honoire (Badessa)
Abbazia di Novalesa
Alta Val Susa
Piedmont
Italia

1939
October 6th.

Dear Sister Minette,

My heart hopes that this letter finds you well. Many months have passed since the doctor delivered your letter, but the content of it yet burns quietly in the drawer of my desk and I can seldom refrain from taking it out to read over. I have not been quiet during this time. I have used it to explore the possibility of granting your wish. I am now informed of a place in the old Chateau on the knoll above your village of La Roque.

Within a gated garden there is a small chapel that has fallen into poor repair. The last surviving son of the house perished in the Great War and who now owns the place I am unaware. No claim has been made on the estate but the chapel was once officially consecrated and as such deserves any attention you can give it. It seems that a M'sieur Godenot has the key. If you can find him, then with his permission and our blessing, you may enter the chapel and redeem it as a place of worship. Please apply directly to myself for any reasonable funding you may need.

I hope that by the time you receive this letter you have resolved any differences with your father, who seems a good man, though afflicted by circumstance and the circuitous nature of less than forthright people. Remember also that he is a doctor. You could not have hidden the Devil's handiwork from him forever. I hope in my heart that this child will shed light into the lives of all who love her.

I wish you God's Strength, The Love of Our Saviour, and our own best wishes to keep you safe throughout this trial.

I have so far resisted Sister Mirais' constant urging to be allowed to join you. Unless you keep me informed of your progress, I may have to accede to her request,

Madre Honoire.

1944

SEPTEMBER 22nd.
FRIDAY

5:57 A.M.

The world beyond the village has been quiet for some days. The shelling has now ceased and the pervasive rumble of war has moved away to the north. The air is cleaner and crisp as the land falls into the softer rhythm of autumn.

It is early yet, the streets are empty and the sun is still beyond the reach of nearby house roofs, trimming barely an edge of sky with a promised pink glow.

Sister Minette is clearing the chapel steps of leaves that have drifted from the alders either side of the lych gate. She scoops a pile into her arms with the aid of a flat board and notices something from the corner of her eye.

In the growing light, a movement has appeared at the bottom of the road. Misshapen and indistinct of colour, it staggers in the shadows. Minette puts down the leaves, takes a step towards the path… then goes back for her brush.

The shape is still approaching but it has not yet entered the light. It comes to a halt many yards away and collapses slowly in a heap.

Thinking it a horse or a donkey, Minette wonders who to ask for help. Most of the village men have been taken by the war in one way or another. Only Auguste of those that are left has enough good sense, but his house is further along, beyond the creature that lies moaning and threshing.

Brandishing the broom before her, she descends the hill.

She begins to notice both grey and brown. As she nears it, her bare feet searching the cobbles for a secure purchase from which to swing the broom, it speaks to her.

'*Kamerad? Hilfen Sie mir. M'aidez.*'

She lowers the broom. The creature has two faces. One of them still and closed, the other looking up at her with an appeal in its eyes.

'*M'aidez?*'

Through the tangle of limbs, Minette can see that one man had been carrying the other on his back. The smile in his eyes searches her face… but in his hand is a rifle. She stands back quickly. His fingers uncurl from the strap and he lets go. Minette darts in to knock the rifle away with her broom.

'*M'aidez?*'

The other body is laid across the speaker, their legs entwined where they have collapsed in the road.

Minette untangles them. With the help of her arm, the soldier climbs unsteadily to his feet. On his cheek is a dark powder burn and his dishevelled *feldgrau* uniform reeks of cordite. He moves to pick up his rifle but Minette gets there first and stands firmly upon it.

The soldier surrenders it to her with a shrug.

'*Haben Sie… avez-vous… eine Zigarette?*' Then he laughs at his own joke. He pats his top pocket and finds a stub which he inserts between his lips.

He stares up at Minette's disapproving face, framed by the black Carmelite hood and white bib, and at the brown habit that barely covers her feet. He notices the distorted foot that is pinning his rifle to the ground and nods sagely.

He puts the stub back in his pocket and grins. '*Ich suchte nach Lili Marlene… und ich habe sie gefunden.*'

Minette rounds on him, brush held high. 'Why have you come here. You are not welcome.'

The soldier shrugs. '*Was? Nichts verstehen.*'

Blood rolls sluggishly from beneath the man on the floor. It is seeping along the tricks between the cobbles, absorbed in places by the dust in the cracks, otherwise pooling and congealing.

Minette pokes him gently with the end of her broom. He moans softly. She drops the broom and kneels beside him.

'He is alive!'

The soldier tries to nudge her aside. She shoves him violently to the edge of the pavement with the head of the broom. He rolls back onto his knees beside her.

'*Ja. Er es nicht tot. Aber, vielleicht…*'

Minette turns the face of the man on the floor. He is clean-shaven with no sign of stubble except a gentle blueing of the top lip under the stain of battle. She lifts an eyelid and a pupil gazes back at her. Clear, brown and wide, it rolls upwards unconsciously.

She reads the insignia on his uniform. 'He is French!'

'… french? *Ach! Ja. Er ist ein Französischer, vielleicht.*'

Minette hits the soldier hard with the flat of both hands, shouting into his face. 'Do not move!'

'*Was?*'

'*Nichts* move!' Minette shouts, knowing it to be in vain. As the soldier reaches for his rifle, Minette snatches it up and points it at him.

'Dear Lord. What on earth am I doing?'

The soldier slides his hand along the barrel to a place beside the bolt while Minette stands mesmerised. His fingers click off the safety catch.

He nods at her and raises his hands.

'*Kamerad.*'

Minette's own hands are alive with tremors, the barrel of the rifle describing loose circles in the air.

The soldier watches the small black hole at the end with

a lack of intensity only war can endow.

He reaches into an inside pocket, draws out a tattered book and offers it to her. He places his hands together as if in prayer then bows his head.

Minette takes the book from him and flicks it open to read the inscription. She lowers the rifle and slips the book of psalms into her pocket. 'Wait here.'

The soldier's face seem much older now in the growing light. His eyes more clear with understanding.

When Minette has gone, he searches the pockets of the uniform the other man is wearing. From a small paper packet he unwraps a piece of stale cheese, then recovers his cigarette stub from the gutter.

6:12 A.M.

'Auguste! Auguste!' Minette clatters into the yard behind the workshop. The vent is convulsing where steam passes through the wall to greet the chill air outside. 'Auguste!'

Auguste Godenot opens the door as Minette threads her way through stacks of seasoning timber, sending some of it flying.

'Sister? Slow down, you will hurt yourself.'

'Come quick. There is a soldier…'

'Sit down a moment, get your breath. Listen to yourself, you sound like my boiler.'

'There are two of them.'

'In God's name Sister, what are you doing with that?'

He points to the rifle that Minette has forgotten she is holding. 'Has the clergy joined the war?'

She thrusts it at him, catching hard at her breath.

'No. I… I took it off him.'

Auguste Godenot steps back and holds up his hands in surrender. 'Maybe you should have joined Jacqueline in the Maquis. You may be our last hope.'

'Auguste! Stop being facetious! You are needed. Now!'

'Sister, I have known and loved you a long time. You do not need to come in here waving a rifle around to give me orders.'

Minette makes a loud, angry sound and throws the rifle into the corner against a stack of timber. It fires with a report that fills the room with the smoke of discharged powder.

The morning light filters in through a new hole in the roof and dust showers down upon them, peppering the surface of Auguste's first coffee of the day with small insects. He tips it into the ash pile by the boiler.

'*Now* you have my attention…'

6:29 A.M.

To Minette's surprise, the soldier is still there when they arrive back at the hill.

He nods to Auguste. '*Kameraden?*'

'*Ja. Kameraden. Deutsche großmutter.*'

Auguste turns to Minette and caresses the large beak of his nose, the prominent chin and deeply carved lines around his eyes.

'Some say it accounts for this.'

'What do they want, Auguste?'

Auguste squats down, eyes level with the soldier's.

'*Was wünschst du hier?*'

The soldier stares directly into Auguste's eyes and there is a sympathy in that gaze.

Auguste feels it supremely misguided but he reaches in his jacket and hands a crushed half-pack of cigarettes to the soldier.

'*Dein Name?*'

'*Kürt. Und sie?.*'

'Auguste.'

The soldier takes the packet greedily. '*Jüdisch?*'

Auguste hesitates a moment, stroking his nose. '*…Ja.*'

The soldier nods slowly. '*Ich verstehe.*'

He gestures with the cigarette. '*Zünde, Bitte?.*'

Auguste offers a match and the soldier draws heavily on the cigarette, the tip glowing brightly. Subconsciously, he cups a hand around the end.

'*Wer sie schiessen? Ich hörte einen Schuss.*'

Auguste laughs out loud. '*Meine Werkstatt hat eine neue Bohrung im Dach.*'

Minette nudges him. 'Auguste, what are you saying?'

'He asks who you shot. I told him my workshop has a new hole in the roof.'

The soldier points anxiously with the lit cigarette. '*Der Junge.*'

Auguste looks more closely at the figure on the ground. '*Junge?*'

'*Ja. Dreizehn oder vierzehn. Nicht mehr.*'

Auguste turns to Minette.

'He says he is just a boy. Thirteen, maybe fourteen. We must get him to safety quickly.'

The soldier moves to help but Auguste points back down the hill.

'*Nein. Jetzt gehen. Schnell! Schnell!*'

'*Meine Gewehr?*'

'*Nein.*' Auguste is glad now that he has taken the time to hide the rifle in amongst the stacked timber. '*Kein Gewehr.*'

He thrusts the pack of cigarettes at him. '*Hier.*'

The soldier takes them and nods gratefully. '*Speise, Bitte?*'

'*Nein.*' Auguste turns away. 'I have no food to spare.'

Minette holds out the book of psalms from her pocket. 'He gave me this.'

Auguste takes it from her, flicking the pages with his

thumb. Inside the cover is a dedication from a mother… it may not even be his… war has a way of shifting allegiances. His eyes will not focus on the long sloping hand. He hands it to the soldier.

'Here… this may be all you need.'

The soldier takes it from him, then slips it back into Minette's pocket.

Auguste follows the exchange with a smile and points a direction.

'Up the hill is a vegetable garden. *Gemüsegarten… essen was Sie wollen.*'

Minette rounds on him angrily. 'That is my garden.'

'Sister, he has just tried to save the life of this boy here so I told him to eat whatever he wants. What kind of a Christian would it make you if you turned him away empty-handed?'

'But he is a soldier.'

'He is a man. With a government that makes him do things they should know better than to make a man do. Help me carry this boy to my workshop.'

SEPTEMBER 22nd.
FRIDAY

7:16 A.M.

Auguste ushers away the people outside his workshop.

'It was nothing… it was an accident. Go home please. Wait… Danielle… Blanche… we might need a hand.'

Minette and Danielle hold the boy between their arms while Auguste sweeps sawdust and filings from the bench.

He pads a clean dust-sheet along its length and they lay the boy carefully on top of it.

Standing back, they can now see that his uniform doesn't fit. The jacket bulges at the sides but the arms are too short. The trousers are held together with string around the waist and the legs show three inches of ankle above a pair of worn-out boots.

Minette's habit and Danielle's hands are drenched in fresh blood. Auguste examines the boy from head to foot, finding a hole in the jacket, right over the heart.

He slips his hand inside the coat and finds a corresponding hole in the shirt, surrounded by a large black patch of hard, congealed blood. He rips at the cloth with his fingers to bare the boy's chest. It is smooth, hairless and undamaged.

'He wasn't wearing this when the bullet went through.'

Auguste turns out the linings of the boy's pockets. The left is empty but tucked in the corner of the right one is a small coin. He holds it under the light but the edges are so irregular and the surface so blurred with age that in this light he can't tell whose face it bears. He hefts it in his hand.

'What is it, Auguste?'

'I don't know, Sister. It's not heavy enough for gold.' He scrapes at it with a fingernail. 'It might be bronze.'

He passes it over to Minette. 'Here… the Church has more need for coin than I do these days.'

Minette slips it into the leather pouch at her waist. 'I will bless you for it.'

'No need, Sister. You do that by your presence. Lend a hand here.'

With Danielle's help they lift the boy up and remove the jacket and the shirt. As they lay him back down he finds his hands slick with blood.

'Turn him, quickly.'

They turn him on the dust sheet. Blood wells from two holes punched deep into his back beside the spine. Auguste measures them with his fingers and realises that they are directly behind the heart.

He shakes his head. 'I am no doctor.'

Danielle turns to a blonde child hovering in the edge of the light. 'Oriel. Go fetch your father, now.'

Auguste stops her. 'The doctor is away on a visit. Jacques Alons' wife breeched last night. They left Oriel with me so it's my guess he's still there. That's twenty miles away.'

He catches Minette's eye. 'I don't think this boy will wait that long. We will have to use whatever skills we have.'

He reaches into a drawer under the bench and removes a bound cloth, unties the strap around it and rolls its length along the bench. Inside it, tools nestle in individual pockets.

He selects a few and passes them to Minette who examines them closely.

'Blanche, fill a pan with water from the boiler.'

Oriel passes her a clean porcelain bowl from the stand in the corner. Blanche snatches it from her hand.

'Thank you. Now go.'

The girl stands rooted, watching the boy's breathing. It

fades, becoming ragged and indeterminate.

'Oriel! Go!'

Oriel retreats into the corner, lean arms held tight against her body. 'You are losing him.' And then as if she can stem the time that is passing from his face, she shouts out loudly.

'Do not lose him.'

Auguste turns to her. 'Oriel...'

'Here...' Oriel reaches under her skirt and rips loose a thin, white cotton petticoat. 'This is clean this morning.'

She pushes it at Auguste. 'Here... use it... please?'

Danielle snatches it from her hand and dips it into the boiled water. She shakes it in the air until it cools a little then cleans the blood from around the bullet holes.

'Do you have more?' asks Auguste.

Oriel loosens her skirt then steps out of it.

With a tool from the roll Auguste slices it into narrow strips, rolling them between his fingers to plug the bullet holes. He pulls out a stool from under the bench and sits down heavily.

Danielle finds a packing case to sit on at the end of the bench. 'There must be more that we can...' She catches sight of the way Oriel is staring at the boy's skin as if it contains a message that only she can read. 'Why are you still here?'

'Leave her.' Auguste pushes away the stool. 'Blanche, go and fetch any bedding you can spare. We need to keep him warm.'

He returns his attention to the boy, adjusting the cotton rolls, covering them with a pad of soft material from the petticoat.

'Minette. Apply pressure to these.'

Minette replaces his hands with her own.

'Blanche! The bedding. Now.' Auguste washes his hands in the bowl, opening the door to throw the contents across the muddy yard. Oriel is standing beside the boy's head, fingertips almost touching his skin.

Minette is watching her intently. Slowly, the fingertips fall until they touch. Oriel's breath stalls in her throat.

Blanche bangs out of the door in disgust.

Auguste passes Danielle a sharp, scalpel-like tool.

'Start at the bottom of the trouser leg and work up.'

Between them they struggle the clothes from beneath the boy until he is prone and naked. Auguste stokes the boiler for more water and throws the remains of the skirt to Oriel.

'Make cloths. It looks like we have a job to do.'

Oriel folds half of the cloth into pads while Danielle soaps and rinses the filth from the boy. She starts at his feet, becoming visibly more reluctant as the cloth is forced to travel above his knees.

Sensing her reticence, Auguste washes around the buttocks, noting the sores there and making a note to salve them later... if there is to be a later.

Danielle cleans around the boy's shoulders, keeping the water away from the fresh dressing.

'Look. There is more blood.'

Auguste pulls her aside, then lifts her hand into the light.

'It is from your hands. go and wash them again.'

'But look. There. By his neck.'

'That's a birth mark, Danielle... and if you don't stop panicking and get moving it will be his death mark.'

'Alright. Let us see if we can turn him. Minette, has the bleeding stopped?'

Minette lifts her hands from the pads over the bullet holes. The blood is congealing darkly on her palms. 'I think so.'

Auguste and Minette lift him slightly from the bench.

Oriel slides the strips of her skirt under him to tie the

pads in place.

Since Oriel's fingers touched the boy, her skin has taken a pale, ethereal glow that Minette cannot look away from.

Auguste jerks her out of it. 'Right, let us turn him.'

Oriel backs away. 'Are the bullets still inside him?'

'They are helping to stem the blood for the moment. When he has recovered enough we will try to remove them.

He beckons her to the bench with a gesture. 'You are needed.'

Oriel remains in the corner where Auguste has hidden the rifle.

He gestures again. 'Do you know what that means, to be needed?' He laughs. 'No, of course you don't. You are eight years old. You only know what it is to need. Come here and find out all that you are afraid of.'

Oriel is shaking with cold or fear, but of which she is not sure.

'You have watched your father, right?' asks Auguste.

'No… only sometimes.'

'Then this will be a lesson for you.'

'Auguste!' Minette speaks sharply to him. 'You cannot expect…'

'Hush, Sister. Put your hands under his left shoulder and hold the pads in place. Danielle, make sure his legs do not twist.'

Auguste heaves with all his strength and the boy rolls slowly over.

Oriel gasps at the sight of him. Auguste takes hold of her arm and shakes her. 'Water. So we can clean the rest.'

Oriel draws more hot water from the boiler and folds the last of the petticoat into two pads.

She passes one to Auguste and keeps the other for herself. She begins to wipe the boy's feet… but that is not where she is looking.

The door swings wide and Blanche enters with an armful of clean sheets.

She holds out the pile of bedding to Auguste without taking her eyes from Oriel's expression. 'Cover him up.'

Auguste folds a clean white sheet over the boy. He pads another under his head, tilting it so that his features take on a shadow, outlining the sunken cheeks and eye sockets. His nose is strong but delicate, almost too delicate for the gaunt pallor and the drawn mouth through which breath rasps occasionally, causing Oriel to start and tremble.

Danielle throws her a bedcover. It drops to the floor beside her naked legs.

'Cover yourself. Where do you think you are?'

Auguste doubles a blanket over the boy's legs. 'Leave her alone, Danielle. She is growing today. She doesn't need you poking and prodding at her.'

'Look at her!'

'Yes, look at her. What do you see?'

'She is too much of a woman to stand around undressed like that.'

'She is eight years old.'

Auguste tucks the blanket under the edge of the dust sheet. His eyes hold Minette's across the bench.

'Oriel, do you have another skirt?'

'Yes, M'sieur.'

'Then go and put it on.'

Danielle takes the remaining bedding from Blanche. 'And then stay away.'

Auguste searches Oriel's face for the child that came rushing in half an hour ago. It has gone.

'No. Then come back. I need you.'

Danielle perches on the edge of a packing case. 'She is too young for this. She should be at home.'

'If she is too much of a woman to stand around with no

clothes, then she is enough of a woman to help.'

He listens to the boy's chest for a moment, then settles again on his high stool.

'Danielle, can you sit with him a while? I am short of my breakfast.'

'So am I, but if you don't care enough then I'll stay with him.'

'Danielle… there are other elements to breakfast besides eating.'

'We'll both stay.' Blanche opens the door. 'Sister, do you not have work at the chapel?'

Minette's thoughts are still with Oriel until Blanche's question snatches at her attention.

'Make sure the boiler stays lit and that it is full. We will not know what we need until the moment comes. If there is any change, send for me.'

Danielle nods wearily. 'We know what we are about.'

Minette studies her curiously. 'Yes, you really think you do.'

6:22 P.M.

Oriel has spent most of the day feeding the fire under the boiler. The vent outside has fumed and drifted the yard with steam continually but is subsiding now that Auguste has sent her home.

Danielle reaches up to switch on the lamp suspended over the bench. She leans over to study the boy's face and listen to his breathing. 'Did you see..?'

'Of course I saw.' Blanche comes to stand beside her. 'So did that fool girl. Did you see her face?'

'Yes, I did.' Danielle stifles a laugh. 'She will find other men something of a disappointment after this.'

Blanche yawns and stretches her arms wide. 'I'm so tired, I'm not really sure that anything I saw was true. That fool

Sister firing a gun! Can you imagine? I haven't been out of bed so early in years.'

'Did we really see it?' Danielle's face colours slightly with the memory. 'Can we be sure?'

'Does it matter? He will be dead soon, and then what good is it to anyone?'

'Blanche!'

Blanche shrugs her shoulders and moves back to her seat on the packing case.

'How long has it been…' Danielle leans against the bench, listening to the boy's shallow breathing. '…since you have seen even an ordinary one?'

Blanche rubs at her eyes. 'I don't know. How long is a war?'

Danielle fingers the edge of the blanket, catching at the stitching with a roughly manicured nail. 'Too long…' She lifts the blanket slowly. 'Ohh…'

Blanche is suddenly beside her. 'Stop that. You must…' She puts her hand to her mouth. 'It *is* true.'

Danielle has already peeled back the blanket. She reaches out with a finger. 'Never in all my eighteen years have I seen…'

'Never in all your *six*teen years have you ever seen one anyway.'

'My father…'

'Doesn't count.' Blanche smiles at her triumphantly. 'It only counts if you see one, as they say. 'in anger'. But in my *twenty* years, I have never seen one quite like it.'

Danielle's finger moves forward until it touches skin. 'It's so soft. The skin is like velvet.'

'If I had one, mine would stay soft if *you* were touching it.'

'And what makes Blanche the expert?'

'I have four brothers.'

'And what happens when you touch theirs?'

Blanche removes her face swiftly from the lamplight.

'I do not!'

Danielle peels back more of the sheet.

The boy's legs are slender and white. The sparse, thin hair surrounding his manhood lacks definition.

Her own translucent hair brushes his thighs as she bends over him. 'Then I dare you to touch this.'

She lays her palm along it so that her fingers run parallel to its length. She closes her eyes and on her skin it feels like something newborn, soft and giving, its warmth filling her hand. She closes her fingers around it as if it might fly away. The boy draws a ragged breath and she jerks her hand clear.

Blanche nudges her aside and takes it between both hands.

'Look…' She eases back the skin. '…it hides in here.'

Danielle bends over to look. Blanche pushes her back out of the lamplight with a thigh and continues to withdraw the skin.

'See how pink it is?'

'It's purple.' Danielle is peering over Blanche's shoulder. 'Are they always purple?'

Oriel eases silently into the room behind them, allowing the door to close against her fingers. From the door she can see between the two women, their hands working together, exploring.

Danielle's movements quicken instinctively. 'See how easily the skin slides?' Her fingers lift the slowly tightening skin up and down.

'Look!' Blanche lifts hers away from where they've been exploring the wrinkled sac. 'It's growing.'

Danielle tries to contain the growth within her hands, to stifle it back into soft acquiescence. The boy groans loudly.

Oriel screams at them from the doorway. 'What are you

doing to him?'

Blanche whirls around in shock. 'What are you doing back here? Get out.'

'No!' Oriel moves around the workshop, her back as close to the wall as the stacks of timber, wire and metal will allow. 'You will kill him if I leave.'

Danielle drags the blanket across him. 'Stupid girl! We have no wish to kill him. Why should we?'

'Look.' Oriel points a trembling finger at the blood seeping out from beneath the boy, turning the dust-sheet and bedding into a scarlet crescent.

Blanche lifts his shoulder and blood pours from the wound where a cotton plug has moved.

'Fetch Auguste.'

Oriel hesitates.

Danielle screams at her. 'Now!'

'But…'

'Is it you that now wants him to die?'

'No… but…'

'Then go… now… and if you ever tell Auguste what you saw…' Blanche looks to Danielle for confirmation. '…it will be you that dies.'

6:33 P.M.

Between them they turn the boy onto his stomach. Auguste removes the cotton plug that has shifted and examines the wound.

'Danielle? How did this happen?'

'We don't know. Perhaps he tried to turn in his sleep.'

'You didn't see?'

'Blanche was resting. I was attending to the boiler. Perhaps…'

'Then why is there no hot water?'

'Oriel didn't come back when I expected her to.'

194

Danielle casts a warning glance to the girl in the corner. 'She was late.'

Auguste snorts in disgust. 'Oriel, stoke the fire under the boiler.'

Oriel crosses to the corner by the door and stops.

'Blanche is sitting on the sticks.'

'Then throw her off. Danielle, fetch Sister Minette.'

Danielle leans on the bench, a proprietorial hand resting on Artus' shoulder. 'Send the child.'

Oriel stamps her foot on the dusty floor. 'I am no longer a child. You said so yourself.'

Auguste pushes Oriel out of the way, grabs Danielle by the shoulder and hustles her out of the door into the yard.

He shakes her violently. 'Do you think I can't imagine what has been happening here?'

'That girl… what has she told you?'

'The girl has told me nothing. One look at your sly face tells me everything I need to know.'

'What about Blanche? It was…'

'Blanche is Blanche, but at least stupidity is honest. Now go and tell Sister Minette her time has arrived.'

Danielle stares at him without comprehension.

'She will know what you mean.'

Auguste pushes her towards the gate. 'Hurry!'

SEPTEMBER 22nd.
FRIDAY

6:40 P.M.

Minette is kneeling before the small altar observing her daily period of Great Silence when Danielle rushes in.

She reaches out to touch the gold-tasselled hem of the cloth and beseeches God to not allow this disturbance to become one of greater note.

She continues in prayer. The candle flickering brightly on the altar still has some way to achieve the mark she has carved into the hard, yellow wax.

An unbound resentment rises within her, not just because this is the time of day she values most, but because the disturbance is represented by Danielle.

Danielle gazes uncertainly around the chapel. This is the first time she has entered since she found that God didn't listen to her no matter how hard she prayed and that certain people continued to live in apparent grace.

The plaster figures in the tiny nave crowd her sense of Godless-ness. Their faces are burnished with expression in the candlelight but she knows that, by the light of day when she has been made to clean them, they are bland and lifeless plaster icons made cheaply in some factory where they run from a production line. With the exception of one.

Behind the altar is a small copy in wood and metal of the Ecstasy of Santa Teresa. Auguste has carved such passion into the features of the Saint as the spear enters her that Danielle hopes it will be mirrored by her own when she too is entered.

'Sister? Sister!'

Danielle is insistent, knowing that, if she fails, Auguste will broadcast his suspicion all over the village.

'The boy is dying.'

Minette opens her eyes, refocusing on the bright flicker of the candle, remembering a lamp lit above a scrubbed wooden table… and a life's flame so easily snuffed.

She takes the old coin from her pouch and offers a silent prayer as she drops it into the empty Offertory Box.

L'ATELIER D'AUGUSTE
RUE COSTE CHAUDE
LA ROQUE-SUR-PERNES

SEPTEMBER 22nd.
FRIDAY

6:55 P.M.

'Bring the light closer, I cannot see.'

Auguste tugs on the wire from the lamp. It gives a few inches more. Minette peers into the deep hole in the boy's back.

'It is closer to the heart than I would like.'

Auguste nods quietly. Minette widens the entrance of the wound with her fingers. 'It is not clear.'

Auguste swabs blood away from the wound. 'Is that better?'

'Yes. I can now see the bullet… I think.'

'It must still be in there, or he would have bled to death by now.'

Minette leans over the wound again. 'Then what will prevent it when we remove them?'

Auguste shrugs, the light from the lamp shadowed by his old, broad shoulders. 'That will be up to God. Let us hope He's having a good day.'

Minette gives a wry smile. 'I was told that it is wrong to ascribe inconstancy to the will of Our Lord.'

'Then I just hope he hears us. After all…' He returns the smile. '…we do have an inside track.'

'Then let me see those tools again. Maybe He will guide my hand.'

From the bowl in which she has earlier sterilised the tools, Minette selects a pair of slender, long-nosed pliers.

'For refitting springs.'

Minette offers Auguste a blank stare.

'Just thought you would like to know.'

'Could be what we need for such a young man. Move the lamp over here a little.'

She reaches into the wound with the pliers. The boy groans loudly, the cavity of his chest reverberating under her hands. He moves and she is forced to withdraw.

'Can't you hold him still?'

Oriel grasps his feet firmly. Danielle and Blanche take an arm each. Auguste leans his weight on the boy's buttocks.

'Try again.'

Through her fingers, Minette feels the pliers scrape against metal. She opens them until they fit the sides of the wound and slides them a little further in. She grasps them lightly and the handles refuse to close.

'I think I have it.'

The pliers lift slowly from the wound. Gripped in the end of the jaws is a small, distorted bullet. She drops it into the edge of the dust-sheet. Oriel quickly rolls a new piece of cotton material and Auguste plugs the hole.

'Let's try the next one.'

Danielle uncovers the second wound as Minette keeps her hands and the pliers clear of contact.

The wound is clean and dry but blood is clotted in the bottom of the hole. Minette drops the pliers back in the sterile bowl and picks out a fine gouge.

With the blade, she clears the clot from the hole. By the lamplight, two shapes reflect at her from the bottom. One, the dull copper of fired metal, the other is a glimpsed white of bone.

'This one has turned. It has hit a rib and been deflected.'

She peers into the hole again. 'I think it is lodged between the ribs and the heart. I cannot do this.'

'Why?' Auguste stands away from the bench to massage his lower back with both hands.

Minette balances the pliers on the boy's skin.

'I may kill him.'

'And if you don't try?'

'The bullet will kill him.'

'Then you or the bullet?'

'The bullet does not have to live with its conscience.'

'Are you sure that is all?'

Minette holds her hands into the light. They are so affected by small tremors that her fingertips describe tiny arcs in the air between them.

'My hands are unsure.'

Auguste reaches for the pliers.

Oriel stands in front of him. 'Everyone knows you cannot see. Leave him alone.'

'Then what chance will he have?'

'I will do it.'

Danielle shouts. 'No!' and releases the boy's arm.

Auguste looks to Blanche for her reaction but she turns her face away in shame.

'I *will* do it!' Oriel displays her hands under the lamp.

To Auguste's surprise they are steady. Minette ties a rag around Oriel's fine, blonde hair and lifts her onto the stool beside the bench. They stare at each other for a moment until Oriel smiles brokenly. 'I *will* do it.'

'Then wait… I learnt this much from… *my* maman.'

Minette swabs the wound and spreads her fingers around it, cleaning and prising as wide as it will go.

Auguste is amazed at how close Minette has come to disclosure. 'If she had done it half so well it may have saved her a lot of trouble.'

Oriel peers into the hole. 'I can see it. It is wedged, but I can see.'

The pliers slip in her grasp, closing emptily. She reaches in again and catches an edge of distorted metal.

She closes the pliers firmly with both hands. Slowly, she twists the bullet out as though it were a screw-thread until it drops onto the cloth beside her.

Auguste reaches for the wound with a pad but Minette stops him. She examines the wound again. Now the bullet is removed she can see the exposed rib has been chipped.

'There is a piece of bone in there somewhere but I can't see it. If we leave it in…'

'Let me try.' Oriel leans over the bench again but the hole keeps filling with fresh blood. 'I can't see anything either.'

Auguste picks up the roll of clean cotton 'Then that is all we can do. We are not surgeons.'

He inserts the roll of cloth into the wound. Blood erupts between his fingers, spilling across the white skin into the dust-sheet below. Auguste presses the cloth into the hole with all his strength.

'Bindings! Get me something to bind this with. Now!'

His hands are slick and red. He feels his grip slipping, his hands sliding on the boy's skin.

Blanche watches the silent flow of pumping blood, finding it impossible to move. Danielle holds firmly to the boy's arm, unable to release her grip.

Minette struggles with a cotton sheet, ripping it lengthwise, filling the air with dust, stopping at a seam and lacking the strength to continue beyond it.

The boy begins to convulse. Strange choking sounds emanate from deep in his throat. A pulse leaps then stops in his neck, starts again then stops.

Minette screams against his ear. *'Stay with us. Stay with us.'*

Auguste snatches a rope from its hook on the wall, passes it quickly under the boy's stomach and ties it roughly.

He knocks Blanche out of the way to grab a piece of kindling from the basket. He inserts it into the loop of rope and begins to twist.

Minette puts a padded block into place over the wound.

Auguste twists violently until the blood slows to a trickle.

The pulse in the boy's neck is erratic, stopping for periods of time.

'He has lost so much.'

The pulse stops abruptly. A single breath rattles in the boy's throat. The convulsions begin again.

'Turn him over.'

They spin him roughly on the bench. Breath wrenches in and out of him then stops again. Minette closes her eyes, waits a long moment for the breathing to restart.

'I think we have lost him.'

Auguste steps away, looking down at his hands, hoping to see enough life clinging there to be able to push some back into this young man on the bench.

He is knocked violently aside as Danielle leaps across him to throw herself at the boy's chest, pummelling it with both fists.

'You cannot do this to me! I will not let you go away! If I have to live with your death, you are going to live it with me!'

Auguste grabs her by the shoulders. 'It's too late, come aw…' She wrenches herself free of him. Auguste staggers backwards to the door. Danielle throws herself at the boy again, screaming at him. '*Stay! Stay!*'

She rains blow after blow upon his chest with both fists, raising them again and again as high as they will reach, bringing them down with all her might.

'Stop!' Minette is surprised at the level of command in her own voice.

Danielle stops, suddenly bewildered.

Minette places two fingers against the boy's neck.

'He has a pulse.'

CHRONICLE

IV

REVERBERATIONS

1941

MAY 10th.
SATURDAY

10:13 P.M.

A quick glance around the empty sky for exhaust flames informs Hess that, for the moment at least, he has shaken off the chasing fighters from *Jagdgeschwader Zwei*.

He is amused by how easy that was but, after all, they were more used to stopping traffic going the other way.

He wonders who saw through his charade at the airfield and alerted them. He relaxes back into the cockpit seat, searching his memory for even a moment of carelessness and finds not one instance.

There remains only one direction from which that alert could have come and, very soon, he will be able to deal with the perfidious element that has infiltrated his very soul.

Quite how he will do that, torn in the way that he has become, will have to wait until the moment.

Below him, *der Nordsee* is flat, black, moonless and without horizon. He drifts across international lines, twin engine exhaust sparks reflecting in the water as he skims low over the surface.

The air is full and vital at this altitude. He removes his oxygen mask and, despite the vapours of spirit and over-heated cockpit leather, the paper still bears a trace of her scent. He lifts the pages to his nose to inhale her memory.

The inscribed hand on the letter is large, cursive, flowing. The red map-light in the cockpit of his Messerschmitt is barely enough to discern the letters…

Since your last letter to Violette I can scarcely keep my breath. She showed me the coded communication from Jacqueline Berniere but would not willingly allow me to read further than my own mention.

Violette is the dearest friend and she insists that 'The Firm' will receive you with all the warmth and respect due to a man of your position.

Gripping the *Steuerknüppel* of his personal Messerschmidt between his knees, he turns the pages, smoothing them flat with a leather glove.

I am filled with anticipation of the small present you are bringing me, the nature of which you are so secretively keeping. Given your position within the Reich... and I know how hard things can be made in Germany at this time... I can only imagine it to be a thing most revealing.

Violette and I have played endless guessing games and although for myself your presence will be enough, please do keep it most cautiously wrapped. I lost track of so many things on that train journey.

Remember to study carefully the poem I sent you in April. If you have been clever with the code I sent earlier then you will see that the words align to the shape of the River Cart.

To the east of the first big house you will find the estate of my close friend, Dougie. You remember Dougie? You met him at the Ribbentrop's soirée in London and again in Berlin. Re-form the words of my enclosed poem and you will see the outline of it.

The house is quite distinctive and at this time of year Scotland barely gets dark. Please do land carefully my dearest, as Lizzie would simply hate to have the Luftwaffe adorning her flowerbeds.

Angelica

He folds the papers back into their envelope and slips it under the string of the parcel placed on the empty rear gunner's seat behind him. In his haste to put the parcel on board undetected, he has caught the paper on the corner of the canopy latch and now a small swatch of blue and taupe flows from the tear.

He hopes she will not be too disappointed.

Another glance around the sky tells him that he is being followed. The British coastal listening posts have picked up the sound from his engines. He has already shed his long-range tanks over the sea and now the fuel gauge is needling downwards.

He zig-zags across the country as much as he dare to confuse the listeners until he reaches the west coast of Scotland.

Above the River Cart, the exhaust on the port engine begins to flash and flicker as the carburettors run lean.

A glance behind reveals another exhaust flare.

The British have found him again. With no time to waste he climbs rapidly and circles above the river before the tank empties.

At six thousand feet he checks his parachute harness and throws back the cockpit cover.

As he tries to clamber clear his foot snares painfully on something in the cockpit. The engines either side of him pop and die. As the plane enters a dive, he ignores the pain and wrenches his boot clear.

In a last second he remembers the parcel and smiles to himself. What good is a messenger who carries no message?

He clutches the parcel tight to his chest and falls into the night.

1950

SEPTEMBER 2nd.
SATURDAY

9:33 P.M.

'Oh… Hello, Auguste.'

'Don't sound so disappointed, Danielle.'

'Where is he?' Danielle is wary in case she's missed the figure of Artus hiding in a corner somewhere. A clock beats time at the end of the bench where it awaits collection.

'He is at home, probably sleeping, as you should be.'

'Only children are in bed at this time.'

'Then why are you not there?' Auguste drops the new spring he has been attaching, the pliers flexing in his hand. 'Instead of interrupting me.'

'Because I am no longer a child.'

Danielle's hair is ash-blonde, thrown with great, studied carelessness over one shoulder; her irises a clear, dawn-washed grey.

Auguste dismisses her. 'Two minutes ago…'

'Auguste… the war is over.'

Untouched by the brief encounter she had with six years of bloodletting, he sees the child still there in the shallow pool of her eyes. 'Also two minutes ago.'

'Five years, Auguste. Five years! Do you not feel it? That half-century spirit? That new…' She spins around on one heel, hair flying. '…I cannot find the word to…'

'Artus.'

She stops to stroke her hair as though the hand belongs to someone else. 'Yes. That will do for now.'

'Danielle, stop fidgeting and go home. I have no doubt he will be here tomorrow.'

The door to the workshop bangs open before Danielle can move. Caught in the light from the bench is the slight figure of a man. His clothes are shabby and oversized for his frame. He affects a large, dark hat, the brim pulled low across his face.

Auguste puts down the spring and pliers. 'I am sorry, but we are closed.'

The man shuts the door behind him without turning, eyes fixed on Danielle's hair.

'I am here to pay an account.'

Over his shoulder hangs a leather bag on a simple strap. He drops it on the bench beside him.

A dawning of recognition is becoming obvious on Auguste's face.

'Danielle. You must leave us.'

'I think I shall stay.'

Danielle's voice trembles but her feet root into the floor of the workshop. She is shaken out of it as the man speaks, his accent obscure and strangely inflected.

'Loyalty is admirable, Danielle, but not here. Auguste and I have things we need to discuss in private.'

He moves away from the door. At a nod from Auguste, Danielle steps around the man and flies through as he holds it open. It closes firmly behind her, leaving her to pick her way through the debris in darkness.

She stumbles along the side alley and round to the main road, climbs the three steps of Auguste's house and knocks on the door. 'Artus? Artus! Wake up.'

Artus peers out of the window into the darkness of the street. The moon is behind him, sinking below the ridge of the house. An edge of it reflects from the window of the Pharmacy across the road with enough power to light the abundant shock of ash-blonde hair by the door.

'Danielle? What do you want at this time of night?'

'Artus… let me in.'

'Danielle… how many times..?'

'No, Artus. This time you *must* let me in… put your clothes on.'

'Well, that will be a first.'

Danielle pushes past him into the hallway as he unlocks the door, snatching a rough working shirt from the rack to throw at him.

'Cover yourself. I need you… now!'

The urgency in her voice has swept aside the last of the sleep clouding his brain. 'What is it? Is it Oriel?'

'Oriel? *Merdé!* Why must everything be about Oriel?'

'Then what..?'

'I think Auguste is in trouble.'

He slides his feet into the shoes she kicks over. 'Then why didn't you say?'

'Because you mentioned Oriel.'

'Only because you…'

Danielle half-drags him through the door into the pitch-blackness of the road. 'There is no time for this.'

The moon has sunk entirely below the roof behind them.

She leads him around the gable and into the alley where she cautions him to be quiet.

Artus pushes her behind him and steers the way through a familiar pattern of abandoned material.

As his hand reaches out for the door to the workshop, she grabs his shirt from behind.

'Listen first. I don't want to look foolish in front of Auguste.'

He prises her fingers loose from the cloth. 'I don't think you need worry about that, Danielle.'

They creep closer to the door until the voices from inside become clear…

'I only ever do my best.'

'But what if your best was not good enough, Auguste?'

'Then it was the best I could do. And if that is not good enough, then maybe the fault lies with the request.'

'My request had been a simple enough one. All I asked was that you unlock the device so it would work.'

'And when it left my hands it *was* unlocked. What you chose to do with it after that is your problem… not mine.'

'It never ceased to be your problem, Auguste.'

The pitch of the stranger's voice lowers until the threat underlying it becomes apparent. 'You took my gold and you lied to me. I warned you what would happen.'

'In the first place it was not *your* gold. It belonged to the Vatican, and as such it was not within your remit to attach conditions. Out of an unusual sense of religious fervour, ably assisted by Sister Minette, I spent what you gave me on the local Chapel. The Pope would have been proud of your contribution… if you had ever dared to tell him.'

Coraloni steps across to the bench. His feet are hesitant on the unevenness of the floor, his gait that of a man never fully recovered from a serious illness. He drags the stool towards him as soon as it is within reach, pulling himself onto the seat.

'Ah… the good Sister. How is little Minette?'

Auguste considers his reply. He hopes the hesitation will not give him away, but this man before him is a pale shadow of the fallen angel he had once been. 'She has died.'

The priest seems affected by that in a way that can't easily be gauged. His head tilts as though listening for an undercurrent in Auguste's last statement.

'Then that is a pity. I had hoped to reacquaint myself.'

He looks up at Auguste then quickly away. Auguste had stared directly into his eyes, the gaze unearthing motives and memories, thoughts long beaten from him.

He hitches himself further onto the stool.

'Let me shed a little light between us, Auguste. It will leave you in no doubt as to why I have returned to carry out my promise.'

9:51 P.M.

Inside the workshop, the priest raises the wide brim of his Saturno. Outside, Artus and Danielle hear a sharp intake of breath followed by Auguste's familiar low chuckle.

In the darkness, Artus tilts a propped paving slab to find an old table leg he has seen there. His fingers fit neatly around the thin end. He draws it without sound from the pile of discarded timbers.

Danielle crowds him to be able to see through the gap in the workshop door. He pushes her behind him to safety. Her hands slip under his shirt to feel the smooth skin on his back, fingers searching for two scars as if the simple touch of them would spin her world.

He tucks in the loose shirt.

They press closer to the door to catch the conversation.

9:57 P.M.

'What can I say? I had no idea… and even if I had I don't know if I would have behaved differently.' Auguste throws up his hands in mock despair. 'So if you have the balls you had better do what you came to do and get it over with.'

The priest places his hat upside down on the bench. From inside the crown he retrieves a thick envelope.

Auguste catches it and holds it under the glow of the light bulb.

'Who is it addressed to? Who is it from?'

The priest brushes the dust from his hat. He caresses the brim fondly before replacing it the right way up on the bench. His hand steals into the large bag he had laid there earlier, returning into sight clutching a small handgun.

Auguste steps back. 'I see… then you *are* serious about this.'

'Seven years ago I made you a promise. I have learned a lot since then about keeping promises… especially to one's self.'

'And you are now going to shoot me without at least giving me the chance to read this letter? Or even tell me who it is from?'

Coraloni picks the hat from the bench and spins it in his hand, smiling fondly at the worn felt crown, remembering each notch cleaved from the brim at irregular intervals around the circumference.

'The letter is from me.'

'From you?'

'Are you going deaf, Auguste… as well as blind?'

'I cannot possibly read this… I need to show it to Sister Minette.'

'I see you are still an ill-accomplished liar…'

Auguste pulls out the stool from under the bench.

'I am sorry… I meant Oriel… the doctor's daughter. I become mixed up between the two. If I am ill-accomplished at anything, it is at being old.'

'Then take all the time you need reading the letter. It will tell you everything you need to know. Did you say that the doctor's daughter was called Oriel? Not a name I would have chosen, but as a bringer of light, strangely appropriate. Does she have blonde hair?'

Auguste stumbles a moment, unsure of his ground.

'Yes… she is also beautiful.'

'As is her mother.'

'The doctor's wife is thin and quite dark, as I remember.'

'Yes… but Oriel's mother was blonde… although perhaps you would not have known that at the time, as it would always be tucked inside her wimple. I thank you for your small indiscretion, Auguste. I can now do what I came to do with a clear conscience.'

Coraloni lifts the gun. Auguste stares at the black hole in the barrel, knowing that a flash will be the last thing he will ever see.

Artus rushes through the door.

As the priest turns, the single overhead bulb brings the black Star of David inexpertly tattooed on his forehead into sharp relief.

Artus aims for it with the table leg.

The gun barrel is still swinging around, Danielle pushing it aside as it lights the room with a bright flash.

Artus continues his stroke, bringing the table leg down with all his might on the centre of the tattoo.

The priest falls to the floor.

The gun clatters into the kindling beside the boiler.

Artus leaves go of the table leg and rushes to grab it.

Auguste stays his hand. 'You will not need that.'

'If he wakes up…' Artus turns suddenly. 'Danielle!' He grabs her from the floor to cradle her in his arms.

Auguste! She is shot. Get the doctor, quickly.'

Auguste bends to pick up the table leg. He places one foot on the priest's forehead and tugs it free. He is certain that in the dark of outside, Artus had not noticed the six inch nail hammered all the way through.

SEPTEMBER 3rd.
SUNDAY

1:41 A.M.

'She will live.'

'Thank you, Doctor Beaufort.'

'There was nothing I could do to save the breast. The bullet tore away the gland tissue. If I had left the remains of it in…'

'I will tell her, Doctor.'

'What will you tell her, Auguste?'

'That life is sometimes uneven… but for all that, it is life.'

The doctor grasps his hand. 'I never realised we had so much in common.'

Auguste is on the sofa he has pushed against the parlour wall to make room for the camp bed. 'But what do we do about our mutual acquaintance. He is still in my workshop.'

'Is the door locked?'

'No. That would be suspicious.'

'And a dead body wouldn't? What if a customer called in?'

'What makes you think I have any customers? The only clock my eyes can see is fifty feet up the church tower. Sit down, Doctor. I have a letter for you to read.'

He pushes back the blonde hair that has drifted across Danielle's face. 'When will she wake?'

'In around four hours, I should think. She may want to sleep straight through the day but I will send my wife to change the dressing at breakfast. If she wakes before then,

215

give her these.' There are two tablets in the palm of his hand. 'You will need to be very gentle.'

'Do you have anything new… for me?'

'I'm sorry, Auguste. All I can do for you now is to help manage your pain.'

Auguste swaps the tablets for the letter.

The doctor hefts it in his hand.

'Whoever wrote this had plenty to say…'

Dear Auguste,

I have returned to complete the promise that I made to you. You may be surprised by this, yet, I assure you, not so surprised as I.

For most of my career I considered the panoply of religion to be my playground. There was no finer student of the privilege it can bring. Ably tutored by my uncle, Cardinal Ullman, I found the ability to twist it to my own ends, weaving a web of deceit in which I finally trapped myself. You have seen the mark that the dark angel left upon me. I will only add that, over the last few years, that mark has been a constant companion along my road to salvation…

'It is late, Auguste. Shall I continue?'

'Of course, Doctor. Danielle is still sound asleep and I know that nothing now will drive Artus to his bed.'

By the time the antidote Angelica gave me began to take effect, the soldiers had disappeared for lunch, leaving me out in unbearably bright sunlight. When they returned with a small hand mirror, I was given to understand how she had also sealed my fate.'

1945

**JANUARY 8th.
MONDAY**

11:43 A.M.

The cattle-car heaves with filth. He stands in a press of other bodies, a pool of faeces around his feet. The slatted floor has long since coagulated over, penetrated only by the occasional wash of urine. Over the last forty-eight hours he has been unable to sit or rest. His legs bear no weight or sensation, the bodies of the others hold him in a state of suspension.

His own gut is empty and now drains only fluid through the once-smart suit. He smells nothing. So used has he become to the eternal miasma, he fears that fresh air will shred his lungs like a knife. The train halts. Through the silent bellow of hot, fetid breath that surrounds him, he hears the clash of steel outside as the door is opened.

11:52 A.M.

The rail within Coraloni's grasp is bent and twisted. The explosive charge has reshaped it into a question of its direction. It is dragged aside, slippery with blood from his hands bound in rag. He turns his attention to a slender section of new steel, brought on the flatcar at the end of the waiting train. As he passes the engine he sees lubricant bubbling from the valve gear. Water is boiling from the seals, sterilising the grease. He rubs it into the rags, hoping later it will soften his skin and give it time to repair.

He lifts the bible from his pocket and scoops up more with the cardboard cover. He closes it gently, retaining as much as he can within the pages… in the camp there are children with unbearable sores.

'*Machen Sie schnell.*'

Having learned that no response is required of him, the padre slides the bible into the pocket of his uniform.

The new rail is too short. The damaged one had been the outside of a bend in the track. The saboteurs must have known this. Coraloni smiles with a new respect. How resourceful these new mice have become, gnawing quietly at the tendons and flexors of the powerful… even to within a half-kilometre of Büchenwald Camp. In the visible distance the entrance gate rears above the track in axiomatic mockery… *Jedem das Seine*… To Each His Own, or, as they have come to understand it, *Everyone gets what they deserve.*

The doors to the trucks are opened. Coraloni staggers back as bodies slide seamlessly onto the track beside him. He searches amongst them for the living, helping the ones he can to their feet. Others lean in dejection alongside the wheels. From the opened doors a slow river drips onto their shoulders.

Coraloni searches the trucks for bodies still warm, for the ones who can't make alone the last effort to daylight.

The vents have been nailed shut from the outside and the trucks so tightly packed it is difficult to tell.

He leans into the cars, heedless of the river flowing sluggishly around him, grasping at hands with lifeless fingers… others just too feeble to return the grip.

A hand takes his. The fingers curl around his wrist and lock. This must be consuming every last ounce the withered body contains. The last four years has taught him that this

response of instinctive energy has only two places in life...
at the very beginning... and at the very end. He returns the
grip and pulls.

The man slides easily across the floor.

Coraloni lowers him down and sits him up by a wheel.

The man's eyes remain tightly closed though every
movement inflicted on him elicits a scream of pain.

Coraloni rips open the shirt. Lice scatter from the light
and the familiar typhus rash is evident across the chest,
welling up from the midriff.

He closes the shirt and takes out his Bible. He smears a
little of the grease on the man's lips to stop the blood where
his screams have cracked them open.

The face is well-bearded and barely human under the
coating of filth.

Coraloni walks up to the engine to cup his hands under
the water escaping the steam drain. It is close to boiling but
there is so much pain inside him that a little more is no
effort. With dipped fingers he clears away the smears of
excrement and grime from the man's face. Underneath, he
finds a smile. The man's lips part and Coraloni pushes dregs
of water between them with his fingertips.

He opens the Bible, selecting a passage from John 14:27.

'I am leaving you with a gift - peace of mind and heart.
And the peace I give is a gift the world cannot give. So be
not troubled nor afraid.'

A hand grasps the wrist that holds the Bible. 'I know
your voice...'

'This is hardly possible...'

'I know... yet... I *know*...'

'All that you need to know are the words of Christ. They
are the Wisdom that will accompany your journey.'

'Not you... not... spoken by you. This is not... my
indignity. It is yours...'

The man's head slumps forward onto his chest. Coraloni pushes it back against the wheel of the car.

In the last four years his hands have touched so many corpses they understand the moment when a soul passes through them.

He lifts an eyelid to find a dark brown iris, the lens occluded like a bright layer of milk. He places his hands on the man's cheeks to push back the growth of beard, smoothing out the ravaged planes of his face into something he can vaguely recognise.

He lays the body down against the track. Against hope he reaches into the jacket pockets.

They are empty. Unsatisfied, he reaches into the ripped linings, the trousers, all empty. He sits back against the rail a moment… reaches forward and lifts the jacket lapel.

Pinned underneath is the faded remnant of a pre-war travel pass… in the name of Karl Ernst Krafft.

1950

SEPTEMBER 3rd.
SUNDAY

3:49 A.M.

...and so you see Auguste, I realised that no matter what reparation I made to my God, I no longer deserved The Kingdom of Heaven. After the liberation I was cast adrift in a world where I found myself having done things I am too ashamed to relate just in order to stay alive.

Eventually, I found my way back into the arms of the church. With a new identity I began again, taking issue with poverty wherever I found it, coming gradually to realise that poverty of the soul is where the real Demons exist. Beside that of every person of worth and honour that I have ever met, my soul will be eternally found wanting. In the event that my better days should provide the excuse for Our Lord to elevate me to the accession of His Kingdom, I have come to you to bear witness. Who better to understand?

In your presence, I will by now have carried out the simple final act that will eternally exclude me from the Gates of Heaven. A fate, it seems, I have striven hard to deserve.

It has been prophesied to me that my tomb shall be of limestone and white marble. I hope that, in some way, however small, you can make this possible. I ask for no consecration... no hallowed ground. The Church will not allow that of a suicide.

In Dei Nomine, I wish you a long and productive life.

In my own name, I also beg for your continued love and care of Sister Minette.

Consummatum est,

Padre Manus Coraloni

The doctor folds the letter back into its envelope and offers it back to Auguste.

Auguste takes it from him with a trembling hand and passes it to Artus.

'Here, Artus. This is your pass to freedom should anyone come asking what happened here tonight.'

Artus takes it from him and stares at the envelope in the pale light of the lamp.

'It is addressed to you, Auguste.'

Auguste shuns the proffered letter. 'It is not a thing I would wish to keep. It holds too many memories. But I think it may be important for you to know some of these things.'

'But I killed him, Auguste.'

'But that was not your intent.'

'The gun? He could have killed you. I only did…'

'Artus, it is not the first time that gunshot has run wild in this workshop, although it is strangely heartwarming that the Church was responsible on both occasions.'

'But I killed him, Auguste.'

'No, Artus. His intent was to die by his own hand. Yours was to preserve lives that you had come to love. That makes you exactly what you were when you first came to us. A good soldier. And if it is of any comfort to you, you have robbed him of his attempt to avoid the Judgement of the Kingdom of Heaven.'

'Do you think he will survive it?'

'I think St. Peter will have to make that uncomfortable decision, Artus. We three have another. Go and fetch the spades from behind the workshop.'

5:15 A.M.

'Does this have to be so deep?'

'There are foxes. Do you want to see your handiwork dragged all over the gardens of La Roque?'

'This is not my handiwork. If only I had been ten seconds later...' Artus rests a moment on the handle of the shovel. 'I didn't know there was a nail. I only wanted to save...'

'I know, Artus, and I am grateful, but you can stop trying now. This makes us even.'

Doctor Beaufort pares away the clay from the side of his boots on a sharp edge of limestone.

'Leave him alone, Auguste...' In the glimmer cast by his kitchen window he can see that Artus' hands are shaking where they grip the handle. '...unless you want to end up digging this yourself. We are all confused... perhaps myself most of all.'

'I should not trouble myself over...'

'Auguste, if you had spent more of your life taking oaths instead of giving them you might understand. Artus? Make this your penance.'

Artus wrests the shovel from the soft earth. 'A few Hail Marys would have been easier.'

Jupiter is watching them brightly from the east above the nearby rooftops, though the windows below are mercifully darkened. The blade bites into a new layer under the weight of his foot. A square of clay lifts cleanly from the Doctor's garden. He sets it aside.

'I think this is as far as we go. It will be light soon.'

The priest's skin is so pale that the dark star with the central black hole stands out in sharp relief on his forehead.

Even though the doctor has closed the eyelids, his expression is still one of surprise.

Auguste drapes a large piece of unkempt rag from his back pocket over the priest's face.

'Now he can't see what we are doing. Carry on Artus.'

Artus passes him the shovel. 'You first.'

'I am too old for a shovel.'

'And I am too young to carry all the blame… take it.'

Auguste takes the shovel with a trembling hand, picks at an edge of the pile of loosened earth. Slowly, he covers the cloth he has laid with a thin layer of soil.

Almost as an afterthought, he reaches down beside him to the marbled pebbles and limestone shards that border the rockery. He grabs a few large ones and places them carefully in a sweeping row across the ground beneath his feet.

He holds up the shovel as he climbs out.

'Doctor?'

'I am not part of this… I only…'

Auguste thrusts the shaft into his hand. 'He is also guilty… who only stands to watch.'

'Wait…' From his jacket pocket the doctor takes the rosary he has kept since his argument with the priest.

He has taken it out on many occasions, struggling with the prospect of revealing it to Oriel, but the cross gleams so cleanly in the dawning light that its potential for disturbing his life becomes untenable.

It slips from his fingers into the hole.

CHRONICLE

V

TERRE MÈRE

CAFÉ DERNOT
RUE DU PORTAIL HAUT
LA ROQUE-SUR-PERNES

1988

SEPTEMBER 15th.
THURSDAY

11:21 A.M.

'He has painted her window… *again.*'

The old woman shakes dust motes from her shawl as she sits, releasing a vivid shock of white hair to spill across her left shoulder, hiding one high, small breast.

'This is the second time in three months… and why does he always paint her shutters with a flower?' She turns away from the thought, savouring the bitterness of her coffee.

Bruno Dernot speaks without looking up from the petit four he is angrily slicing into one quarter each for the women. 'Help me out here, Danielle… I am making notes… how does one spell *'euphemism'*?'

Danielle sits straight-backed in the wicker chair, arthritic knuckles gripping hard on the side rails.

'You think you are clever, Bruno, but you are not as good as Albert, your father. The only notes he needed to make said 'francs' on the front, but what Artus has *ever* seen in that woman I will not understand.'

Bruno clatters the plate with the squared petit-four onto the table.

The women wait until he is out of earshot, eyes glancing, pecking at the small white cups as if they are the bones of unspoken conversation.

From the corner of his eye, Bruno regards the woman outside his door. This is the fourth time this week she has appeared.

He watches her hesitate, scanning the faces of the crows at the table. When Danielle had dropped her headscarf, the woman had taken a step forward.

Bruno offers her an uncharacteristic smile through the glass. He notices pale skin drawn tight over high cheek bones… but no returning smile easing its way to her lips.

She turns her face away, but not before he realises that she is not as old as he at first thought. She turns completely away, then back again. As she approaches the café, he notices that she favours a slight limp.

Holding in a breath, in case her sudden resolve should evaporate along with it, Mignon Merle pushes open the door.

A bell jangles loudly above her head, jolting her memory back into years of uncertainty…

1981

**MARCH 3rd.
TUESDAY**

4:43 P.M.

Mignon is wrapping elastic bands around a freshly-wound hank of green wool. The bell jangles and the door bangs against the wall as Chrétien enters the shop.

His presence begins an interminable jangle in her head.

Hanks of wool are stacked in boxes half-way around the shop, the rainbow of colour beginning at one end and arcing around to the space by the till.

Chrétien waits impatiently, turning this way and that.

Mignon keys in an amount and hands a customer the change.

Chrétien's hands are deep in the wool now, disturbing the strands and making it difficult to ball later. He looks up as the customer leaves and waves a hand to encompass a rack of lurid book covers along the far wall. 'Do people actually read these?'

Before Mignon can answer, even though she has learned better than to respond, he continues. 'I mean, do people actually waste their time… reading?'

Mignon remains behind the till, the only place of comparative safety in the shop.

Chrétien paces around, pretending to study the mystery of lettering on the book covers. He leans over the counter.

Mignon sidesteps out of reach as he lunges behind the till with one hand.

'Come here, you ungrateful bitch. What kind of wife are you to run away from her husband?'

Mignon stays out of reach. An ingratiating smile flickers across Chrétien's lips. 'Has the old whore paid you yet?'

Jacqueline Berniere comes through from the back room with two mugs of coffee.

'No, M'sieur Merle. The old whore hasn't paid her yet. So what else can we do for you?'

Chrétien stares angrily from the owner to Mignon. 'Then where is her money? I need it now.'

'All things have their time, M'sieur Merle, and I have not yet been to the bank.'

'Bank! Pah! Take it from the till.'

Jacqueline nudges Mignon protectively away from the till towards the door into the rear of the shop. As she touches her arm she can feel the tremors that fill Mignon's body from head to toe. She presses a key on the till and the drawer balloons open to the bright sound of a bell.

She peers in then closes it again. 'There is not enough.'

Chrétien faces her over the top of the register, cheeks crimson, knuckles white, gripping tight to the sides of the machine.

'Give me what there is.'

'M'sieur Merle, this is my shop and if anyone makes demands in here it will be me. Please leave now before I call the police.'

Chrétien reaches for her over the till and misses, his hand clawing empty air as she steps back. He thumps the keys on the till and the drawer shoots open. His hand reaches in to grab the handful of notes he knows will be in there.

Jacqueline slams the drawer shut on his hand and leans her weight against it.

Chrétien screams at her. 'It is my money. I give you my wife to work for you so it is mine!'

Jacqueline leans harder against the metal edge of the drawer, her face pale and angry, pressing up to his.

'It is my money until I decide to pay her. Then it is her money. If she then gives it to you she is a bigger fool than in all of Christendom!'

She gives the drawer one last hard push. 'Do not ever come into my shop again!'

Chrétien throws a punch with his other hand. It catches Jacqueline full in the face. Blood pours from her nose as she staggers away from the drawer.

Chrétien wrenches his hand free, clutching a small bundle of notes. He stuffs these quickly into his pocket.

'Do not ever try to tell me what is or isn't mine!'

With one last kick he sends a pile of wool flying across the shop. The bell jangles loudly behind him.

Mignon throws her arms around Jacqueline then takes her face in her hands. She can see that the top lip is split, but there is more blood than substance in the injury.

Jacqueline's nose is slightly out of shape, but then again… it always was.

'Here.'

She leads Jacqueline through to the kitchen and sits her down at the small table by the stove. The water in the kettle is still hot. She cools it with a splash from the tap and wipes away the blood with a clean kitchen towel. 'I am so sorry.'

'So am I.' Jacqueline grins crookedly as Mignon wipes gently around her nose. 'I should've broken the bastard's hand while I had the chance.'

Mignon sits on a stool beside her.

'Whatever he has taken, please take it out of my wage. Then it won't be stealing… will it?'

'Mignon.' Mme Berniere takes the towel from her and dabs the colour from her cheeks with the cooling cloth. 'Why do you continue to protect that bastard?'

Mignon closes her eyes, shaking her head uncertainly.

'I… I do not know… perhaps…'

Jacqueline watches Mignon visibly closing down, all the shutters behind which she hides dropping silently into place.

'Perhaps… when you have been moved about as often as I have, never knowing how or who to give your love to, then any kind of stability is better than that. Perhaps I am just tired of moving.'

Jacqueline takes her hand. It flutters within her own like a bird being taken. 'I think you will have to move again.'

Mignon gives a short, guttural laugh. 'I don't think that I can.'

'You must.' Jacqueline grips her tightly, trying to force some of her own strength through the skin into Mignon's despair. 'Or he will kill you.'

Mignon shakes her head. 'I am pregnant.'

Jacqueline is shocked, then her features fall into lines of concern. 'Do you think he will even notice that?'

'He must. He is…'

'What kind of father looks for his children in the bottom of a bottle?'

'Perhaps a lost one. Perhaps it is my fault. If only I…'

'Mignon!' Jacqueline lights the gas under the kettle. 'For God's Sake wake up!'

'But he will be fine now, it is only when…'

'He is his own internal punch bag! Can't you see that? I knew his mother. Now there was an old whore! Tarred and feathered and tied to a streetlamp for days after the Germans left.'

She rinses cold coffee from the mugs gathered off the counter. 'I also knew his father. He would have made an old whore of me, too.'

'As I said… it is not his fault.'

'Mignon… Mignon. How many times can you delude

yourself? I am astonished at your capacity.'

Mignon stands the mug upside down on the draining board.

'Mme Berniere, you have been so kind that I don't know how to begin to thank you.'

Jacqueline waves it away, dabs at a fresh streak of blood issuing from her nose, looks at the towel and throws it in disgust into a corner by the door.

Mignon rinses her hands under the tap, drying them on her skirt.

'Please, Mme Berniere, I give you whatever Chrétien took from my wages. If there is any left you can keep it for the trouble I have caused you.'

Jacqueline leaps from the stool to shake Mignon violently by the shoulders. 'If it would only knock some sense into you I'd hit you myself. How can you be so stupid? Why is it *you* that has caused the trouble, instead of that bastard that you are unfortunate enough to be the wife of? Tell me that?'

'Perhaps if I was a better wife... perhaps if I did the things...'

'Get out! Get out of my shop now! I don't need this kind of stupidity.'

1988

SEPTEMBER 15th.
THURSDAY

11:22 A.M.

From the last of her reserve, Mignon Merle summons a first step into the café, her head turning this way and that, her breath short and shallow.

'I am sorry…'

Bruno Dernot ushers her to a solitary table in the corner.

'I am most days. Don't let it make you feel special. What do you want?'

'What do you have?'

He drops a menu in front of Mignon and walks away.

She looks up, surprised, to find the blonde woman at the next table staring at her, but not unkindly.

The woman inclines her head to indicate Bruno.

'He isn't always so polite.'

Mignon places her handbag in her lap and reaches down to straighten the hem of her rough felt coat.

'What is good here?'

Oriel Beaufort indicates her plate with a small silver fork.

'This. I always have it.'

Mignon leans over until the table stops her.

'Here…' Oriel picks up the plate and comes over to sit with her. Mignon moves her bag to the floor as she studies the cake.

'What is it?'

'It's called '*Mort par le chocolat*'.'

Oriel turns in her chair. 'Bruno? Another fork, please. Oh, and two coffees.' She smiles at Mignon. 'You do drink coffee?'

'Yes. Yes… but how do you have it?'

'Black.' Oriel looks curiously at Mignon's fingers where they dance uneasily along the edge of the table. She places a hand on them and feels them subside under her touch. 'You will have yours black too. It's the only way.'

Dernot returns with a fork and Oriel passes it to Mignon.

'Here… try a little of this. If you like it we will get you a fresh one.'

'No, no. I couldn't. Not… this is…'

'Don't be silly.' Oriel takes the fork, carves a small piece from the side of the cake, scoops up some of the excess chocolate and points it at Mignon's mouth. 'Open up.'

Mignon cannot speak. From the moment the chocolate hits her taste buds she is in shock.

Oriel turns around. 'Bruno? Another one.'

He returns with two cups of black coffee. Mignon picks hers up immediately. Oriel puts a hand on her arm.

'Not yet. Bruno always makes it too hot.'

The cup rattles back into the saucer.

'Have you not been in here before?'

Mignon slides her finger from the handle of the cup.

'No.'

Dernot brings the plate of chocolate dessert to the table and Mignon feels his no-nonsense face searching fearlessly for her eyes. His once-lush dark hair, the harsh but heart-shaped features, all combining to undermine the courage she has had to find to enter the café. He pushes the empty chairs around them in order.

'She has been looking in my window these last few weeks. I did wonder…'

There is a look of astonishment on Mignon's face.

Oriel turns in her chair. 'Since when was it a crime to look in your window?'

'I was just saying…'

'See?' Oriel touches Mignon's hand again. 'Ignore him. It's just words. Tell me your name.'

To Mignon, the lines that appear around this woman's mouth and eyes as she smiles suggest great confidence. They are symmetrical, like the veins in a butterfly's wing and, in a world where symmetry means normality, she recognises how much she has lost.

She glances down at the soft shoes she is forced to wear, the twist in her ankle. 'Merle… Mme Merle.'

Oriel is glad that she has never seen this level of insecurity in her own mirror.

'Well, I am Oriel… Mme Beaufort… but you must call me Oriel.'

There is no immediate reaction from Mignon, yet there is something behind those sharp, grey-blue eyes that Oriel finds reassuringly expansive. 'How long have you been here?'

'A year, I think.'

Bruno shouts from the door to the kitchen. 'And never been in here once. Just looking… always looking.'

Mignon lifts her head to look Oriel in the eye. 'Time passes differently when you are afraid.'

'Of what are you afraid?'

Mignon opens her purse, searching it for coins to leave on the table. 'Will that be enough?' She pushes the coffee away.

Oriel nods, staring blankly at her.

Mignon picks up her bag. 'Mme Beaufort, may I call on you?'

Oriel snaps back to the moment. 'What? Of course… yes. What about?'

Mignon adjusts her coat against the wind that is driving leaves around the square outside.

'Daughters.'

'I'm not sure how I can help with that.' Oriel softens at the look on Mignon's face. 'But… do you know my house?'

Mignon lifts her collar. 'Yes. Your father's… the Old Surgery?'

'You know it?'

'Yes. It's the one with freshly painted windows.'

SEPTEMBER 16th.
FRIDAY

4:55 P.M.

The season is closing in and the rain captures only a little of the warmth of the air through which it drifts. It drenches Mignon Merle's black coat, releasing kitchen odours from the cloth. She descends three streets to where the road winds with houses on one side and the causeway by the river on the other.

The river is flowing well today. Mignon leans to watch the water dodging rocks and debris, flowing around an old bicycle bell lodged between two stones and long, braided fronds of mermaid hair whipping in sharp twists.

Leaving the familiar comfort of the river to her right, she turns away to where the road steepens to climb anti-clockwise up the hill. At the fourth house along she stops.

She tries to look up but is afraid the rain will sting her eyes as she searches for the small, monogrammed Iris.

There are steps to the yard at the rear. Mignon climbs them, unfastens the string that latches the gate and begins to count the doors.

The pathway is broken in places and through the gaps come shoots of fresh mint, a root of sage, sprigs of thyme and parsley.

She pauses to rub some between her hands and onto the lapel of her coat. At the fourth door along she knocks.

There are no lights in the window beside it, despite the falling greyness of the day. She turns to leave, then hears footsteps making their way down a stair.

Mignon can see that Oriel Beaufort is surprised to find

her there. 'I can come again some other time… if it will be more convenient?'

'No, no. Not at all.' Oriel stands away from the doorstep and beckons her in. 'I said you could call.' She closes the door behind them quietly. 'I just didn't expect it to be so soon.'

'I really can…'

'Shush.' Oriel nudges her arm. 'Go through into the sitting room and take a seat. The one by the fire is the most respectable.'

Mignon smiles shyly. 'Then we should save that one for you.'

'It is reserved for honoured guests.'

Oriel lights the gas with a match and it pops, burning yellow, blackening the sides of the kettle. 'I really must get Artus to see to this.'

She leans in the doorway watching Mignon perch nervously on the overstuffed chair by the hearth, bag clutched firmly on her lap in both hands, coat still fastened, one end of a bright scarf protruding from the collar.

'I know how you take your coffee… but how do you take tea?'

'As it… as it…'

Oriel smiles warmly on her way back to the stove.

'I think I know. Take off your coat. That's if you are stopping?'

She pours the tea, slits two fresh slices from a lemon so that they hang on the rim of the small cups. Buttering the end of a fresh baguette she cuts petite roundels onto a plate.

By the time she takes them through Mignon has removed her coat but still has the scarf tied tightly around her neck over a heavy woollen cardigan. The buttons are fastened all the way to the top.

'Are you cold?'

'No, no.'

Several watercolours decorate the wall opposite the fireplace, engaging Mignon's immediate attention.

Other drawings fit between them, soft pencil sketches, filled with movement and fragility.

'I like your house. You have nice things.'

'Do you know why I have nice things?'

Mignon shakes her head, unable to make sense of the question.

Oriel lays the tea service on a side table in front of the hearth. 'It's because I have no-one to break them for me.'

She sees a look of consternation cross Mignon's face as she passes her a cup.

'Sugar?'

'Yes… I suppose…'

'One lump?'

'Please.' Mignon fusses with the cup. The lemon always seems to be on the wrong side.

Oriel takes the chair across the fireplace from her, trying hard not to stare at the poor quality clothes, the heavy, dark stockings, the twist in her leg that becomes apparent by the time it reaches her ankle, the splay of her foot across the silk rug. She offers fresh tea from the pot.

Mignon waves in protest. Oriel catches the hand. 'Then tell me how you like it. And I'll have the same.'

Mignon fusses with the buttons of her cardigan. 'Can I have a little milk, please?'

'Milk! Why didn't you say?' Oriel pulls a face all the way into the kitchen.

'Is that better?'

Mignon sips gratefully at the tea. 'Yes, thank you. Much better.'

Oriel observes her obliquely for a moment. The woollen cardigan, second knit she guesses, at least. On a drier day, the dark brown polyester dress will cling to her legs.

She feels emotion rise within her and hopes it isn't pity, but recognises that when it finally surfaces, it is the one most likely.

'Are you sure you're not cold?'

Mignon sits with both hands around the cup, shoulders drawn inwards. 'I'm alright, thank you.'

Oriel comes to sit beside her on the floor, eyes fixed on the dead embers in the grate. Her short sleeved blouse and print skirt shed a summer tint into the growing spectre of autumn slowly becoming resident in the room.

She is many years older than Mignon, but the light seems to seek her out first, nestling in the pellucid depths of silvering blonde hair caught tightly in a bun at the nape of her neck, accentuating the fine bone structure of her face.

'I don't even know your name.'

'Mignon.'

Oriel feels herself being studied so intently by Mignon that she can't allow it for a moment longer.

'Daughters?'

As Mignon pulls at an errant cardigan button, Oriel realises how slender she must be under all those clothes. She is reminded of a half-feathered chick she found in a rain-washed gutter… strings and fragility never meant to be sustained by anything more substantial than air.

Mignon pushes away the half-empty teacup. 'I have a daughter, you see.'

'I don't understand why you think I can help.'

'I don't know who else to ask. Everyone in the village seems so intimidating.'

Oriel draws her knees to her chest, folding her arms around them tightly. 'What about the school?'

'Raoul goes to school. He is doing well, but Fabrienne is beyond teaching… for now.'

Oriel considers this, rocking against her heels.

'Have you reason to believe that will change?'

'I have a hope she will speak again. It may not be a real hope… but until she was three she made all the usual noises, the gurgles, the laughter, the first words.'

'Then what happened?'

'We had to move.'

They sit quietly for a moment, thoughts sketching the air between them as if they are each searching for the loose thread of a voice.

Mignon lifts the decorative teacup and sips it dry. Oriel watches the fat from the milk swimming in hers.

Outside, the light is fading. Rain clouds swirl a sky that barely clears the trees down by the river. A pattering begins on the glass behind them as the wind swings around to the east, peppering crumbling stonework with dark circles.

Mignon starts to fuss the tea things onto the tray, making room for the sugar bowl. 'I'm glad I brought my coat.'

The bread with butter sits untouched on a matching side-plate.

Oriel stretches out her legs. 'Leave them. I'll do them later after I've made a fire.'

Mignon sits back in the chair, regaining possession of her handbag as if it were filled with demons she dare not loose. 'If you are sure?'

Oriel nods. 'You are my guest.'

'But I'm used to doing everything myself, you see.'

'What about your boy, what's his name… Raoul?'

Mignon nods anxiously. 'Yes, that's it. Raoul. He's a good boy.'

'And Fabrienne?'

Mignon pauses to consider how much time has passed since she left the children in the house preparing vegetables for the evening stew. Fabrienne will have eaten most of what she has been given to peel, but Raoul will be delicate and accurate. He is so deft with the knife that she will find swedes and onions cut into perfect dies, beans sliced and tailed in equal rows.

'I give them little things I know they can do... but Fabrienne? I don't know what to do. That's why I need your advice.'

'I have no experience of...'

'And I have only love. But perhaps I have too much. That's what I wanted to ask. I think you have lived more than I... I'm sorry... I didn't mean it to sound like that... and I wondered if... if she has spent too much time with me alone. But then how should we have spent it? I thought you might know.'

Completely misreading the look of concern on Oriel's face, she rushes on. 'I'm sorry, I shouldn't have asked. I'll go now. Where did I put my coat?'

Oriel places a hand on her wrist, massaging it gently.

'No, no. Stay where you are. This is why you came, isn't it?'

Mignon's knuckles are drawn white by the way she is clutching the bag. She stares at the half-empty fire grate.

Oriel briefly squeezes her wrist. 'Wait there.'

She pulls herself to her knees by the arm of the chair, crumples a few sheets of newspaper from the hearth and pushes them amongst the dead embers in the grate, laying short, brittle lengths of kindling on top before she turns to Mignon.

'Do you have a match? No, of course you don't. I'll get one from the kitchen.'

The rain has taken away most of the light but this room is so comfortable that Mignon begins to feel less insecure.

By the time Oriel returns, she has found her coat and is fingering the black serge to see if it is still wet.

Oriel lights the paper and sits back on the floor. Their shadows flicker, keeping quiet time around the walls.

Oriel is unsure quite how to phrase this, but one of them has to make a beginning.

'*If* I had some time…'

'Would you? Would you?' Mignon perches the edge of the chair as if she is about to throw herself on the mercy of the wind.

Oriel is taken aback by the speed of her response. 'If… *if*… I had some time to spare… do you think Fabrienne would help me tidy my garden?'

'Would there be something that she could eat?'

Oriel frowns at the question, glancing out of the window at the lowering sky. 'At this time of year there is little left in the garden. Onions mostly… but there may still be some of the berries. Why?'

'It is how I get her to do things. If she can eat it, she can see the purpose in it. If not, she may run away.'

'And if she should run away, where would I find her again?'

Mignon sways slightly in her seat. Her stone of anxiety is rolling unstoppably downhill… to exactly where she needs it to be.

'Don't worry. Children always find *you*.'

'I have never had to be responsible for children.'

'She is no longer a child.'

Oriel's eyebrows lift in surprise, remembering her last glimpse of Fabrienne in headlong flight down the hill outside, the sound of her feet pounding the river bridge and the palpable rush of air as Raoul thunders past the window in pursuit of her.

'Since when?'

'Since the day before I met you in the café.'

For Oriel, the first pieces begin to fall into place.

'I see… but she seems so young… and you want me to tell her what is happening to her body?'

'Yes. Yes. That too… if you think you could.'

'Why not tell her yourself. You are a woman… and you have two children.'

Mignon tightens her grip on the bag.

'I find such things difficult.'

Oriel tongs large pieces of coal onto the kindling. The wood shifts and spits, angry at being disturbed. She pushes the pieces around until they fit. The light dies as the flame drifts to blue and licks the edges of the coal. A tiny pocket of gas whines into absence like a last wasp of the season.

The shadows in the room have become muted and vague and Mignon allows the tension in her shoulders to fall away.

'Yes, I have two children, and I have my experience… but no-one ever explained it to me in a way that I could properly understand.'

'Your mother?'

'No. You see, Mme Beaufort…'

'*Oriel*… please.'

'Mme Beaufort… I am a foster child.'

Oriel observes her silently, searching her face for tell-tale emotions that may stray unbidden to the surface, trying to tease out more pieces of this uncomfortable jigsaw in her comfortable chair where no-one else has ever managed to seem so ill at ease.

'Then perhaps your foster mother..?'

'Which one?'

'There were many?'

'I can't remember them all. And there are some that I can that I do not wish to.'

Oriel finds herself irresistibly drawn to touch the hem of the serge coat Mignon has hung over the chair back.

The wool is coarse and unrefined, yet there is a warmth

reflected in the touch.

She cannot imagine Mignon wearing anything else.

'Do you remember your real mother?'

'No, but I know who she is.'

'You *know* who she is? How is this possible? I thought these things were held secret?'

'When I was old enough that everyone had forgotten about me, I took a job as a cleaner at the Agencie in Pont-Saint-Esprit. In a uniform no-one cares who you are. I had every night for a year to search.'

Oriel draws her knees to her chest again, clasping them tighter. Mignon jumps as a coal splits with the sound of a distant rifle. A candle of flame leaps from the crack and the colours of Oriel's dress flare briefly as an Indian summer.

The embers of kindling fall shimmering below the grate as Mignon studies Oriel's face.

'I have known where she is for many years.'

'Where? Here in the village?'

'Yes.'

'Does she know that you are here?'

'I think she has forgotten that I exist.'

Mignon's eyes brim over with tears. They streak her face, tracks shining and reflective with firelight. She dabs them with the end of her scarf, shrugs her arms into her coat and picks up the bag.

'I'm sorry. I should go now.'

Oriel stops her at the door.

'Wait a moment… have you thought of speaking to her about this?'

'Mme Beaufort, I have thought of little else.'

1:30 P.M.

Oriel answers the door to discover the tiny figure of Fabrienne. In her hand is a hoe with a shortened shaft, the end of the timber pale and freshly cut. She is dressed no differently than at any time Oriel has seen her… broken shoes, the same dark skirt and non-descript blouse under a shabby lemon jumper, collar half-in, half out… though her most striking feature, her smile, is lost today.

'Come in.' Oriel beckons her into the kitchen. Fabrienne shakes her head theatrically and points to the garden.

Oriel reaches for her hand, watching her all the time as she might something brought in from the wild.

'Not yet.'

Fabrienne follows reluctantly, a narrow smile breaking on and off her face as she steps across the threshold.

'That's it. That's it.' Oriel coaxes her into the kitchen where the kettle purrs on the stove like an ancient cat. A pan of culled greens bubbles quietly beside it, gas flames licking hungrily at their sides.

Fabrienne lifts her hand from Oriel's grip and walks over to the stove. She reaches up and turns it off. The flames die away and the kettle falls silent. Fabrienne turns around… and now the smile has returned.

'Would you like a drink?'

Fabrienne shakes her head and points to the back door.

Oriel points to Fabrienne's muddy shoes. 'You need to take those off in here. There's time for the garden later. Let's sit for a minute.'

She is surprised when Fabrienne kicks off her shoes and puts them by the door.

'You can understand me? But I thought… Oh, I see.

That will make things easier. Here…'

Oriel pulls out a stool. 'Sit down with me.'

Oriel sits across the table from Fabrienne, studying the face smiling back at her with its green-flecked, grey-blue eyes, the unruly mop of dirt-filled hair and the wide, forgiving mouth that overrules any other feature of her face, unfairly drawing attention from the fine snub nose and elfin ears.

Fabrienne leans forward until their noses are a hairsbreadth apart and something jumps the gap between them like a spark.

Oriel takes a deep breath and sits back. Fabrienne rubs her nose with a grubby hand. With the other, she points at Oriel's mouth, making fish-like movements with her own.

'You want *me* to talk?'

Fabrienne reaches out to touch Oriel's face, the grubby fingertips gently tapering her skin, experiencing the soft white down on her upper lip.

Oriel speaks softly, exaggerating the movements of her mouth.

'What is it you want me to say?'

Fabrienne takes her hand away, places it on her own lips and replicates the movements with her mouth. Suddenly tired of the game, she leaps from the stool, grabs the hoe and points to the back door.

Oriel catches her arm. 'No. Not yet. We have to get you properly dressed for gardening. Come with me.'

Fabrienne stands stock still, looking at the dark timber door panels as if she can see directly through them into the yard beyond.

Oriel opens the stair door. 'Come with me.'

Fabrienne resists as though her life depends on it.

Oriel throws open the back door and swings the stair door wide to give her the choice.

'Here… I won't hurt you. You can come with me or you can run away. I don't mind.'

Fabrienne stands a moment longer, looking out at the garden with its rough-and-tumble bushes and the fading vegetation, then slowly closes the back door.

1:40 P.M.

From the inside of the opened wardrobe Fabrienne pulls out the hem of a cream wedding dress.

Oriel gently removes her fingers from the silk. The letter she has patiently sewn into the bodice crackles under her fingers as she irons the creases with her hand.

'No. Not that. Here… let's try these.' From the top shelf she takes down a pair of faded brown dungarees. 'Take off your skirt.'

Fabrienne stands silently.

Oriel kneels to undo the fastenings on the waistband and lets it fall to the floor. Fabrienne puts her arms around Oriel and squeezes tightly, pressing her cheek into Oriel's neck.

Oriel waits a moment before disentangling herself. She holds Fabrienne at arm's length. 'Here. Let me look at you.'

Fabrienne lifts her arms and poses, face breaking into the warmth of a smile.

'No, turn around.'

Fabrienne shakes her head. Oriel indicates a spin with her fingers. Fabrienne shakes her head again, the smile crumbling into watchfulness.

Oriel holds out the dungarees. 'Then step into these.'

Fabrienne steps into them and Oriel tugs them around her waist. They are enormous on her. Oriel ties knots in the straps and rolls half the length of the trousers into a neat cuff.

'Take a look at yourself.'

Fabrienne walks uncertainly over to the mirror, takes a

brief look then runs back to Oriel, flinging her arms around her once more.

Oriel takes her hand. 'Come on, back to the kitchen. Mind the stairs. They are steep.'

From behind the curtain that cloaks the space under the sink, Oriel passes her a pair of tall rubber boots. Between them they fold the trouser legs inside the tops.

Fabrienne grabs the hoe and opens the kitchen door

Oriel looks around as they walk up the path. 'Now then, where do we start?'

Fabrienne is already digging.

2:23 P.M.

Oriel has amassed a pile of dead leaves at the top of the garden. Fabrienne has a large hole between the redundant sweet pea canes and a broad gooseberry bush. When she jumps in the bottom she disappears to her waist.

Oriel pulls off the gardening gloves and bangs the dirt from them on her thigh. 'I think that will do for today. Wait there, I have a treat for us.'

She returns carrying two large glasses of homemade ginger beer from the flagon clearing under the kitchen sink.

The garden appears deserted. The hoe with the short shaft has been thrown across the stems of laid-up onion sets. Earth is crumbling back into the edges of the large, freshly disturbed hole.

She turns to go back to the kitchen and trips over Fabrienne.

'There you are. I wondered where…'

Fabrienne dives headlong at Oriel, sending the glasses flying. They wrestle into the leaves that Oriel has amassed, arms and legs flailing.

Oriel is forced onto her back, legs folding beneath her. She struggles them free, one shoe held by the soft, moist earth and manages a grip on Fabrienne, who is squirming, playfully punching, coating them both in fresh dirt.

Without warning, Oriel collapses into laughter. Her hands set Fabrienne free to do whatever she will but finds the small arms wrapped tightly around her. She takes hold of a wrist but it is beyond release. From every place this small, shaking body is in contact with hers, Oriel finds the movement shuddering in her blood.

She kicks off her shoe, abruptly aware of the absurdity of earth that clings to their clothes and skin, the ridiculously perfect shape of her own foot held in the air and the blind stupidity of skies that circle above them, watching without comment.

2:48 P.M.

Fabrienne kicks off the rubber boots, still laughing. Since she began out in the garden she has not stopped. Now, in the kitchen, the sound has become horribly discordant.

Oriel unbuttons the straps from the dungarees and puts a finger to her lips. Fabrienne stops as suddenly as she began. Oriel tousles the leaves and dirt from her hair as she watches silently, her eyes locked on Oriel's, unmoving and impenetrable.

'Wait until I tell *maman*. She will be so pleased.'

Fabrienne pushes her away sharply, touches her own lips with a finger and reaches across to touch Oriel's.

'Me… You.'

Oriel grabs her by the shoulders. The bones are slender and fragile, barely below the surface. Her musculature is little more than a thin cover and she wonders what has enabled her to dig so fiercely.

'But I must tell your maman.'

Fabrienne shakes her head slowly, running a finger across the width of her mouth like a zip. She touches Oriel's in the same way.

Oriel lifts Fabrienne's chin with a finger until their eyes meet. Fabrienne's are a beautiful grey-blue, with that slight green fleck in the left iris, much like her own. But in the way they stare there is a wildness that Oriel has not seen before.

'Can I tell her… later?'

Fabrienne nods assent.

'Tomorrow?'

Fabrienne shies away again.

Oriel tugs her back, searching for the next piece of this puzzle. 'Will you tell me when I can?'

In her ear, she hears the whispered, 'Yes.'

She grabs a cloth from the sink and scrubs the dirt from Fabrienne's hands and face.

'Right, my little silent Mademoiselle, upstairs and get your skirt.'

Fabrienne makes a dash for the stairs. Oriel reaches out to slow her down and the jumper crumples in her hand.

She holds Fabrienne firmly on the third step, level with her eyes. The hem is raised, exposing Fabrienne's lower back.

Quickly, she covers it again.

2:50 P.M.

For three days, Oriel has prayed for Fabrienne to return.

She crosses her hands over the end of the rake handle and rests her chin on them. When she opens her eyes again, Fabrienne is staring silently at her from the bottom of the path, watching to see if her grimace will soften into a smile.

When she smiles, Fabrienne rushes towards her, feet flying, scattering broken acorns into the air. At the last second she leaps, cannoning them both into the garden.

The mulching leaves are wet, slick as a second skin.

Oriel folds her arms around Fabrienne.

'I can see I shall have to teach you how to shake hands.'

She struggles to the door with Fabrienne still attached, shucks off her shoes at the entrance and steps inside.

Fabrienne's grip relaxes and Oriel allows her to slip to the floor. She motions her to the bottom step.

'Shoes!'

She pulls Fabrienne's cracked leather shoes from the small, perfectly shaped feet. She has no socks and the spaces between her toes are black and filled with earth. The toenails are long and roughly broken at the ends and her skin is so bitterly cold Oriel holds a foot between both hands to warm it.

'Wait here…'

She fills a kettle and sets it to boil.

Fabrienne has retreated to the furthest corner of the step and Oriel reaches down to lift her, gratified by the way Fabrienne's hands reach up.

The fire has faded in the grate, leaving the sitting room warmer than outside but not by much.

Oriel carries Fabrienne to her own favourite chair and

tucks a throw around her. Fabrienne's feet stick out of the bottom, pale and white only where the shoes have rubbed the dirt off. Oriel places a small log on the fire and watches for a moment as the flames play in Fabrienne's eyes.

She has refilled the kettle and left it to simmer. Gently lifting Fabrienne's feet into a bowl, she scrubs warmth into the cold skin with an old piece of wet flannel. The soap lifts the earth out from between the toes and fine lines appear in the soles. From scabs on her ankles, dried blood dissolves into the water.

Fabrienne sits quietly, watching the flames dance and shiver, turning suddenly to watch her own shadow at play amongst the drawings and watercolours. Fascinated, unable to turn back to the flames, she lifts her hand from under the throw and points.

'Do you like them?' Oriel allows Fabrienne's feet to fall free. 'Which one?'

Fabrienne points to a faded watercolour of the river.

Oriel slides it onto Fabrienne's knees and watches the child's face as firelight deepens the pigment.

Fabrienne traces the rocks with her finger, making tiny scuttling movements over the paper, emulating the movement of the water around them. A smile spreads slowly across her face.

'Shhhhhh…'

Oriel is jolted by how closely the sound resembles that of the river she hears when she wakes in the night.

'You want to draw? Pictures?'

Fabrienne stares at her blankly, returning again to trace the path of the water with her finger.

'Wait a moment…' Oriel returns from the sideboard with a pencil and paper backed by a stiff card. She pushes the pencil into Fabrienne's hand.

'Here… you try.'

Fabrienne stares blankly at the pencil in her fingers, then carves bold, striking lines across the paper.

4:36 P.M.

Oriel has carried Fabrienne outside to sit in the last of the sun on a stiff canvas sheet sketching birds, fallen leaves and the faded husks of once-bright summer flowers. With each stroke Fabrienne seems to push more life into them than they had ever possessed.

Oriel lies back, staring up at ebullient storm clouds, high anvils catching the bright sun as it slips to the horizon. The roofs and gutters are limned in surreal golden light as the sun bleeds beneath a lowering sky.

The first drops of rain hit the pad in Fabrienne's hand, shuddering the paper into ripples. Before either can stand, the sky opens. The strange light gilding the edge of the house collapses in a loud crack above their heads. Their skin crawls with wild electricity.

Oriel grabs at Fabrienne, board, pencils and all, to dash toward the house. She barely has her feet under her when the rain descends. Fabrienne casts away the board and pencil, throws her arms up into the sky and opens her mouth, letting the downpour splash across her face. In an instant she is soaked to the skin. She begins to spin, jumping up and down in the falling water. Oriel joins in, whooping loud as a night-fox… Fabrienne a dervish beside her.

The rain stops as suddenly as it began. Feeling a little foolish in the silence, Oriel watches its shadow march across the land beyond the oak tree, the edge of the storm trailing a grey mist.

For a moment they are both silent, watching the cloud-burst torture the crows in the trees over the valley.

Turning away, they catch sight of each other.

Oriel is the first to giggle.

'Will you help me?'

Fabrienne nods eagerly.

In the hearth, logs crack open in small explosions of light. The rug is warm and dry beneath their knees.

Oriel has removed her dress. Fabrienne has taken off her cardigan and they kneel together, shivering, as heat builds into the room around them.

Oriel turns away so that Fabrienne can reach the clasp that holds her hair in a bun. Released, it cascades into the firelight, burnished by the colours of the flames.

Fabrienne runs her fingers through it, casting it into pale rivulets over Oriel's shoulders. The fire catches brightly, heat scorching the thin skin over her nose and cheekbones.

Oriel touches her arm, drawing her attention from the flames. 'Your tee-shirt. Take it off.'

Fabrienne shakes her head. Oriel takes hold of the hem.

'You must. You'll catch your death…'

Fabrienne screams loudly.

Oriel takes her by the shoulders and shakes her until she stops. 'I have already seen!'

Fabrienne still shakes her head although she now stays silent.

'Fabrienne! I know… I have seen your drawings. Here…'

She rummages in the bag stashed behind the chair, tugs loose a handful of folded paper and pushes it at her.

Without looking, Fabrienne throws the pictures into the flames. Oriel reaches quickly but is too late. Small pieces of ash writhe up the chimney, leaving behind scars of pencil on ghost paper glowing red on the hearthstone.

Without lifting her eyes from Oriel's, Fabrienne takes hold of the hem of her tee-shirt. She pulls it slowly over her head and allows it to drop to the floor between them.

Oriel drapes it over the arm of the chair where the fire can tease the rain from it.

Gently, she turns Fabrienne around. The firelight lifts her scars into high relief. In places where the skin has stretched and torn it is livid beyond belief, as white as snow in others.

Fabrienne takes one of Oriel's hands and places it gently amongst the scars. She continues to stare at the light from the hearth, her back in shadow while Oriel's fingers trace the contours. The pain trapped within this tiny body transmits itself through Oriel's skin, lodging deep in her heart.

Fabrienne sits back, spooning her body into Oriel's. They slip sideways onto the rug, folding together under the heat of the crackling timber where firelight flickers their skin.

Oriel puts her arms around her and holds tight.

After a moment… she realises that Fabrienne is crying too.

7:56 P.M.

The fire has died and the room turned cold. Outside, the last of the light is gone and the window is a black square in a room lit vaguely by sparks.

Oriel gets up quietly without disturbing Fabrienne, lifting the tee-shirt on the arm of the chair to check it has dried. So has her dress where it hangs behind the door.

She slips it over her head and goes through to light the gas under the kettle. She returns to the sitting room with her old housecoat and drapes it over Fabrienne, tucking in the edges.

Behind her there is a knock at the door. When she answers, it is Artus.

He smiles at the way her hair is disturbed, the obvious sleep still closing the corners of her eyes.

'I came to see to the gas.'

She pulls him into the room and closes the back door.

'Shhh.'

Artus is suddenly uncomfortable. 'I'm sorry, I didn't know you had company. I can come back later.'

'You silly man, come here.' She grabs him by the lapels of his work jacket and kisses him.

Artus staggers back. 'What was that for?'

'For you. Who else?'

'I don't know. You were shushing me… and your hair…'

Oriel grabs him again by the lapel. 'Be quiet. I have something to show you.'

She leads him to the door into the sitting room.

The fire has died but the ashes glow fitfully and by their light Artus can make out the shape of someone on the floor, tucked under Oriel's old housecoat.

'Who…?' then he notices the wilderness of hair wisping out from beneath the coat. 'Fabrienne! I wondered…'

'What did you wonder? Did you wonder if I had someone else in here?'

She punches him softly, pushing him steadily backwards, playfully teasing colour into his cheeks. 'A lover, eh? Is that what you thought, you *ancien chèvre*?'

Artus holds her punching fists in his own large hands.

'No… I meant…'

'What? That you don't trust me?'

'No, no, no. I am glad that she is here. I wondered where she was, that's all.'

'And why should you wonder that?'

Artus draws a chair out from under the table to sit down

'She has…' He hesitates, knowing that, even though it is with Oriel, he is betraying a secret. 'She has been working with me.'

'Working with you? Doing what, sweeping up? It's about time someone did. Your workshop is a disgrace.'

'No. She has a talent. One that is unlocking an old secret.

If only Auguste were still here.'

'What kind of a 'talent'?'

'If you have never seen her with a pencil in her hand, you could never understand.'

'Wait here. Make the coffee.'

Oriel steals quietly into the sitting room, eases open the drawer and takes out a handful of papers. Artus has poured water into the pot and as they sit to wait for the grounds to settle she pushes the drawings across the table at him.

'Like this, you mean?'

Artus sifts them through his fingers, stopping only to admire the pin-feather detailing of a sparrow, the droplets of water cast on a spider-web.

'These are beautiful…' He spoons two lumps of sugar into his cup in preparation. '…but this is not what I mean.'

He lifts the lid of the coffee pot and holds it out, rim facing her. 'She can draw a perfect circle.'

'Anyone can.'

Artus replaces the lid.

'Freehand? In any way I can measure, it is perfect. I cannot better it with a compass.'

Oriel pours the coffee and wonders at his amazement. After all, it is not unheard of, only rare.

'How many perfect circles do you need?'

Artus stirs in the sugar until it has disappeared and he can no longer find the grains with the back of his spoon.

'That's not all. I tell her how many teeth to place on the outside of it and there they are! Neat and regular, correct in size and number like the teeth in a dragon's mouth. When I think of the years I have spent marking out cogwheels, I could…'

'You know you love it.' Oriel places a lump of sugar the size of the end of her thumb behind her teeth and sips at the coffee. 'You could never be anything else.'

'I know.' Artus smiles a half-secret, wishful smile 'But if I'd had that talent, my clocks would have graced the halls of Kings.'

'But then you would never have graced mine.'

He reaches for her. 'I would have found you somehow.'

She pushes him back. 'Not now, old goat. I have a job for you.'

He lifts the cup of hot, sweet, black coffee. 'The gas seems to be working well enough.'

'Not the gas. I need you to take a message to Fabrienne's mother.'

'Should I not take Fabrienne, too?'

'No, she is fast asleep. The child is exhausted.'

Artus puts down the cup, refills it from the pot and reaches for the sugar. Oriel stops him, patting his waistline.

He drops the spoon back into the bowl.

'What have you been doing to her?'

Oriel drops one lump of sugar into his cup, stirring it quickly for him. 'It is what she has been doing to herself.'

'Like what?'

'Like opening doors.'

'And what is this important message that leaves you no time for me?'

'I want you to tell Mignon that Fabrienne is safe and to ask if she can stay the night because she is already fast asleep. Whatever you say, do not tell her that Fabrienne has been working with you. Not yet, anyway.'

'Why?'

'Trust me! Don't say more than you have to.'

'It would be just as easy for me to carry her.'

'Just go!' She punches him playfully again. 'The sooner you go, the sooner you will be able to come back.'

'You mean… I can come back?'

She ushers him through the kitchen door into the night.

'You dare not!'
Artus wedges his shoe in the door.
'Are you sure? I mean…'
'Of course I'm sure.'
A smile spreads across his ageing, weathered face.
She lifts his foot from the doorstep and pushes him out.
'How else am I going to get my gas fixed?'

7:13 A.M.

By first light, Fabrienne's shoes are missing from the foot of the stairs. Oriel wraps her housecoat tightly against the cold and goes through into the sitting room. The cardigan, skirt and tee-shirt are also gone. She rushes upstairs to the box room. The cot she made up last night for Fabrienne is empty. She shivers, looking around for a sign or a clue, then hears the sharp chink of metal striking stone out in the garden. She opens the curtain and smiles with relief.

Fabrienne is out in the garden, soil flying from the blade of the hoe, frantically enlarging the hole she began the day before.

Oriel watches her a moment.

The child is totally absorbed by the displacement of the earth, not caring where it flies. Oriel sees it lodged in the spines of the gooseberry, in darkly rich clumps along the entire length of the path, but mostly it is in Fabrienne's hair.

Her legs are splashed from yesterday's rain that has sat against the surface, unable to drain into a sub-soil already in capacity.

The hearthstone is still warm, but the embers are grey and lifeless. Oriel replaces them with sticks from the basket.

She fills a large pan with water and places it on the stove beside the kettle. She taps on the window with her fingers but Fabrienne ignores her. From behind the pantry door she unhooks a large tin bath and carries it in front of the fire. By the time the fire has warmed the room, the pan and kettle are simmering on the stove.

She slips on her shoes. 'Fabrienne… Fabrienne!'

Fabrienne stops, eyes wide with pleasure.

She points down into the hole. In the bottom are flat

moons of marble and limestone, unearthed by the energy of her digging. They lay on edge in a curved row, like the vertebrae of a dinosaur, undulating across the base of the excavation.

Fabrienne grins broadly and continues to dig the hole, scraping earth from the sides with the hoe.

Oriel leads her down the path and into the house.

'Clothes off.'

Fabrienne stares blankly at her.

'Now… please?'

Fabrienne sits on the bottom step. Oriel kneels down to take off her shoes and realises that she isn't wearing any. She peels away the large clumps of muddy earth that are stuck to the bare skin.

'Where are your shoes?'

Fabrienne raises her eyebrows by way of reply.

Oriel takes hold of the cardigan buttons, then pulls it directly over her head instead and drops it on the mat by the door.

In the sitting room, the logs have caught and the room is filled with a humid warmth that cloaks the window panes with a fine breath. Fabrienne is quite still as Oriel undresses her and points to the bath.

'Get in.'

Fabrienne shakes her head. Oriel shakes her gently by the shoulders. 'You must. If you could see yourself…'

She tries to pick her up, but Fabrienne squirms out of her grasp.

'What's the matter? Don't you like to be clean?'

Fabrienne shies away from the bath, the surface rippling from where she has kicked the side in her struggle with Oriel.

'Water.'

'Yes, I know it is water. That's how you get clean.'

Fabrienne turns her back to Oriel, bending her spine so that brittle knobs of bone show through the scar.

Oriel spins Fabrienne back around. 'But the rain is water too. You enjoyed that, didn't you?'

Fabrienne grins broadly, her mouth wide with pleasure.

'Rain… is… rain. Water… is… water.'

Oriel considers that for no more than a moment.

'Fabrienne, do you trust me?'

Fabrienne whispers. 'Yes.'

'Then hold my hand and close your eyes.'

Small fingers intertwine with her own, filling the missing places until she feels unaccountably complete. Slowly, she dips their joined hands towards the bath.

Fabrienne hesitates, jerking Oriel to a stop.

Oriel's hand is becoming insistent. 'Trust me.'

Their hands slip silently through the surface of the water and heat soaks through their skin into the cold bones beneath. Fabrienne's other hand finds Oriel's shoulder and, without opening her eyes, she steps into the bath.

Oriel steadies her as she sits, flinching at every sudden movement of the water.

'There… now don't move until I come back.'

Oriel returns from the garden, pausing in the kitchen to pick up a towel and soap. She hands the bar to Fabrienne who studies it suspiciously until it slips from her hands.

Oriel dips her watering can into the water, pouring it slowly over Fabrienne's hair. The water clouds instantly. She finds the soap and rubs it into the mass of tangled wet hair, her own hands turning black in the process. She rinses it clear and sits back, amazed. Under her hands, Fabrienne's hair has turned from dirty brown to a glorious blonde.

Fabrienne shakes her head like a dog, stencilling the fireside with drops of water that hiss and spit on the hearth.

Oriel scrubs her face with the towel, then sets about the

rest of her.

Under the dirt, her undamaged skin is pale and soft. Oriel lifts her to her feet and pours a full can of water gently over her head, watching it trickle her skin, flowing between the other places where it is covered in scratches, knocks and small bruises.

'You are beautiful.'

Fabrienne smiles and hugs her, heedless of the water splashing between them.

'*Rain.*'

9:00 A.M.

Oriel wraps the towel around her, avoiding the obvious bruises and scratches, then sits her into the comfortable chair.

'Let's see about some clothes for you.'

She returns from the bedroom with an old wrap-around skirt and a warm jumper. The waist of the skirt fits around twice and the waistband is folded over until Fabrienne's feet show beneath the hem. The sleeves of the jumper are rolled to the elbow. Oriel's winter socks hang off the end of Fabrienne's feet, no matter that the tops are turned right down.

Oriel hands her the pad and a pencil.

'Draw me something. I have a job to do.'

She gathers the discarded clothes from the floor and dumps them into the bathwater, turning it black and gritty as she folds, wrings, soaps and scrubs. Every time she looks up, Fabrienne is watching from the depths of the chair.

'Draw! I want a picture.'

Fabrienne rips off a sheet and tosses it into the flames.

As it burns, Oriel catches the brief outline of herself kneeling beside the bath, hair pushed behind her ears. The flames take it quickly away.

The clothes are as clean as Oriel can get them. As she wrings the water from them, seams burst under her fingers.

The undergarments are more hole than substance, but these too she hangs up to dry.

Fabrienne is scribbling away with the pencil. Oriel leans over to see what she is doing. On the page are two arcs of a circle, they are poised, as incomplete as brackets, a gap at top and bottom but Oriel can see that if they were joined with two similar arcs, they would be perfect. In the centre of them Fabrienne has written in a beautiful hand the word… '*Maman*'.

Oriel shakes her head. 'I don't understand.'

Fabrienne returns the pencil to the paper. Completing the top arc with precise lettering, she writes… 'Oriel'. It sits perfectly on the page like the jewel in a ring. Oriel taps the gap at the bottom.

'Where is your name? Why is it not complete?'

Fabrienne looks deep into her eyes. Oriel feels her soul sifted and evaluated under that gaze, unable for a moment to tear herself away from the pale, grey-blue eyes with their solitary fleck.

There is a knock at the door. She blinks and the spell is broken.

'This will be maman looking for you.'

Between Artus' hands is a small brown paper parcel.

Oriel cannot conceal her surprise.

'Artus? I thought it was… shouldn't you be working?'

'Who did you think it was? Your lover from last night, eh?'

'Then I would have been right… no?'

Artus blushes slightly, a fragility that has always endeared him to her. 'Here.' He pushes the parcel into her hands. 'I have work to do. I hope these will be alright. I took them last night.'

Feeling the hard soles of shoes through the bag, Oriel throws a quick glance towards the sitting room. 'I wondered where they were. You've just saved me from digging up the garden.'

Artus smiles wickedly. 'Save your energy for later.'

'Look…about later… can you call at Mignon's to see if Fabrienne has more clothes?'

'Shall I ask Mignon to fetch her home?'

'No. Not yet. I will take her when she's ready.'

'Shall I come with you?'

'No. There are things I need to ask.'

'Ah! I see. Women's things.'

She leans out for a kiss on her cheek but he has gone.

9:23 A.M.

Oriel fetches bread and jam from the kitchen and they sit beside the fire. Fabrienne is watching patterns in the flames. Oriel is watching jam spread across her face.

Artus has returned empty-handed and gone away again.

When the ruined socks are dry, she slips them onto Fabrienne's feet, kissing the small toes that protrude while Fabrienne giggles at the attention. She wipes the jam from Fabrienne's face with a damp cloth and pulls the tee-shirt on over her head. The skirt and cardigan have shrunk and barely cover the bruises. The shoes have been freshly soled and heeled, the leather reinforced and polished with new, soft insoles slipped into place.

Fabrienne keeps lifting each foot off the floor in turn to stare at it.

Outside, the wind has risen, with leaves climbing the spirals at the corner of the street. Oriel finds an old jacket and hangs it around Fabrienne's shoulders. She cinches the narrow belt.

'There. Maman will not know you. Wait…'

She tucks Fabrienne's hair into the woollen beret she has found in the jacket pocket, pulling it down to her ears. 'Now she would walk past you in the street.'

She shakes her own winter coat from the cupboard, winding a scarf loosely around her neck.

'Are we ready?'

Fabrienne hands her the drawing pad. In the space at the bottom of the arc she has inscribed the word. 'Artus'.

LA MAISON DE MIGNON
CHEMIN DE RONDE
LA ROQUE-SUR-PERNES

SEPTEMBER 24th.
SATURDAY

11:33 A.M.

The carrots clutched in Mignon Merle's fingers swing by their green tops, showering the mat with small dark spots. She pads barefoot into the kitchen and drops them into the sink. By the door to the street she notices a small white envelope.

She leaves the carrots to soak and picks it up, staining it with water from her hands. On the front is her name, correctly spelled, with ink now running into the finger marks. Her hands tremble as they open the paper. In her experience, letters have always been demands for money or orders for eviction… but this one is from Oriel.

She sits down at the table to release the breath she hadn't realised she was holding until she saw the signature on the page.

SEPTEMBER 24th.
SATURDAY

11:58 A.M.

Mignon stands outside the café door, unwilling to enter unless Oriel is already there.

Bruno Dernot watches her curiously as she moves up to the glass to peer in. He shouts to her from behind the counter.

'Twice in one year. Be careful not to overdo it.'

Oriel waves her over. 'Bruno! Behave. She is my guest.'

She pushes a chair free for Mignon. 'I am glad you could make it. What will you have?'

Oriel is already half-way down her coffee and cake and Mignon is made sharply aware of how little concept she has of time.

'I'm sorry… am I late?' She looks around for a clock. There is a small one on the wall behind the counter but she cannot make it out at this distance, her left eye will no longer travel its full orbit.

'No, I was early.' Oriel pats her hand. 'Bruno?'

Dernot looks up from quartering a petit-four for the crows by the door.

'Bruno? I think we will have…' She waits a moment as Mignon seems lost in indecision. 'I think we will have… coffee.'

'No! Wait.' Mignon jerks suddenly to life beside her. 'We will have tea, please, with lumps of white sugar.'

'Milk?'

'Yes… wait… No. We will not have milk.'

Dernot rips the page from his pad, crumples it into the

air and disappears into the back room.

Oriel finds herself in sympathy with Mignon's emotional plight. She has come to realise that she is barely scratching her surface and is half-scared of what she may find beneath.

'Bruno can be so disrespectful. I can't think of anyone he hasn't offended. Would you like something to eat with your tea?'

Dernot shouts through from the back room. 'I was going to ask but life is too short.'

Oriel laughs out loud. 'Bruno! You are disgraceful!'

He brings the tea through and lays it at their table. 'Then maybe I am in good company.'

Mignon settles her handbag in her lap, gripping the clasp tightly with both hands. Oriel takes it from her and sits it on the empty chair beside them.

'Leave it. Relax. Enjoy your tea.'

Mignon places her hands together in her lap as if the handbag had never been removed.

'I'll be alright in a moment.'

Oriel reaches over to unbutton the top fastening of Mignon's coat. Mignon turns quickly away, clasping the collar with one hand.

Oriel takes her hands away. 'I shouldn't have done that. I apologise. It's far too familiar. It's just that it's warm in here.'

'No, no. You're right.' Mignon fiddles with the top button, turns the collar down flat against her shoulders and rearranges the scarf around her neck. 'That's better.'

'No. You don't feel comfortable here. Perhaps it would be better if you came back to my house?'

Mignon lifts her teacup and reaches for a lump of pale sugar.

'I'll be fine in a minute. I just need a drink.' She sips the tea through the sugar without difficulty, then stops and smiles. 'I've been practising.'

Oriel covers her expression behind the tilted rim of the cup. 'Have you any idea why I asked you here?'

Mignon swallows the last of the sugar. 'It must be Fabrienne. I know she has been to see you every day for the last two weeks.'

Oriel is taken aback, but decides to let the inconsistency pass. 'Yes, you're right.'

'How are you...? How do you...?'

Oriel smiles and holds her cup in the air for a refill.

'Oh, we're fine. We have quiet conversations about...'

She stops as a look of shock spreads vividly across Mignon's face and remembers her promise to Fabrienne.

'In our own way, of course. She talks to me in many ways. Sometimes just by the way she listens to something she likes.'

She shakes her head, sensing her own unworthiness in this situation, holding back from Fabrienne's mother the most precious piece of information she could possess.

Mignon's fingers unlock their grasp on thin air.

'For a moment... I thought you meant... You would tell me, wouldn't you?'

Oriel knows that in time she will come to pay for this moment.

'Of course I would.'

Folded into her pocket is the drawing that Fabrienne made by her fireside. She can almost divine the detail and precision through the skin of her fingertips.

She takes a deep breath and takes it out, then pushes it straight into her bag beside the chair. Now is not the time... and here is not the place.

'Finish your tea.'

'Pardon?' Mignon is alarmed by the peremptory nature of the demand. Oriel stares at her unwaveringly across the table.

'Bruno? *L'addition.*'

Bruno drops a wrinkled piece of till roll on the table between them, '*Oui, Madame!*'

Oriel touches the sleeve of Mignon's coat in what she hopes will be a reassuring gesture, sensing again the rough weave between her fingers.

'We need to talk...'

The café falls suddenly silent. Her voice drops to a whisper as she casts a glance around the room, watching the crows gathered for their ritual morning coffee, waiting until they have begun to chatter again amongst themselves.

'... but not here.'

'My house...' The women by the window fall silent again. Mignon drops her voice to the merest breath. '...is just around the corner.'

The café remains silent as they leave. All eyes turn their way until they round the corner of the square, where Oriel slides her hand through Mignon's arm.

Mignon smiles up at her... and grips it as tightly as her bag.

SEPTEMBER 24th.
SATURDAY

12:36 P.M.

'You must take me as you find me… I didn't expect…'

Oriel follows her into the cottage, wiping her feet on the clipping rug just inside the door.

Mignon hangs their coats on a peg at the foot of a steep staircase, pushing open the door into the parlour.

Oriel peeks in. The room is almost bare, but fastidiously clean. Under the window there is an old settle with a pale yellow throw folded neatly over the arms. A wooden chair with a tall rail back waits beside an unmade fire. The carpet is also clean, but the weft shows through the faded colours. The firedogs gleam with black-lead but the hearth is empty and cold.

Mignon half closes the door. 'We can sit in there if you wish. As you can see, we have very little, but I can light a fire…'

Oriel smiles at her and draws the door firmly shut. 'I am a kitchen person.'

'But *your* sitting room…'

Oriel backtracks with remarkable alacrity, considering what she is here to ask. 'I mean in other people's houses. It says so much more about a person, don't you think?'

'I don't know.' Mignon leads them through into the kitchen.

The stove is on a slow burn and an aroma of simmering vegetables pervades the air.

The kitchen is stripped to bare necessity yet, to Oriel, the scent of cooking fills the entire room.

'To have someone to cook for is a great luxury.'

Mignon fusses in the drawer under the table for a spoon.

Oriel takes a hard-bottomed chair, convinced that it had once belonged to Artus. 'I have no-one, you see.'

'You have M'sieur d'Horo. I'm sorry... that sounds like I am prying. I didn't mean to.'

'Artus and myself are no secret in this village. The only secret is what has taken us so long, but then... we were driven apart many years ago. It's funny how things like that matter less as you get older. What herbs do you have? The stew smells marvellous.'

Oriel gets up from her chair and opens the little cupboard in the corner. Inside are three plates, three cups, three saucers and a small collection of battered saucepans.

'There are no herbs. Where do you keep them?'

Mignon takes a bright print pinafore from the table drawer and slips the ties over her head. 'Outside. I only pick them when they are fresh. I hate the dried ones, don't you?'

Oriel leans her arms onto the scraped-clean table top. Her fingers insinuate themselves together without thought or purpose.

'I wish I could say that I cared.'

'Perhaps...' Mignon moves the kettle across to the boiling plate with a hand wrapped in the bottom of the pinafore. 'No ...this sounds silly...'

Oriel watches her, wondering how she is going to steer this conversation around to where she wants it to be.

'I won't laugh... I promise.'

'Then perhaps you could cook... for me.'

Oriel sits up sharply. 'Of course, but you have seen my kitchen. Did you not notice how barren it is? Don't you think that says something about me?'

The words spill out of Mignon quite uncharacteristically although she tries but fails to bite them off short.

'And what does mine say about me?'

Oriel relaxes her shoulders, her arms follow. The sense of ease traverses their length until her fingers disentwine of their own accord. The pungent, herb-driven scent of the stew re-awakens in her senses.

'Yours says that you have made a home. Something I never have.'

Mignon rattles the lid of a teapot in the sink, rinsing it under the tap, afraid to turn and face the compliment, afraid as always that she falls short of what might be achieved with just that extra little bit of effort.

Oriel watches the set of her shoulders from behind. Gravity has assumed great proportion in this woman's life or, heavier still, something that may be missing?

'Do you have lemon?'

'There is one on the shelf over the stove. In the blue pot.'

Oriel reaches it down. In the bottom is an obviously fresh lemon. 'I see you have started to take lemon with your tea.'

'No. I still prefer milk... sorry.'

'Don't apologise. You're free to take it how you like. Shall I put this back? Were you going to cook with it?'

'I bought it for when you came round for tea.'

'Why should you think that? Not that I haven't thought of it myself. I was waiting for the right...'

'I know these things... sometimes. Don't ask, I can't explain. I just know... sometimes.'

Mignon hands her a small painted tea caddy from the shelf. Oriel opens it to find rock sugar. In her saucer is a wedge of fresh lemon and an old apostle spoon.

The tiny figure on the handle seems as shrunken as a mummy but its arms are wrapped so closely around itself, Oriel is reminded of Mignon.

'Then you also know why we are here?'

'Maybe… I don't always know the why.'

Oriel reaches into the bag beside her for the folded drawing that Fabrienne made. 'Mignon, sit down.'

Mignon places the teapot between them. Oriel takes her hand and guides her to an old wicker-bottomed chair.

'I want you to tell me about this.'

Mignon's eyes are fixed on the folded paper between them.

'Is it a letter? No good ever came of a letter.'

'That's not true. What about mine?'

'Well… I'm not sure… yes, it was a very nice letter… but where is it leading me? They always seem to bring trouble.'

Oriel covers the drawing with her hand, thinks for a moment to return it to the bag unopened but she has come too far for that, there are too many questions.

'I can't promise that this won't. But you need to see it anyway.'

Her fingers twist open the folds of paper. Mignon sits up to the table, turning obliquely so that she is watching from the corner of her eye. Oriel presses the drawing flat across the table with the palm of her hand.

'Oh, my God!' Mignon backs away.

Oriel turns the paper so that she cannot escape from the picture it contains. 'It might help if you tell me about it.'

Mignon shudders visibly. Fabrienne's hand unmistakably present in the confidence of line, the subtlety of shade and light, the bright glisten and shatter of thrown liquid.

'Children have such imaginations.'

Oriel pushes the picture closer until it is as inescapable as the pungency of herbs that now permeates the kitchen.

'There is something else you should know.'

Mignon pushes the paper away as far as she can reach across the table.

Oriel stops it with her hand. The paper crumples and folds between them. 'It is too late for that.'

Mignon continues to stare at the paper, broken now into unrecognisable lines and creases.

Oriel pushes it back towards her.

'I have seen the scars on Fabrienne's back.'

Mignon recoils. 'She has *shown* them to you?'

'I saw them by accident. I thought you might tell me how this happened.'

Mignon turns the paper over on the table top. Some of the shading is still visible through the blank side. She pushes it away again.

Oriel folds it back into her bag. Mignon relaxes as the paper disappears, then her arms begin an uncontrollable vibration. Oriel steadies her with a hand.

A smile shakes its way across Mignon's face. 'So these are the conversations you have been having. What else did she tell you?'

Oriel reaches into the bag at her feet where her fingers find the other drawing she has brought, but finds herself too afraid to complete the action.

Mignon stands to untie the strings of the pinafore. 'Did she tell you about this?' She lifts it over her head, unbuttons the front of the grey wool cardigan beneath and pushes it aside. Her fingers hook into the hem of the loose black top she is wearing.

Slowly, she lifts it.

The bared skin of Mignon's midriff is ruched and as vivid and angry as the scars on Fabrienne's back.

To Oriel's surprise, Mignon allows her touch.

Oriel closes her eyes. Beneath her fingers is the bright surface of the moon, rilled and cratered starburst scars that terminate in a clean line below Mignon's breasts.

She feels the breath quivering in and out, the tremor of

Mignon's stomach, the warmth passing through her finger tips into her own body as if the heat of the boiling liquid is still desperately seeking a way out.

She experiences Mignon's sharp intake of breath and wonders what she is about to say.

Mignon holds it tightly within for a moment, the scars hardening above the undamaged muscle, then releases it suddenly.

'Did she also tell you that I owe my face to my daughter?'

Oriel lifts away her hand, but it hangs in the air between them.

'She didn't need to. The drawing said everything except why.'

Mignon allows the top to fall from her fingers.

'Perhaps I wasn't a very good wife.'

CHRONICLE

V1

SEXT

1984

APRIL 21st.
SATURDAY

5:30 P.M.

Raoul's hand searches out hers and tugs on her fingers.
'*Maman*? I am hungry.'

Mignon looks back along the breadth of Place Jacquard. Most of the flea-market has packed up and gone, the few bright awnings remaining twitch violently in the throes of being taken down. The sun has left the side of the Place where their apartment sits and, inside, the walls will be downcast with early hues of grey.

These meagre rooms are all they can afford. This too is her fault, along with becoming pregnant with Fabrienne.

It is three years since she gave up her job at the wool shop below out of shame. What little money they have now comes from odd jobs that Chrétien does for the local shops, a little from Raoul at the weekend when he delivers for M'sieur Anton and whatever she can scrape from cleaning and mending aprons at the bar.

Time passes quickly as she sits like this, head slowly emptying of all thought… Fabrienne chasing pigeons… Raoul stalking his reflection in the shop windows over the road. She glances at the church clock and realises that she has stayed away too long. She gathers up Fabrienne, catches hold of Raoul and walks quickly along the street.

As she approaches the apartment, she sees Chrétien once more outside the bar. His back is to them and he seems to be studying the bottom of an empty glass. Hoping he hasn't noticed their approach, she propels the children quickly into the hallway and up the stairs. She has barely had time to lift the casserole from the searing oven when she hears the landing door slam.

Chrétien is bleeding from a small wound to the side of his head. He sits down heavily at the table. 'Food.'

'It won't be long. I just have to heat some…'

'Why is it not ready?'

'It will not be long.' Mignon is frantically shelling peas, the carrots already sliced into the pan.

'What have you been doing all day?'

'Looking after your children.'

'They are not my children.'

Chrétien's arm wavers uncertainly in the direction of Raoul and Fabrienne where they stand peering through a bedroom door held ajar.

'Not mine. I don't want them to be mine.'

'I still have to look after them. They are children.'

'And what about me? When I have been out trying to earn a living in this shithole of a town and I come home to no supper? What about me?'

Mignon puts a large plate on the table in front of where he sits.

'It will not be long. Why don't you have a wash?'

'There is no hot water.'

Mignon touches the side of the kettle with the backs of her fingers. 'It will not be long.'

'Is that all you can say? Is the record stuck?'

She puts a knife and fork beside him. He grabs her wrists in one hand and drags her down until her face is pressed tight against the plate. He picks up the fork and pushes it hard into the soft, fleshy underpart of her eye.

The four tines draw sharp dots of fresh blood. 'Perhaps

I should eat you. Who would blame me? Answer me that?'

Mignon knows that by this point only silence will save her from greater harm.

'Perhaps if I turned you out on the street with only one eye you could beg for a living, eh? Shall we try?' He pushes the tines deeper and blood flows like tears down her cheek.

Suddenly, small fists rain down on his back.

'No! No! Leave maman alone!'

Chrétien throws Mignon away from him and she falls to the floor, partially under the table.

'The bastard speaks!'

He turns rapidly and with one sweep of his arm sends Raoul crashing into the corner.

'I will see to *maman*. I married her. That gives me the right, although I must have been drunk at the time. Or bewitched…'

He drags Mignon out from under the table by her hair, aims a kick at her face, his features contorted with anger.

'Bitch? Witch? What are you?'

A wasted lifetime fleets blindingly before his eyes. 'Do I have to kill you to remove your spell?'

Raoul picks up a chair, the slender muscles in his arms trembling with fear. He tries to hit Chrétien with it, but finds it wrenched from his grasp.

Chrétien pushes him back into the corner.

'I'll show you how to use a chair.'

He raises it over his head to bring it down on Mignon.

As it passes the table one leg catches. The chair shatters in his hands, pieces raining on Mignon's head, puncturing the skin, adding to the blood already on her cheek. He raises it again. Fabrienne dives into the room to land on top of Mignon.

Chrétien halts mid-strike. Throwing the remains of the chair at Raoul in the corner, he staggers over to the stove and grabs the large iron dish. The heat of the handles burns straight through his flesh but he is too locked into the patterns of his own past to notice.

He swings it around and throws it over Mignon and Fabrienne, scattering vegetables and steam all around the room. The child screams as the thick boiling liquid sticks to her back, preventing it from spilling across Mignon's face. The rest of it drenches Mignon's midriff, making her cry out in shock and pain.

She pushes Fabrienne under the table out of the way and lurches to her feet. 'Bastard! Bastard! Your own child!'

Chrétien fells her with one punch to the side of her face.

She collapses in a heap, legs strewn across the hearth, skirt above her waist, the bared flesh of her midriff and thighs scouring bright pink from the burn.

Fabrienne is screaming violently beneath the table, trying to reach around to her back where the stew in her clothes is still burning.

'Shut up! Shut up! Shut up!'

Fabrienne is silenced immediately by Chretien's voice.

Raoul glowers at him from the relative safety of the corner, clutching defensively in his hand a piece of the broken chair.

Mignon is sprawled unevenly across the floor. Chrétien kicks her hard between the legs.

'Is that where your spell lies?' He kicks again, forcing more vehemence into the swing of his boot. 'Well, you won't bewitch anyone else after this.'

He stops mid-swing, his boot hovering above her.

He sees the lie of her leg over the hearthstone. He brings the boot down and bones crack sickeningly under the blow.

Mignon snaps momentarily into consciousness before her eyes glaze over again.

Chrétien looms above her. 'Now you can't run away when I tell you to stay home.' He grabs the fork from the table. 'And no-one will ever look at you twice again.'

He pulls her head back by a hank of hair and rolls her onto his boot to hold her still.

Raoul leaps from the corner, broken chair leg in hand, the end of it sharp and wickedly pointed.

He plunges it at Chrétien's back but it will not puncture the heavy shirt he is wearing.

Chrétien shrugs him away, oblivious to all pain except his own.

'You are next, little bastard.'

Under the table, Fabrienne's legs jerk like a broken automaton, trying to scramble her body further away.

6:47 P.M.

Mignon wakes to find herself in darkness. Her whole body is numb, but in the same instant she realises she is badly damaged.

She runs her hands over her face, reopening wounds.

'Rao… Raoul?'

Raoul answers her softly from the corner by the window.

'Maman?'

'Fabrienne?'

'She is alive, Maman.'

The apartment is grey and silent. Mignon has lapsed back into unconsciousness on the floor. Raoul has poured cold water onto his sister's back and is now sitting in the corner, watching them.

His maman is breathing steadily. There is rapid eye movement under the closed lids and her limbs twitch.

Fabrienne is under the table, drifting in and out of awareness.

Chrétien is where he has fallen, half across Mignon.

The serrated kitchen knife that a stray kick from Fabrienne's threshing feet had pushed across the floor to him is still in Raoul's hand.

He has tried… but finds it impossible to put it down.

There is blood between his fingers from where his hand slid down the handle until he was grasping the blade, the steel coming to rest against the white of his bone from where it could slip no further.

Even though he has watched the body convulse and retch, Raoul finds it impossible to believe that Chrétien is dead and so he sits, watching him, knife high and ready again as the room grows dark.

7:30 P.M.

In the shop below, Jacqueline turns out the lights, reaching up for the switch that operates the lending library sign in the window of the apartment above.

Raoul hears the door close and the key turn in the lock. He stays still until she has moved away along the street.

As the light from the sign turns everything around him into contrasts of red and black, Raoul climbs from the bits of broken chair with which he has surrounded himself.

He takes the stair slowly, hoping not to hear Chrétien following.

Once outside, his legs begin to fly under him. He runs heedlessly, feet shifting the cobbles and causeways behind him in a blur to the end of Rue Praire, where the lights of the square shine more brightly.

A boy shouts to him… a friend from school… and his feet accelerate more quickly than he thought possible.

Across *Jean Jaurè*, two steps, three at a time over the plinth of the Church. He darts through the evening traffic, horns blaring, faces mouthing mindless violence behind sealed-shut car windows, across the pavement, and a sharp turn into Rue de Lodi.

RUE DE LODI
ST. ETIENNE
LOIRE
FRANCE

7:40 P.M.

In the shadows Raoul stops, panting, to bang loudly on a door. A window above rattles upwards in its sash and Remi Anton leans out.

'I am closed. Come back in the morning.'

Raoul gathers his breath. 'M'sieur Anton. It is me. Raoul.'

Raoul steps away from the door to where the light filters through from the main road. 'It is me. Please help.'

Remi Anton smiles willingly. Raoul is always a pleasure, even if he never does keep his promises. Then he notices the glint of the knife clutched in Raoul's hand.

'Don't move.'

Footsteps clatter down the stairs. The door bursts open and Remi drags him in. In the darkness of the hallway, Raoul realises they are not alone. He flinches away from the hand on his shoulder.

'Martha.' Remi resumes his grip. 'Turn on the light.'

Raoul stands there, dishevelled, his face red from the pace he has maintained all the way to the greengrocer's shop.

Remi holds out his hand. 'Give me the knife, boy.'

Raoul stares blankly at the knife he has forgotten.

He tries to let go, watching his own blood dripping from the pointed end of the blade. 'I can't.'

'Easy, boy.' Remi takes the handle sticking out beyond the clenched fist. With his other hand he peels away Raoul's fingers from the blade. 'You're safe here. Whatever it was can't hurt you now.'

Martha strokes his hair, finding a large lump on his skull.

'Remi, the boy is hurt.' She parts his hair. The lump is already showing luminous blooms of purple and yellow.

'That may be the least of his problems.' Remi opens Raoul's hand slowly. Fresh blood flows from the opened wounds.

Martha leads him by the shoulder up the stairs while Remi studies the blade in his hand and wonders who else's blood it is that has already hardened on the steel.

Martha pours salt and water into a bowl and submerges Raoul's hand. He cries out from the sharp shock as it enters the wounds.

Remi holds him firmly by the shoulders until he stops shaking.

'Raoul? Is there anyone else?

'*Maman.*' Raoul grits his teeth against the pain. 'And Fabrienne.'

'Are they…?'

'Leave the boy alone for a minute. Can't you see he is hurting?'

'He will mend. It is others I am more concerned about.'

'Then go and see!'

Remi hesitates a moment, leaning over Raoul's shoulder.

'Chrétien… is he… is he?'

'He is gone.' Raoul cries out as Martha dresses his fingers with a clean piece of bandage. The blood soaks immediately through the cloth.

'Gone?'

'Yes, M'sieur. I think he is quite gone.'

'Will he be coming back?'

Raoul's shoulders begin to shake under his grip.

Martha searches in the table drawer for an extra pad of lint.

'Don't be such a coward, Remi. Get over there now. Mme Merle may need help with Fabrienne.'

'But Chrétien…'

'Everyone knows he is too much of a coward to attack a grown man.'

'As long as *he* is aware of that…'

PLACE JACQUARD
ST. ETIENNE
LOIRE
FRANCE

8:11 P.M.

The red light from the Library sign in the window paints desperate shadows across the pavement as Remi ventures into the hallway, feeling high up and to the left. His fingers find a conduit and trace it to the switch. The hall floods with light and to his overwhelming relief it appears normal, apart from a darkening smear down the wall at waist height as he climbs the stair.

The landing door is closed against the spring, but unlocked. Beyond that, the apartment door is wide open.

Inside, red light from the sign casts impenetrable black shadows. He reaches round the frame and locates the switch.

His first instinct is to run, but that is far beyond anything his legs will allow, his second is to turn quickly and vomit loudly onto the floor of the landing.

He wipes his mouth on the back of his hand, checks again to confirm what he thinks he has seen, and steps cautiously into the kitchen.

The exposed skin at the side of Chrétien's collar is cold. His checkered work shirt has holes in the back, too many to count. The blood has pooled into one stream down the side of his waist.

Remi's shoes stick to the worn linoleum. He takes an old newspaper from beside the stove and throws it down to stand on. Locking his fingers into Chrétien's collar, he heaves him away from Mignon.

Her clothes are dragged up above her waist and the slender legs he has so often admired as she leaves his shop are now red and blistered. There are puncture marks on her face below the left eye.

He pushes the discarded fork away in disgust and pulls down her skirt. Suddenly she rears from the floor, fists flailing the air around his face.

He lays her down gently.

'Quiet, now. It's M'sieur Anton. You are safe.'

Her eyes flicker open. He smiles down at them. They close again as she drifts back into unconsciousness.

He slides a cushion under her head.

'Now… where is Fabrienne?'

He searches the bedroom without success. He tests the spring on the landing door and safely assumes that she could not have opened it unaided. He returns to the kitchen and searches through the wreckage of the furniture, finding her laid soundlessly in a pool of congealed blood under the table. He sits down heavily on the hearthstone.

Moving Mignon's leg carefully to one side to make room, he feels it twist and notices the crazy angle it now assumes.

'Oh, Christ!'

His head falls forwards until it is cupped by hands still covered in the blood from Chrétien's shirt. He drops to his knees and reaches under the table to Fabrienne.

She is warm to the touch. Her eyes are open, watching his every move as he pulls her out carefully. Her clothes are soaked with a thick, dried stew and the remains of under-cooked vegetables. Where she has been laid she is covered in blood. Relieved, he traces the pool back to Chrétien.

He tries lift Fabrienne's cardigan from her back but it is stuck to her skin and one edge shows the angry pink of a large broken blister.

He picks her up in his arms, shocked to find her staring directly at him, eyes empty and unwavering.

He holds her close, face buried in his shoulder, swings his boot down hard on Chrétien's distorted features then turns out the kitchen light and makes his way carefully down the stairs.

RUE DE LODI
ST. ETIENNE
LOIRE
FRANCE

8:38 P.M.

'Dear God! What has happened to you?'

Martha rushes up to Remi. Bars of blood streak his face, hands and clothes. The child in his arms is bathed in it, her clothes stiffening as they dry in the warm night air.

'I am alright.'

'You are always alright. I was talking to the child. Give her to me.'

Remi hands her over. 'Be careful, she is badly burned.'

Martha undresses her, gasping at the size of the wound.

'Where is he, the bastard who did this?'

'He is gone.'

'Gone? Gone where?'

'Gone where no-one can touch him.' He nods to the knife on the draining board.

'Good! He does not deserve to live after this!'

'Shush. The boy...'

Martha punches him sharply in the chest. '...has done the world a favour! Why did you not bring Mme Merle?'

She stops, realising that she may have just unearthed something that she would never wish to hear, no matter how many times she has been jealous of the way Remi looks at her. 'No! She isn't...?'

'She isn't. But she is badly hurt. I left her sleeping. She needs a doctor.'

'Then what are you waiting for?'

'I'm not sure I can do this on my own. I need to think...'

PLACE JACQUARD
ST. ETIENNE
LOIRE
FRANCE

9:33 P.M.

Remi has dragged Chrétien aside to get at Mignon. Her eyes are closed and her breathing is regular. The bruises on her face are fast turning purple and the skin around her left eye is bloodshot and swelling.

'Paul... what shall we do?'

'She needs an ambulance.'

'Yes, but…'

'We don't know what other injuries she may have. I'll go home and call one now. You stay with her.'

'Wait! The ambulance will bring the police… and what will they say?'

'They will say that someone killed him.' He nudges the body of Chrétien with his shoe. 'They will say it was self-defence.'

'You don't defend yourself by stabbing someone in the back. That's premeditated.'

'Just look at her face. He gave her plenty of reason. It was a *crime passionnel*.' He sloughs away the responsibility of making a further decision. 'She will get away with it.'

'She didn't kill him.'

'Then who did?'

'Raoul.'

'He told you this?'

'He had the knife.'

Paul turns Mignon's face with his hand. It rolls on the cushion, undamaged side uppermost.

'Handsome woman. Why can't some men see what they have?'

Remi shakes his head in despair of the once-fine bone structure, the delicate arch of brow; the long lashes, the wide forgiving mouth.

'Remi… look here.' Paul lifts a hank of soft black hair. He tilts her head gently into the light so that Remi can see.

'She is really a blonde! Can you imagine that?'

Remi closes his eyes. His memory returns in minute detail to her movements as she leaves his shop. 'Yes, I can.' He snaps back quickly. 'But what do we do about Raoul?'

'Nothing. This is even better. He is too young for the police to prosecute.'

'But they may still take him away… and these are good

people.'

'There are many things we could do, but making criminals of ourselves is not one I would recommend.'

'I was not suggesting for a minute…'

'No…' Paul hunts around for a cover, drags one off the settee and lays it carefully over Mignon. '… but if I give you a minute you will.'

He turns her head again so that the bruised side is uppermost. and sits back on his heels to study her.

'Such a beautiful tragedy… I'd better get the ambulance.'

Remi grabs his arm. 'Just wait for a minute One minute. Let me think.'

'It's never been your strong suit. It's why you're still a greengrocer.'

'And you run *Le Grande Boucherie*, I suppose?'

Paul taps his foot. 'I'm waiting.'

'Just a minute. Why did she stay with *him*?'

Remi indicates the crumpled shell of Chrétien in the corner by the window.

'How would I know? What reason does a woman need?'

'Because of the children, you old fool. There is no stronger bond.'

'So?'

'So what will happen if the police are involved?'

The history of the last hours seems a tangible thing, imprinted upon the fabric of the air. Paul observes it as he might if he had a suspicious nature which, since the end of the war, the police seem to have cultivated to excess.

'I think they would say that she had killed him.'

'And what would they do about it?'

'They would investigate, of course. Ask all the usual questions.'

'And while they are doing this?'

'Well… I suppose the children would be taken into care.'

'And if they find her guilty?'

Paul closes his eyes in frustration. An emotional net is closing around him the way it does every Friday night when he wishes to go home and Remi convinces him that what he really needs is one more drink and another hand of cards.

'Just get on with it, Remi.'

'I'm saying that whatever happens, the children will end up in care.'

There is a chair lodged under the edge of the table, its one good leg pressing against Mignon's side. Paul reaches under to pull it clear. Pointedly, he throws it into the corner where the body of Chrétien is heaped in disarray.

'That is not our problem.'

'Then what is? We have both helped this woman in the best way we could. A *chou…* a *poulet* here or there.'

'Remi… I suspect your motive in this.'

Remi laughs away the sting of the suggestion. 'So what's a little lust between friends?'

Paul kneels down beside Mignon, noticing the sudden flickering of her eyelids.

'She is coming round.'

He puts his hands beneath her head to cradle her. Her eyes flicker open, filling instantly with fear. He watches it fade as she recognises his face.

'It's alright. You are safe. There's just me and Remi.'

Mignon's mouth opens raggedly, blood issues from where her teeth have torn open the inside of her cheek. Her spine stiffens as she raises herself from the floor.

'Not… not… in care.'

She collapses into the support of Paul's hands, her lips moving silently. Her eyes close and she slips away again.

'You see!' Remi grabs him by the shoulder. 'I was right. She knows what will happen.'

'Remi, there is more at stake here than facing down our

wives at three o'clock in the morning.'

'Then for once in your life do something important. If we tie her legs to a piece of broken chair, we can roll her in a carpet and carry her across to my shop.'

'And him?' Paul indicates the body of Chrétien beneath the window.

Remi rummages amongst the shattered chairs, looking for the longest straight length of unbroken timber.

'He will be your penance.'

'*My* penance?'

Remi places a section of chair firmly into Paul's hand and rips a strip from the threadbare tablecloth on the floor by his feet.

'Tie her legs with that… and I apologise… to a friend who has no need of redemption.'

Paul stares at him curiously. 'It seems not. Until now…'

Remi moves the table aside, lifting it carefully over Mignon's legs.

'I promise you, this will be the most Christian thing you have ever done.'

'This is Christian?'

'This is nothing. It is what comes next that is.' Remi indicates with a nod of his head the body of Chrétien.

The full impact of what they are about to undertake lodges itself behind Paul's breastbone as a solid ball of acid fire. His stomach heaves, the movement readily apparent on his face as Remi maintains a smile.

'I thought you were *Le Grande Bouchier*?'

Paul concentrates on tying Mignon's legs tightly to the chair rail, realising that if he doesn't empty the contents of his mind, the contents of his stomach will soon follow.

'And what do we say happened here?'

'We say only that we saw Chrétien running away up the street. Beyond that we know nothing.'

'Won't they pursue him?'

'Why? Has he killed somebody?'

Paul shifts his attention away from his hands to the silent, pain-free expression on Mignon's face. The bruising is spreading a rainbow across her cheek. 'What about this?'

'What about it? Beating up on your wife is a national pastime. If they pursued every drunk that beat his wife then we'd all end up on the run.'

'Except you.'

Paul finishes the knot with unusual concentration.

'What do you mean by that?' Remi lays out the carpet beside the still figure of Mignon, pushing Paul out of the way.

'I mean… with you it might be the other way around.'

'I beg your pardon?'

'Nothing… nothing.' Paul fusses around with Mignon's skirt, making sure it will remain hidden within the rolls of the carpet.

Remi stops him with a hand. 'Wait… What are you saying?'

'I'm only saying what everyone else is saying.'

Paul is ashamed now that he has brought this up, but the way Remi has applied hidden leverage to the crime they are committing offends his sense of natural justice.

'I am saying that if the police were to pursue anyone it would be your wife.'

Remi sits back on the carpet. Paul nudges him playfully with a fist.

'Your Martha is not the quietest of women. At first we were envious. We thought you were making mad passionate love.'

Remi takes a deep breath. 'At first we were.'

10:02 P.M.

'Lift her. Carefully!'

Paul and Remi ease the carpet from the floor.

Martha tugs it away to one side, seeing the blood matted in Mignon's hair.

'Dear God! What am I going to find in here?'

Remi touches her shoulder. 'Take it easy. She is still alive.'

Between them they shuffle away the last layer to reveal Mignon. The roll of carpet has smeared Chrétien's blood all over her. Martha gasps but Renée pushes her aside.

'It is no worse than one of Paul's aprons. It always looks more than there is. Get me that water you cleaned Raoul with.'

Martha remains static. 'Look at her legs!'

'The water! Martha! Move! Remi! Scissors! Don't just stand there…'

Remi thrusts a pair of scissors into her waiting hand.

Renée hefts them with a growing confidence, lifting the hem of Mignon's skirt.

'Well? What are you two waiting for?'

Paul and Remi are transfixed by the unfolding of this terrible plan they have so recently conceived.

'You two. Get out. I am not going to undress this woman in front of you. It will have to remain in your dreams. Take the children through and settle them in your bed.'

Renée cannot help a small tingle of satisfaction as the scissors bite down into the material of the skirt then, as the unexpected layers peel away, feels it replaced by a sense of pity.

Exposed, Mignon is so frail. Her legs are blistered vividly above the knee. Her ribs lift, gaunt, into the light with each breath, each side carrying marks of old injury washing out to palest blues and yellows, yet nothing where it would show except for the fresh marks to her face.

Her breasts are separate, small and pale, their tips a pale rouge. The blistered skin across her midriff has burst, becoming angry and shrivelled where the boiling stew has penetrated the layers of her clothing.

Renée rocks back on her heels. 'What is it about this woman?'

Martha gently pulls out the soaked remains of clothing from beneath Mignon and studies her face closely.

'I don't know. Her hair?' She lifts a soft black hank to reveal the roots. 'She is a blonde, but you and I have always known that.'

There is a knock from the bedroom. The door opens a crack. Renée shouts. 'Get out!'

Remi's voice filters through the gap. 'Paul was just asking about her leg. Perhaps the doctor should be called now?'

'Wait until we get her cleaned up, then we can see the damage. Close that door.'

Between the bruising, Mignon's undamaged skin glistens in the lamp light. There is something pure and simple here that Renée senses but cannot connect with.

'I still don't understand.'

Martha dries the pale skin around Mignon's perforated cheek with the dragged edge of a clean tablecloth.

'You're not meant to.'

'What do you mean, I'm not meant to?'

'Renée...you're a woman. It's not supposed to work on you.'

'What isn't?'

'The... I don't know the words... the *magic*.'

'Magic?'

Martha throws her one end of the bedspread, they pull it taut between them and fold in the sides.

'Whatever it is some women have that sends men crazy.'

Renée lays out the bedspread, covering Mignon's breasts and tucking it around her shoulders. 'When was the last time *your* husband went crazy?'

Martha washes the blood from her hands in the sink, watching thoughtfully as it swirls around the drain.

'The first time this woman walked into our shop.'

PLACE JACQUARD
ST. ETIENNE
LOIRE
FRANCE

11:05 P.M.

It is late, but the bar owner has telephoned Jacqueline to say that she has seen two men stealing a carpet from the apartment. Suspecting that it may well be Chrétien selling her furniture out from under her, Mme Berniere has made the short journey from home to put a stop to it.

She opens the door to darkness, feeling along the wall for the light switch. She clicks it on. The stairwell is quiet. The door above is slightly ajar. She stops to listen. Only silence. There is a dark stain on the pale green wall beside her. She licks a finger and rubs at it. It streaks red. She wipes her finger on the old coat she has thrown on to make the journey and teases open the landing door. She is dismayed, but unsurprised, at the pool of fresh vomit beside it.

A strange mixture of smells is radiating from the kitchen, sweet and bitter at once, with a sharp tang of copper. The room beyond the door is dark.

She reaches around the corner for the light.

304

Light from the apartment window is reflecting in the shop glass across the road.

'Remi? Did you leave the light on in the apartment?'

'I don't think so. I don't know for sure. You were the last out.'

'I think it was off. What shall we do? Run?'

'Where to?'

'Anywhere but here…' Paul prods at the bulge of apron and boning knife under his coat. His eyes begin to roll. 'How do I explain this?'

Remi clutches at him quickly.

'Calm down. No-one knows anything about this.'

'Perhaps we were seen.' Paul's breath hisses out between clenched teeth.

Remi can feel the blood pounding through Paul's arm, the tightly bound muscles. 'Breathe!'

'What?' Paul stares around them in panic.

'Just breathe. Look… slowly… in… out… that's better.'

'Than what?'

'Than panicking about something we don't yet know.'

'But the light…?'

Remi drags him into the doorway. The door swings easily open.

'Did you close this?'

Paul shakes his head wildly. 'I don't remember!'

'Wait here until I call you. If you hear me talking to someone, go quickly as you can back to my shop and tell them to prepare for the police.'

'But…'

'No buts. Just wait… and listen.'

Remi takes the stairs two at a time. He pushes the landing door wide and steps into the kitchen then, without further thought.

'Oh, Dear God. Whatever next?'

He hears the outer door slam shut below. He rushes to the open window in time to see Paul set out at a pace he never thought the butcher capable of, his bulk swaying on and off the pavement in the red glow from the Library sign.

'Paul!' he tries to bring his voice down to a controlled hiss and manages an absurd stage whisper. 'Paul!'

Further down the street the footsteps stop. Remi hears them shuffle for a second or two, then return to the splash of light below the window.

Heavy footsteps climb the treads until Paul peers around the doorframe.

'Come on Remi, before she wakes up. Let's go.'

He reaches into the room and tugs at Remi's sleeve.

Remi shrugs him off. 'No. Come in. Close the door.'

Paul takes a last look down the stairwell then closes the door quietly. 'What?'

'We wait.'

'What for?'

'We wait for her to wake up. Meanwhile…'

Remi claws away the remains of the chair thrown on top of Chrétien. He grabs his legs and straightens them out. They spring back slightly.

'The tendons…' Paul gulps at the night air drifting through the open window. 'They tighten, you see.'

'Then where's your knife?'

Paul holds tightly to the wrapped bundle under his jacket. 'This is too much. What about her?'

Jacqueline Bernier sits where she has slid down the wall in shock the instant the bulb flickered into life. The damaged valve in her heart is picking up now, repairing the lost circulation to her brain. The breath emitting from her wide-open mouth is ragged and shallow, accompanied by a faint snore. Her eyelids twitch and flutter without fully opening.

Remi grits his teeth and slides the knife raggedly through the material of Chrétien's trouser leg.

Paul hops from one foot to the other, turning around to watch Mme Bernier's face for any sign of wakefulness.

'The shoe, Remi. Take off the shoe first. Oh God! What am I doing here?'

Remi slips a shoe and throws it across the floor to Paul.

'Find a bag. Anything.' He throws the other one. 'Look under the bed. They must have a suitcase. Everyone has a suitcase.'

The screech of dragged furniture awakens Mme Bernier and, as her eyes open, she sees Remi poised above Chrétien with the knife.

'You!' She straightens her back against the wall. 'So it was you. Why have you come back?'

Remi hesitates, lowering the knife.

'Hello, Jacqueline. And no, it wasn't me. What are you doing here?'

'Someone saw him stealing my carpets. Is he as dead as he looks?'

'Absolutely. And, by the way, it was me stealing your carpet.'

There is a loud rumble as a bed is pushed across the floor in the next room. Jacqueline jerks fully awake.

'Where's Mignon?'

'She's safe. We carried her to my place in the carpet.'

Jacqueline struggles to her feet. Leaning against the edge of the door she takes in the chaos of the flat with one swift glance.

'The children?'

'That's another matter.'

She leans heavily on the edge of the table.

'Oh, God, Remi. I always thought he'd kill her… but not

the children.'

'He hasn't.' Remi rinses a cup from the drainer and passes her a drink of water.

She gulps it down greedily. 'You're not just saying that?'

Remi shows a wry expression.

She nods. 'Of course not. You wouldn't do that.'

'I never let the truth get in the way of a good lie, you know that, but the children are safe. Damaged... but safe.'

'Who killed the bastard, then?'

'You don't want to know.'

'How else will I know who to pin the medal on?'

She stands away from the edge of the table. Her legs wobble slightly and Remi reaches out a hand. She flinches and Remi realises he is still holding the knife.

She pushes his hand down to his side. 'You can tell Paul he can come out now.'

Paul opens the bedroom door slowly and peers round the edge. 'Hello, Jacqueline. I... we...'

'Shut up, Paul, and come in here. What's that you've got?'

'A suitcase.'

'What are you going to do with that?'

Paul chokes violently, hand to mouth, holding down the contents of his stomach.

Mme Bernier watches him thoughtfully.

'Remi? Why did you bring him?'

'He's my friend.'

'I know, but...'

Remi turns the knife around in his hand. 'No 'buts'. He's my friend. We're in this together.' He shoves the handle of the knife at Paul. 'Here...'

Paul backs away as far as the wall will allow. 'I don't think I can.'

Jacqueline Bernier snatches the knife out of the air.

'Move...'

Remi catches her arm. 'He's the butcher.'

She stares him briefly in the eye. 'Strange… that *he's* now '*Le Bouchier*'. Tell me again why I'm doing this.'

Remi drags Chrétien into the centre of the room by his legs. 'To keep Mignon and the children together.'

'So she did for him at last, eh? I didn't think she had it in her. Good for her.'

'It wasn't her.'

Jacqueline shoots a quick glance between Paul and Remi.

'No, no.' Remi shakes his head. 'It wasn't either of us. We're just trying to sweep up the mess.'

Her mouth drops open in shock. 'No. It can't be… not little Raoul? My God, Remi…' She gives a sharp, brittle laugh. 'A Frenchman with balls for once.'

Paul throws the suitcase down, the clasps fly open and clothes cascade out onto the floor.

Mme Bernier picks up a jumper and examines it between her fingers. 'Look here. Worn out… and I happen to know this was her best.'

Paul kicks the suitcase violently. The lid snaps shut again.

'How can you…? A man's dead for Christ's sake! How can you…?'

'Paul, for God's sake shut up! Remi, close that window if this fool is going to tell the neighbourhood.'

Paul quietens down, staring fixedly at the knife in Jacqueline Bernier's hand where she stands poised over the body of Chrétien, determining where to begin.

'How can you?'

'I admit…' Jacqueline Bernier massages the ache out of her knee. '…I was more at home with throats than legs… but I'm never too old to learn.'

Paul rages at her. 'Do you know what you are doing? We will go to prison if we are caught!'

'For what?' Mme Bernier slits the belt of Chrétien's trousers, continuing downwards with the tip of the blade. 'For killing a dead man? Even the Germans didn't have a law against that. Ah! It is as I thought.'

Paul moves into the light. 'What is it?'

Remi waggles the little finger of his left hand.

Paul pushes him away in disgust. 'Here… give the knife to me. There is only one thing I need to know.'

He closes his eyes and presses the knife to the grey, dirty skin and stops when he feels the blade encounter bone. He opens his eyes and begins to slice flesh away from the joint.

Unexpectedly, the contents of his stomach settle. Under his hands, Chrétien has become just another carcass as the blade flenses deftly, paring away flesh and tendons until he can see the set of the bones, the pure mechanism of the joint.

'That is enough. I think I know how to set Mignon's leg now.'

He hands the knife back to Remi. 'You two can finish off here. I'm going back.'

'Wait…' Remi grabs Paul's apron as he rises. 'Where can we put the rest of him?'

'In the cold locker at the back of my shop for now.' He throws Remi the keys.

Remi looks briefly at Jacqueline. 'I don't think we can carry him.'

'Then don't put all of him in at once.'

APRIL 22nd.
SUNDAY

12.28 A.M.

'She is still bleeding.'

Renée cleans around the top of Mignon's legs with a damp cloth. It comes away bright red. 'On top of all this she gets the curse!'

'I may still have something. I'll go and look.'

Renée shouts her back.

'I don't think that will help. Here... look. The bruising. There... just coming.'

Renée parts Mignon's flesh and Martha's breath catches in her throat. Mignon stirs and twists her thigh.

Martha peers more closely. 'If he wasn't dead already I'd kill him myself.'

Renée takes away her gentle fingers. 'I can't see any major damage. Maybe it's just the swelling that makes it look so bad, but can you imagine how this will feel when she wakes up?'

'Let's hope she doesn't feel anything. Not for a while anyway. I have some painkillers for my arthritis. She can have those when she's awake. Let's get her wrapped up and keep her warm.'

The door bursts open and Paul rushes into the room, forehead bursting with sweat, his face crimson.

The first thing he notices are Mignon's feet protruding from the bedspread. They seem pale and lifeless.

'Is she...? Is she...?'

'She's fine... well?'

Martha sees the fresh blood on Paul's apron, the tremors passing in waves through his body. 'Where's Remi?'

'He won't be long. He's just tidying up. Jacqueline Bernier is with him.'

Martha and Renée glance at each other across the table.

'They seem to know what they are doing.' Paul pauses a moment, remembering the ease with which his knife had passed between them. 'So why does that worry me?'

Renée notices the look of concern that flashes across Martha's face. 'He'll be alright. Remi knows things.'

'It's not *what* he knows that worries me.'

Paul pushes them abruptly to one side. 'In the name of Chri… they are cutting up a corpse! What did you think they were doing?'

He bends to examine the angle at which Mignon's feet protrude from the bedspread, then scissors through the bindings holding the splint and throws it angrily into the corner.

'Here… hold her thighs tightly… like this…'

Martha and Renée apply their weight to Mignon's legs above the knee. Paul traces his fingers along the length of the bones. His hand strays above the knee joint, teasing fit and arc from beneath the skin with his fingers.

'If you let her move it will ruin everything.'

His fingers return to her ankle. Thankfully, the bones there are firmly socketed in place. The fractures are further up, at around the midpoint of the shin, the tibia showing as a distinctly sharp lump.

Grateful for Mignon's unconsciousness, he feels around for the parted edges.

The breaks feel reasonably clean.

'I think I can do this.'

'There should be a doctor. She needs…'

'Renée! Listen to yourself. A doctor means police and

then where will we be?'

Martha laughs ironically. 'In jail. Just a bit sooner, that's all. You don't think we can get away with this, do you?'

Paul wipes the sweat from his face with the back of his forearm. 'We better had, or this is the last time Remi talks me into *anything*. Now *hold* her…'

He takes the ankle in one hand, moves the other along the fibula, inserting his fingers between the overlapping calf muscles to find the bone buried in there. He pushes upwards, and at the same time tugs hard on the ankle.

There is a slight twist of bone. Mignon cries out and bucks wildly on the table.

'Hold her!' Paul grabs Mignon's good ankle to stop it hammering up and down beside her damaged leg. As quickly as she awoke, Mignon slips back into unconsciousness.

Paul reaches further under the cover. The ankle and the knee are now aligned. All that remains is to set the shin in place. He stretches her toes to extend the muscles then lifts her foot with his thigh until the gap between the bones closes. He keeps the pressure on until his fingers tell him that they are as close as his limited skill will allow. The hard lump of displaced flesh has disappeared.

Her leg is now almost as smooth as the undamaged one. He tenderly strokes the skin of both, one after the other.

Renée reaches for his hand until he shakes her aside.

'How else can I..?'

'As long as that is all you are doing…'

'Jesus, woman, I am…' Paul raises his hands in the air, a sudden flush of sweat standing out on his skin. 'Pass me something to tie the splint again.'

Renée hands him the broken chair leg. 'There must be something better than this.'

Paul sights along it as if it were a rifle. 'No. The shape is perfect. Since when did you know anyone with a straight leg?

Put this between her legs and tie all three together. She must not be able to move it for a few days.'

'This will be difficult.' Martha begins to scissor an old pair of curtains into long, thin strips. 'What about her toilet?'

Paul takes off his apron, rolls it into a dirty bundle and throws it at Renée.

'I should ask Remi and Jacqueline. They seem to be good at clearing things up.'

RUE ROGER SALENGRO
ST. ETIENNE
LOIRE
FRANCE

4.22 A.M.

Amplified by fear, each clink of the spade echoes wildly in Paul's imagination. Remi snatches it from his hand.

'Here… my turn. Rest a moment. You can fill it back in.'

They have dug a large circular hole between the bushes, missing the tangle of roots that inhabit the rest of the fruit garden.

Remi stands waist deep in dark earth, the moon sinking above him through the branches of a nearby oak.

'I think this will do.'

Paul agitates beside him in the darkness.

'No. No. Deeper!'

Remi rests a moment on the handle of the spade. 'But we don't have to lay him out…'

'I don't care!' Paul's agitation is sending thick clods of earth back into the hole.

'Deeper! I want him where I don't even think I can see him.'

'Paul, Paul…' Remi stands erect in the hole. 'It won't matter. Once we've re-planted that blackberry over the top of him, no-one will ever suspect.'

'Do you think I won't know? I won't always remember?'

Remi sends the spade deeper into the earth.

'We will laugh about this in years to come.'

'Ha!' Paul turns away from him, scanning the furthest corners of his garden for other eyes.

Remi throws a spadeful of earth across his shoes.

'See, you've started already. What a resilient thing the human soul is.'

'Remi! Stop it! I cannot see any reason for humour. This is a man…'

'Was a man…' He wiggles his little finger. '…and not much of a one at that. Is there any of him left in the locker?'

'No.'

'Then this is deep enough. The bush will cover easily by autumn. We can watch the sun go down and remark on how much body there is in your blackberry wine.'

The contents of Paul's stomach finally lift into his throat. He spins around and pours them noisily into the hole.

Remi moves aside quickly.

'A fitting tribute. You always rise to the occasion, Paul. I've long admired you for it.'

'Shut up! Remi! Shut up! Remember this is my garden. It will be me they guillotine for this.'

'Only if we get caught. Pass the suitcase over.'

'No, Remi. Deeper.'

The ball-ends of bones flensed from their sockets reflect the light of the moon as they tumble from the suitcase.

Remi covers them with a few quick shovels of earth.

'The sooner we cover him up, the safer you will feel. Oh, and while we are doing it, just in case someone should come digging…'

'Who? Who will come digging, Remi?'

'Stop it! Just in case someone comes digging, you should

always leave them something to find. Then they will not dig further, you see? Have you got an old tin box we can put a few francs in?'

'No, I have not. And I am not putting my money...'

Remi sifts through the wallet in his pocket. 'Look, just fetch your old cash box and I will put in the francs. Get on with it.'

The old battered tin drops onto a layer of earth scattered above Chrétien.

Paul wipes the sweat from his palms. He stops, noticing that Remi is looking at something far above him.

'My God, Remi...'

They watch in silence as Martha turns Fabrienne away from the window overlooking the garden.

Remi hands over the spade.

'Here. Finish off. I will return in the daylight to replant the blackberry.'

'Remi? You can't leave me to...'

'I have to talk to the children. For everyone's sake, Mme Merle must never know what happened here tonight.'

CHRONICLE

VII

COMPLINE

1989

**SEPTEMBER 22nd.
FRIDAY**

10:18 A.M.

Spinning rapidly in Artus' lathe is a slender length of hollowed olive branch. He lays a gouge against the tool-rest and forms a decorative ring in the wood before moving along to shape the end into the slightest of flares.

'Why did you not tell me you were supposed to be working in the garden with Oriel?'

Fabrienne returns his question with a blank stare.

With a narrow blade Artus cuts each end of the flute almost through as it spins. He kills the motor and opens the drawer beneath the bench. Fabrienne dashes a hand inside to pull out the pad and pencil.

Artus trims the fache until the flute comes away cleanly in his hands. He throws the cut ends into the kindling box by the boiler.

'I wish you understood.'

Fabrienne rewards him with a smile. He pokes at her hair with his fingers. 'There... that's better.'

She shakes her head and her hair returns to its natural condition, loose spikes hanging over her eyes while the rest loops wildly about.

Fabrienne has returned to stalking the woods behind the cemetery and half of it seems to be still in her hair.

Artus smiles in return and pulls up the tall stool he has made for her. 'Sit.'

He opens the frame of an old case clock and leafs out a small sheaf of papers, spreading them across the bench.

'Here… let's see what sense we can make of these.'

Fabrienne points with a finger from one circle to the next. There are several pages of circles, none of them numbered or in any resemblance of order. On a separate sheet is a series of numbers. '76'. '19' and '223'.

'I wonder what Auguste meant?'

Artus' hands are shaping the mouthpiece of the flute without conscious thought. Fabrienne is ignoring the question, her own fingers sifting quickly through the papers. Artus takes the one with the numbers. Fabrienne snatches it back and places it above the others where she can see it. She stops a moment and sits back on the stool, eyes moving constantly, never leaving the field of papers.

Artus is marking out the positions of the finger holes.

'Auguste never mentioned these drawings. I only found them when I was clearing out. I almost used them to light the boiler.'

Fabrienne's concentration remains centred entirely on the papers.

Suddenly, she snatches one from the pile and places it separately on the bench. On the paper is a single large circle.

Drawn many years ago by Auguste, the pencil line has become smudged from the number of times Artus has tried to decipher this collection. It seems too large to fit against any of the others. Fabrienne sifts again through the scattered papers until she picks up another. She places this above the first one. Imprinted on it is a much smaller circle.

Artus winds the vice gently closed on the length of the flute and takes up a hand-brace. He slots a narrow drill into the chuck and nips it tight with his hand.

'No, that wheel will never fit. The clock would be huge.'

Fabrienne draws small but perfect gear teeth around the

outside of the smaller circle, finishing exactly where she began.

Artus takes it from her and counts the teeth.

'No. Neither '76'. '19' or '223'. So it doesn't make sense. Neither does the '86' he has written at the bottom.'

Fabrienne begins to fit teeth into the inside of the large circle.

'Ah! Now I see.'

Fabrienne's small fingers twitch the pencil tip in and out until she has completed the sequence of gearing. She pushes the paper into his hand. As he studies it, she reaches into the drawer and takes out his toolkit. She unrolls it across the papers, takes out the knife file and thrusts it into his other hand.

'What? Oh, I see. Maybe later when I have nothing more important…'

Fabrienne slams the door on her way out.

Seconds later, Raoul walks in. 'What's the matter with Fabrienne? What have you said to her?'

Artus is taken aback by Raoul's thinly-veiled aggression.

'I haven't said anything. Not that she would understand if I had.'

'Then what have you done?'

Raoul's whole body language demands attention. Artus quickly realises that he is no longer a boy, despite the still-soft skin and the smudge of feature that he knows will harden over the next few short years leaving him looking… well… perhaps a little like himself at that age.

'Oh, come in and sit down, Raoul. You know I wouldn't hurt her. I think she wanted me to do something in a hurry… and you know what I'm like at that.'

Raoul's arms swing awkwardly from his shoulders as if they belong to someone else.

Artus spreads the drawings on the bench again.

'Sit down. Being angry doesn't suit you. Here… I'll show you…' He points to the ones on which Fabrienne has drawn the teeth. 'She wants me to make these.'

Raoul's shoulders ease, his hands find their sullen way into his pockets. 'So?'

Artus hands him the knife-file. 'Remember this?'

Raoul nods. Artus gives him a piece of thin brass plate.

'Then I think you've just found yourself a job.'

OCTOBER 9th.
MONDAY

2:32 P.M.

'Fabrienne… stop sulking and mark out the next cog.'

Raoul hands her a small sheet of brass and a sharply pointed scriber. 'See if you can do it before Artus comes back from his lunch.'

Fabrienne nudges him out of the way and unclamps from the vice the small piece of metal that Raoul is filing. She drops it onto the brass plate he has given her and with the scriber reproduces the dimensions of one tooth. She pushes it aside, leaving it for him to reinsert. Raoul shakes his head and clamps it in the vice, turning it slightly. If his hands remain steady, he knows he will finish perfectly behind the first… for this is her talent… and he wishes it were his.

Fabrienne spreads her small hand across the metal plate in a spider's stride, holding it firmly to the bench as the point of the scriber moves deftly between them, identifying the points. The teeth form a serration on the inside of this wheel. When finished, it will be sleeved to a carriage that in turn will be screwed into the framework of the emerging device. The cog under Raoul's hands will become a planetary, traversing the inner orbit of the plate she is now marking.

In Fabrienne's mind the device is already complete.

From studying the drawings made by Auguste she can see where the end lies. She has been in pursuit of it since she marked out the first set of teeth for Raoul.

This is their spare time pursuit, whenever she can nudge Raoul into action. He doesn't experience the urgency passing from the metal directly through her fingers the way she does, or she wouldn't have to sulk to get him to work on it.

There is a resentment in him that she fails to understand.

She reaches out to touch the skin of his forearm with her finger, even though she knows this doesn't work on Raoul… he is too closed… as rigid in his defence as she knows the framework of this device will need to be.

Raoul pushes her away, forcing the hand holding the scriber back to the metal. Fabrienne's grip judders under the swiftness of the rebuff. Under the weight of Raoul's hand, the scriber impales her index finger, passing easily through the flesh to come to rest against bone.

Blood spreads quickly across the brass plate, following the inscribed lines until the whole wheel is sharply defined.

Fabrienne pulls the scriber loose and throws it across the bench.

'*Merde!*'

Raoul halts the file for a moment… then carries on working as if he hasn't heard. Fabrienne lifts her injured fingers slowly to her mouth and inserts them. Her lips close around them, allowing the blood to flow into her mouth, tasting copper-iron on her tongue.

Raoul stops the file.

'You don't speak to me for years and the first word you say is 'Shit!'. Perhaps you have been trying to save us all from the embarrassment of your vocabulary?'

He twists around on the stool to face her as she studies his eyes for an answer. 'Don't expect me to look shocked. Mutes don't talk in their sleep.'

Fabrienne removes her fingers from between her lips. The flow has stopped and the holes appear tiny, like the holes Raoul will drill for the rivets in the now blood-red cog wheel.

'I talk in my sleep? Does Maman know?'

'Of course she does. We are not stupid… only patient. We agreed to wait you out… even though we had begun to think that maybe…'

'Maybe what?'

'That maybe you preferred things this way… I mean… the old way. Without words you hold all the power.'

'And in my sleep… what do I say?'

'I am not sure that you ever said anything. These were conversations. Sometimes they seemed to be around you… above you… or about you. They came through you… but I never thought they were *of* you. Do you understand?'

Fabrienne allows her hand to fall to the bench… the slowly congealing blood is blackening on the bright brass… her fingertips resting where it had spilled. The metal sings to her in a way that it has never done before… in a way that she could never describe to herself… let alone to Raoul. Buried deep in its song are voices.

'Fabrienne… Fabrienne…' Raoul shakes her by the shoulder. 'Take yourself home and get that cleaned up properly.'

Fabrienne stares unbelievingly at the injury to her finger. The hole is closing rapidly and cleanly. 'I… it will be alright.'

Raoul shakes her again. 'Home… now. You have a job to do… unless you want me to drag you there?'

Fabrienne distances herself from him. 'No. I have to do this on my own.'

'Good.' Raoul turns away from her and back to the bench.

'Do it well… and remember… words are like money… spend as little as you need and it will be enough. And stay away from…'

He turns back to find he is alone.

OCTOBER 9th.
MONDAY

3:16 P.M.

'Fabrienne? I thought you were at…?' Mignon grabs her by the hand as she passes through the hall into the kitchen.

Fabrienne's hand and arm are streaked with the black of dried blood. Mignon holds it into the light from the window over the sink but can tell little from what she sees.

'What is it…? Who? Is it Raoul?'

Fabrienne turns on the cold water and rinses the blood away into the sink. 'No, *Mamie*. It is only me.'

'Only you…'. Mignon's leg splays into an uncomfortable angle beneath the table as she sits heavily on the stool. 'Only you…'

Tears well in her eyes and spill without fear or shame across her smile. 'Only you…'

Fabrienne dries her hands on a teacloth and reaches out for Mignon. She stands against the stool, Mignon's cheek held firmly against her body where she cannot mistake the words that reverberate through her chest.

'Yes, Mamie. Only me. Mamie? I love you.'

Mignon slides a hand between Fabrienne's rough shirt and the skin of her lower back, placing her hand without sympathy in the middle of the scar. With the other, she draws Fabrienne's hand to touch the pale, unblemished sheen of her own cheek. 'You are the only person in the world who does not need to tell me that.'

She holds Fabrienne by the shoulders at arms length. 'Who else have you told?'

Fabrienne hides her face in shame. 'Only… only…'

OCTOBER 9th.
FRIDAY

3:40P.M.

'How could you not tell me? I trusted you like no other…'

Oriel holds the door open, allowing Mignon into the kitchen. Wrapped in Mignon's old coat is a person she barely recognises, but one she has known she would have to face at some time, just not so soon. Not so soon after the letter of release from Sister Mirais and not when Artus has just asked her again… and finally…

'Why should you trust me with something so important to you?'

Mignon presses her back against the door, closing it behind her, the gesture shunning the world outside, circling her resentment into the small space between the cooker and the sink, the door to the stairs and the open space into the sitting room.

She braces her anger against the dark wood, fear stiffening her spine against the hole that is opening up before her and yet… is this not exactly where she has always wanted to be? Inside her, the stone she has carried for years reaches the foot of the slope… and stops.

'Why could you not trust me in return?'

Oriel turns away, unwilling to meet the eyes behind the question she knows full well that she deserves.

'Because I have betrayed the trust of too many children.'

Mignon's fingers flex, automatically grasping after the handbag she has forgotten in her downhill flight to Oriel's door.

'But you have only ever betrayed the trust of one.'

Oriel keeps her eyes downcast. The black of the kettle seems to absorb her attention. She wishes it lit again and bubbling with happiness in the way she had found herself in those precious moments with Fabrienne.

'Even one is too many.'

'I know, and that is why I have come to redress that… *Mamie.*'

1989

**OCTOBER 10th.
TUESDAY**

2:18 P.M.

Artus gathers the tools that lay scattered across the bench. These are fine tools in every sense of the word, so he wipes them with an oiled cloth to preserve the sheen of the steel. In each handle is an inlay of white beech. 'Auguste Godenot: Horologer'. He strokes the letters with his thumb.

Each day for forty-four years he has remembered the first time he was shown them...

1945

JANUARY 15th.
MONDAY

12.32 P.M.

Auguste Godenot unrolls his toolkit. Artus stands beside him, trying to make sense of the love the old man obviously feels as he lifts each of the tools in turn.

'See this? This is a knife-file.' He places it into the boy's hand. 'See the edge? The way it is shaped like a blade?' He slips it back into the pocket in the cloth. 'With this you will learn to cut the teeth of cogs and the barbs of escapements.'

Auguste smiles quietly, noticing discomfort in the way Artus handles the file. This will change. He understands the boy beside him as a blank canvas, one that he has waited for all his solitary life. He hesitates a moment more, realising that Artus cannot possibly take all this in, given his present condition.

'Does it hurt to stand?'

Artus shakes his head.

Auguste settles onto the padded high stool beside the bench. 'Well, it hurts me. But then I am no longer fourteen.' He looks up into the boy's face. 'And I no longer remember that I ever was.'

He turns away from the tools to study the boy beside him, the inequities of leg and arm to torso, the slight stoop towards protection of his damaged shoulder.

'What is your real name?'

'I don't know, M'seiur.'

'If we are to work together, as it seems we must, then

you must call me Auguste.'

'Thank you, M'sieur.'

'Do you know why you were given the name they chose for you?'

'No, M'sieur.'

'Well, it is both joke and compliment, take it whatever way you will. It is the name of a mythical English king who withdrew his great sword from a stone, and with it brought happiness and good fortune to those around him. The women of La Roque hope you will do the same for them with yours.'

The boy ponders a moment, lightly touching the handle of a metal punch, flinching as it rolls away from him across the bench. 'I have no sword.'

Auguste shocks the boy with his outburst of laughter.

'These are women, Artus, and one must always be careful of that breed, for the story of the King is also one of feminine deceit and great tragedy. But you do have fresh eyes and, for that at least, I shall be truly grateful.'

Artus runs his fingertips over the opened tool roll, barely touching the surfaces of the handles, collecting a fine film of oil on his skin.

Auguste nudges him to one side and opens a drawer under the bench, drawing out a long, serrated knife.

'Do you know what this one is for?'

Artus shakes his head again.

Auguste nudges him towards the workshop door.

'It's for cutting our lunch.'

1989

OCTOBER 10th.
TUESDAY

2:42 P.M.

In that same drawer beneath the bench now lie another set of tools, quite the equal of the ones he is wrapping. Inset into each handle is 'Artus d'Horo', the name given him by the village, his original still firmly lost in the darkness of the war.

He rolls Auguste's tools in the cloth and places them carefully into the drawer beneath the bench. He sets aside a dismembered clock, laying the severed hands into a small tray. He picks up a twisted escape mechanism and ponders why, since his arrival, he has never found his own.

Oriel has asked him to make her a present of a chiming clock. It is the only thing he has ever refused her. How can he tell her without seeming insane that every night, as he slips into sleep, he hears the single toll of a distant bell, and that it accompanies his awakening to the day? That single sound fills him and drives him. To create more would seem a dilution of himself. He hopes for her forgiveness.

He moves out quietly amongst the evening pavements and cobbles of La Roque. Over one shoulder, he carries a wooden pole ladder. Its timbers are old, bleached and dry. In another hand is a half-filled paint kettle and from the pockets of his jacket poke the tips of paint tubes and numerous small brushes.

OCTOBER 10th.
TUESDAY

3:15 P.M.

Artus stops beneath a bedroom window long enough to raise the ladder, select a brush from an inside pocket, and begin to climb.

At the top, a bitter-sweet floral scent assails him. He stands a moment… transfixed by the promise that the scent carries… then begins to apply fresh lavender paint to the summer-chined wood.

5:37 P.M.

As he paints the final shutter edge, a hand appears holding the stem of a wine glass… a low ray of sunlight catching fire in the bowl. A finger lifts and beckons. Behind the louvres, a glimpse of white-blonde hair sways in the filtered darkness.

He descends the ladder to lay it flat beneath the next window, where it will wait safely until morning, unattended.

Oriel Beaufort removes her wedding dress, returning it to its scented linen shroud in the wardrobe where it will hang in silence until tomorrow. She smoothes the fine silk between her fingers, caressing the hand-stitches that hide the letter that brought her a moment of such sorrow… and this chance of a long-awaited freedom.

She lodges a book behind her bedroom shutters so that the wind will not collide the freshly-painted surfaces. In the bottom left corner she knows there will be a small, painted monogram of a blue iris, and she knows that it will be perfect. The accompanying leaves will be a blush of green, the blues of the flower delicate, shading to yellow and white, and that it will drive Danielle to desperation and that, like Artus, it will not fade in the summer light.

9:45 P.M.

The room has grown dark by the time Artus enters. A window in the far wall has shutters opened the slightest crack, slicing an early retroussé moon into slivers, yet this is enough, as his eyes become accustomed, to know the slow sheen of silk counterpane and the absence in the corner where the old wardrobe absorbs light as if the ends of worlds were within its capacity.

The door swings gently shut behind him.

From the centre of the room he knows that two steps to the right will bring him to the wall, three forward will take him to the window, one to the left will reach the bed. He unfastens the top button and pulls the shirt over his head, allowing it to fall to the floor. The rest of his clothes fall into a pile at his feet, where the moonlight through the shutter ribs them neatly.

Artus stretches his arms upwards to relax his shoulders. and, from the bed, Oriel sees his late paunch retreat almost half a century. His manhood is cloaked in pale light, as it was back when it had been no more than a fleeting visitor in this room.

She reaches a hand to touch the cloth of his garments, drawing past comforts from the soft wear in the corduroy of the trousers between her fingertips, the harsh cotton present of the shirt she has recently bought for him.

She slides a finger down the back of his leg as he stands, rewarded by the slight tremor this still produces. She reaches further and pulls him to the bed. 'Turn around.'

He lowers himself to sit beside her.

She turns her attention to his shoulder, hands spread and searching. Three fingers down from the arc of the scapula she finds what she is looking for.

Two small, puckered scars like pursed mouths.

She traces them with a fingertip.

'I am just making sure.'

'After fifty-three years?'

'Moments… my love… just moments.'

Artus rolls into bed to find her trembling.

She climbs astride him, then leans forward to reach around and press her fingers against the twin scars.

She sees him again, bleeding, rolled and washed, bullets teased from his back, chest pummelled, the dust of ripped cotton sheets, the sweat of desperation, the copper-iron tang of blood, women shouting, the sound of life retching from him.

She shudders violently as she slides against his skin until he lets out a long ragged moan and his breathing settles to an even pattern.

Before she settles, she weaves her fingers into the harsh grey hair of his chest. 'You are an old dog.'

'Woof…' He speaks to the darkness in the room.

She slips toward sleep. 'Saturday you will be an old *married* dog.'

'Woof Woof.'

Oriel closes her eyes over the knowledge she has kept from him. She releases a smile, imagining his face when he finds out in church that her bridesmaid, Mignon, is his daughter. The hairs on his chest curl against her smile. She teases them with the corner of her lips. Artus rolls away and as he falls quietly into sleep, she spoons into his back, reaching up with her lips to plant a kiss on the lozenge shaped birth- mark at the nape of his neck.

3:36 A.M.

Artus' eyes open suddenly in the night, then close again. He smiles in the darkness, holding secret the sudden, inner revelation of his true name. He can hardly wait to tell her at the altar. This could change everything.

He turns over towards her, pushing his arm under her head to hold her tight against him.

The muscles between his shoulders flex, moving forward an old sliver of bone… to where it meets an artery…

To Be Continued…

In…

MEKANISMO

JOURNAL

II

ARGO NAVIS

BY

CYBERMOUSE BOOKS

ISBN: 978-1-0686097-1-8

AFTERWORD:

Wandering the back streets of a southern French village one warm summer evening, we came across a row of terraced cottages beside a river.

Two of the occupants, both elderly ladies, were sitting outside on their doorsteps. We exchanged nods, that being the extent of my French, and walked on until I stopped at one particular house.

The curtains were open as was the door and, although the light inside was very dim, it was reflecting from the dials of many clocks of all sizes.

This image was to become the house of Auguste Godenot.

The river beside the houses was not much more than a dry bed but there were many signs that on occasion it could be much more than that.

We suggested that it might become 'a torrent in winter'.

This became my first working title for the book.

Around this time I became aware of the Antikythera Mechanism through a magazine article. It absolutely captivated me in a way that few things do. I still find it astounding that medieval civilisations lost the artistry to create such intricate aids as this, given the trouble that the initial investigation of it caused, namely to Valerio Stais, its discoverer.

He was labelled a hoaxer and allowed to go to his grave with that as an epitaph before the emergence of the truth.

The thing that caused Stais a problem was the discovery, by early X-Ray, that the mechanism contained a differential with a planetary gear system. These systems were not thought to have been invented until at least fifteen hundred years later.

Carbon dating, shortly after its invention, restored its validity to the date of 86 B.C. and also to Valerio Stais' reputation, although many years too late.

I began to wonder what would happen if there were more than one Mechanism. Would a machine such as this have the capacity, in the right hands, to do more than calculate? Perhaps it could also predict. Even if that were no more than a possibility, how would the powerful react to the potential of that. One can only imagine the advantage it could create.

For this novel, imagining that is exactly what I did.

In the 2010's we drove many miles around Europe and the idea for this story followed me wherever I went.

The picture was slowly building inside me all the time I was there and has continued up until today as I write this. I don't think there has been a moment since that warm summer night that this idea has left me entirely alone.

As the story began to build in my imagination and across the page, I realised that it encompassed more than one timeline. In fact, there are many. You will need to read this book and Volume II, 'Argo Navis', and Volume III, 'Ophiuchus', to discover all of them. They are not of necessity sequential, but I hope the links make them emotively so.

When the writing of this first Journal was almost complete I realised that I had the opportunity, while attending a wedding in Certaldo, Italy, to personally visit all the other places across Europe that my protagonists visit in the book.

We varied our route home to encompass Val de Susa, Italy, where we found a beautifully decorated Monastery which became the Abbazia. We have walked along the platform of the Stazione in Susa. We have heard the incredible roar of the waters at Rheinfall am Main, and traversed the Lötschberg tunnel. I became locked in a restaurant toilet above Frutigen and was forced to telephone my way out. We have stayed overnight at the Hotel Rugenpark, Interlaken, (and in here have made an accurate description of it as it was then), taken coffee at the Altstadt Tearooms there (without arsenic, so it couldn't have been a Friday) beside the raucous turbine grind of the Elektrizitätswerk. We have sailed Thunersee on a paddle steamer and experienced all the European points in the book but, the main event, although not on the same tour, was our later trip to Athens and Antikythera. That journey is a complete story in itself and for that, you will need to find...

'Mekanismo', Journal II, 'Argo Navis'

(Cybermouse Books 2024   ISBN 978-1-0686097-1-8)

I hope you have enjoyed this first part of the story and the places and times it has taken you to.

Best Wishes,

Bill Allerton

Other Books in the Cybermouse range:

Bill Allerton;
Novels:
The Fox & The Fish   (ISBN 978-0-9548373-2-7)
Magpie   (ISBN 978-0-9930424-5-4)

William Allerton;
Mekanismo Journal I: (ISBN 978-1-0686097-0-1)
Mekanismo Journal II   (ISBN 978-1-0686097-1-8)

Short Fiction:
Firelight on Dark Water   (ISBN 978-0-9930424-4-7)
A Day for Tigers   (ISBN 978-0-9930424-3-0)
Watch & Wait   (ISBN 978-0-9548373-1-0)

Childrens Books:
Foxes, Frogs and Rice Pudding   (ISBN 978-0-9930424-6-1)
Sir Tingly - The Quest for The Dargon (ISBN 978-0-9930424-8-5)
The Time Mouse   (He's running late!)

Bryony Doran;
The China Bird   (ISBN 978-1-7392643-2-1)
The Sand Eggs   (ISBN 978-1-7392643-0-7)

Sara Jane Harding

My Brilliant Boobs   (ISBN 978-1-7392643-7-6)

Sylvia Wright;

My Crazy Brain (A Life with M. S.)   (ISBN 978-0-9930424-7-8)

Audio: (Available free on Spotify and all podcast stations)

Urban Tiger Radio (Mature fiction, Music & Poetry)
Urban Tiger Radio Childrens Hour (5 to 12 yrs.)